About the Author

James Ellis lives in Bath and writes fiction.

He has published a number of flash fiction and short stories including *The Fire Diver's Assistant*, *The Therapist* and *A Rare Bird*. *The Wrong Story* is his first novel.

THE WRONG STORY

THE WRONG STORY

JAMES ELLIS

This edition first published in 2017

Unbound

6th Floor Mutual House, 70 Conduit Street, London W1S 2GF

www.unbound.com

ISBN (eBook):978-1-911586-18-0

ISBN (Paperback):978-1-911586-11-1

Design by Mark Ecob

Cover image:

© Shutterstock.com
© iStockphoto.com

Printed and bound in Great Britain by Clays Ltd, Elcograf S.p.A.

To Sally, without whom I would not have written this book, to my father, who didn't live to see me write it, and to my mother, who never once doubted that I would write it.

Dear Reader,

The book you are holding came about in a rather different way to most others. It was funded directly by readers through a new website: Unbound.

Unbound is the creation of three writers. We started the company because we believed there had to be a better deal for both writers and readers. On the Unbound website, authors share the ideas for the books they want to write directly with readers. If enough of you support the book by pledging for it in advance, we produce a beautifully bound special subscribers' edition and distribute a regular edition and e-book wherever books are sold, in shops and online.

This new way of publishing is actually a very old idea (Samuel Johnson funded his dictionary this way). We're just using the internet to build each writer a network of patrons. Here, at the back of this book, you'll find the names of all the people who made it happen.

Publishing in this way means readers are no longer just passive consumers of the books they buy, and authors are free to write the books they really want. They get a much fairer return too – half the profits their books generate, rather than a tiny percentage of the cover price.

If you're not yet a subscriber, we hope that you'll want to join our publishing revolution and have your name listed in one of our books in the future. To get you started, here is a £5 discount on your first pledge. Just visit unbound.com, make your pledge and type SCRAPS17 in the promo code box when you check out.

Thank you for your support,
unbound-signatures-for-letter

Dan, Justin and John
Founders, Unbound

Super Patrons

Sue & Colin Allan
Hazel Barkworth
Victoria Bennett
Miguel Blasco
Vivien Boast
Angharad Brown
Susie Campbell
Paul Campy
Louise Casey
Pauline Casey
Jason Cass
Amal Chatterjee
Charlotte Clifford
Hannah Collins
Benny Collins
Dan Coomansingh
Alexandra Coulton
Mungo Coyne
Rachel Darling
Mark Davis
Laura Deutsch
Yvonne Dewing
Harminder Dhillon
Barry Dodd
Sylvia Ellis
Michael Ellis
Lauren Ellis
Dan Ellis
Joe Ellis
Andrew Ellis
Linda Ellis
Brian James Ellis
Giana Elyea
Oli Gill

Rory Gleeson
Heidi Godfrey-Jones
Mark Goody
Roger Gray
Sam Guglani
Manish Gupta
Shahla Haque
Kiran Hargrave
Katie Hawksworth
David Hetherington
Mary Hopcroft
Maggie Hunt
Alice Jolly
Elena Kaufman
Dan Kieran
Ollie Landerer
Declan Logue
Simon Lovell-Smith
Julie Mansfield
Ruth Marks
Kate McCombe
Sally McGuire
Barry McGuire
Patricia McGuire
Charlie McIntosh
Moira McKendry
Gordon McMann
Dale Melita
John Mitchinson
Leonard Montgomery
Patrick Neil
Adrian Pasciuta
Dominic Perry
Roy Plummer
Justin Pollard
Gordon Porter
Sue Ransom
Becky Ravenscroft

Tom Ravenscroft
Bill Rees Lewis
Amelia Rowe
Phillipa Ryan
Graham Slater
Christiane Travers
Oliver Tuhey
Nicola Turnbull
Dorothy Turner
Christian Uta
Kevin Venus
Rachel Louise Venus
Neil Ward
Gemma Warriner
Darla Warriner
Lois Warriner
Chaz Warriner
Fiona Wiltshire
Keith Woodgate
Anthony Woodgate

With grateful thanks to
Sally McGuire

'Don't you ever wonder what happens in between the frames? What happens in that dark line that separates one frozen moment from the next?'

Tom Hannah

Contents

Prologue

Part One

The Feint

7

Part Two

The Draw

65

Part Three

Bang

145

Epilogue

Acknowledgements

217

Patrons List

219

Prologue

Later, he would remember this: there was no cushion of air to carry him safely to the ground and, if there had been, it would have been too thin to take his weight. Instead, he saw the concrete cap above him recede at speed and felt the warm wind push past him in an upward rush. There were no thoughts and no past life flashing before him; only a tumbling and a reaching out for what wasn't there.

ii

weekendingnews.com/news/cart_survives/280223/

Cartoonist Falls Off Car Park Roof

By Robert de Moor – Monday, 13 April 2015

SOUTH LONDON – An accident closed off a South London street yesterday morning. Tom Hannah, best known by his professional name, Tash, the creator of the cartoon strip *Scraps*, fell 60 feet from the top of a five-storey car park and landed on a market stall. Despite the drop, Hannah survived.

Witnesses described the cartoonist as being in the air for a few seconds, seeming to hover for a moment before falling backwards towards the ground. Paramedics said that the combination of the market stall's canvas roof and the collapsing effect of several crates of bananas slowed his fall sufficiently to prevent serious injury.

'See those crates? He blew them apart like a bomb,' said Parks & Open Spaces gardener Peter Hobbes, 27, who was one of the first to go to Hannah's aid. 'The roof vanished and bananas flew up in the air and people were running all over the place. Lucky the earth had been dug over and was soft – otherwise he would have broken every bone in his body.'

A spokesman for the council said that market stall-holders were strictly prohibited from setting up on the municipal flower-beds and there would be an investigation into why this rule had been flouted. A spokesman for the Market Stallholders' Association said that compensation would be sought for the loss of produce.

The cause of the accident is currently unknown.

iii

#tashfalls

Charles & Hermione *@charleshermione*

Who is this idiot anyway? weekendingnews.com/ news/cart_survives/280223/ **#tashfalls**

Loosey Lucy *@FootballPuller*

Is it a stunt? **#tashfalls** *#PlausibleImpossible*

Brant Hart *@DoodlingGeek*

@charleshermione Thomas Arthur Stevenson Hannah – moustache man who draws a cartoon about a fox #moustache **#tashfalls**

Captain Padlock *@captainpadlock*

Anyone know which hospital he's in? **#tashfalls** *#hermit*

Gerard Borkmann *@BorkmannCreativeAgency*

@charleshermione Tom Hannah created the #scraps comic strip. Speedy recovery, Tom. **#tashfalls**

Brant Hart *@DoodlingGeek*

@BorkmannCreativeAgency Is he still drawing? Haven't seen anything in a while **#tashfalls**

Loosey Lucy *@FootballPuller*

@BorkmannCreativeAgency Zoicks! Is that the one with the cat and the pelican? I love animal art **#tashfalls**

Gerard Borkmann *@BorkmannCreativeAgency*

@FootballPuller Yes & a hedgehog & an always-angry restaurant owner. Terrific work by a modern master **#tashfalls** *#scraps*

Charles & Hermione *@charleshermione*

@FootballPuller Some say dots and lines ain't art, baby **#tashfalls**

Loosey Lucy *@FootballPuller*

@charleshermione Some say some people should wind their necks in #windyourneckin **#tashfalls**

Captain Padlock *@captainpadlock*

@charleshermione Did he jump or was he pushed – any witnesses? **#tashfalls**

Gerard Borkmann *@BorkmannCreativeAgency*

@captainpadlock Can I refer you to the official

channels? *Speculation on social media is #nothelpful*
#tashfalls

Captain Padlock *@captainpadlock*

#officialchannels *#nothelpful* **#tashfalls** *#Why-
DidTashFall*

Gerard Borkmann *@BorkmannCreativeAgency*

@captainpadlock Is that you Germaine? **#tashfalls**

Part One

The Feint

He was woken by a dog barking. With his eyes closed he thought he could be buried in a box or in a morgue or in a womb about to be born, although when he moved he felt sick. So not dead, then; but not ready to be awake either. He listened for the dog, waiting for it to bark again, but it was quiet now and he could hear nothing except the hiss in his ears and the sound of blood pumping from somewhere deep inside him. Perhaps it had been a dream dog or a cough or a door banging, but it had sounded real so that's what he chose to believe. He had been woken by a dog barking: a dog barking in the distance, a real dog with a real bark. It became a fact, a truth, a recorded memory.

It was warm and quiet and comfortable and he was already drifting off again, sinking back through his pillows into a darker place where more disturbing memories waited: a shape moving across an expanse of shimmering white concrete, a bird flying over the edge of a wall, a cold punch of something hard hitting his face, blood in his mouth. Faces looking down on him; a pressure inside his head. And voices.

Are you all right?
Stay still.
Are you in pain?
What's your name?

The next time he awoke there was light from fluorescent strips on the ceiling and light from outside, too: daylight, wide and bright. Also noises: rattling trolleys and people talking and telephones ringing. He lifted his head and saw that he was in a bed that had padded side rails that kept him in bed rather than on the floor. There was a man pushing a trolley with drinks and newspapers and magazines on it, and there were nurses in a group by a desk.

He tried to say, 'Hello?' but nothing came out other than a hiss

7

and a crackle. He moved his tongue backwards and forwards, exploring and lubricating his mouth, and found he had a broken tooth at the front. The gum surrounding it felt raw and red, and a warm liquid oozed from it. It tasted sweet. He felt pressure against his eardrums as if he were under water and there was a noise inside his head, a rise and fall of something deep like an engine switching on and off.

He wriggled his toes and fingers and found that everything moved except the thumb on his left hand, which was bandaged and stuck out at an angle – like the hand of a mummified hitchhiker. On his wrist was a white plastic band. He held it up to his eyes and squinted at the words printed on it.

Thomas Hannah.

They were familiar words. He had seen them drawn in a childish hand in orange crayon, typed on labels, carved in wood, doodled on books, signed by him on documents, on drawings, on photographs.

What's your name?

Thomas Hannah.

It was his name and with that knowledge came a sense of being. He reoccupied himself. The little boy at school who had drawn a picture of a house and grass and sky was now a big man with a big moustache that tickled his nose, lying in a hospital bed; a behemoth; big bones, big hands, big feet. He looked down at his spreading stomach and the bedclothes that covered him and, although he still felt woozy, everything seemed to be in the right place: his face was correctly stretched across his skull, his neck was taking the weight of his head, his heart was beating, his lungs were breathing. He was intact. He was Tom Hannah.

'What happened?' he whispered.

There were needles in his left arm, one of which had a tube that ran to a bag on a pole. He found another tube, thick and greasy, emerging from beneath the bed covers. It was attached to a bag that hung from one of the side rails. There was a support collar around his neck, and a bandage around his head with a pad beneath it beside his right eye.

'Hello?' he said again.

He moved his head from left to right and his skull felt tight as if it had shrunk in the wash. Dormant aches and pains shifted deep inside his body like slumbering giants kept under lock and key, and his but-tocks, which felt sore, were supported by a rubber ring.

'Hello? Hello?'

A young woman with a round face came over from the nurses' station and looked at him from behind thick glasses.

'Good morning,' she said. 'My name is Maggie.'

He nodded. He tried to speak but it felt as if there were a blade in his throat. Maggie half-filled a plastic cup with water from a jug on the table by his bed.

'Have some water.'

When he drank the cup bumped against his swollen lip and his moustache – his moustache was enormous. He could see it on the edge of his vision and he could feel it pushing up against his nose, his swollen lip extending it beyond its normal range. The water stuck in his throat and dribbled down his chin onto the sheets.

'Thank you,' he said.

'You're welcome.' She wiped his mouth and called to another nurse. Her name was Bianca and she told him that he could call her Bee.

'Everybody should have an animal name,' he whispered and his voice sounded distant and weak.

'You're still waking up. You've been out all night. Do you know where you are?'

'Hospital?'

'Yes. You're in Halverson Hospital. This is Meadow Ward and I'm the ward manager.'

He nodded and closed his eyes.

'Try to stay awake,' she said.

She took his blood pressure and measured his temperature and then they adjusted his rubber ring and hauled him up the bed until he was sitting upright.

'We'll need a longer bed,' Bee said.

Maggie lifted his hands and feet, let them drop and then wrote in a blue folder that was lying on his table while Bee rearranged the bed covers and the cotton gown he was wearing.

'How do you feel?' Maggie said.

'Sick.'

'Nauseous sick or going-to-be-sick sick?'

'Sick sick.'

'Tell me if you're actually going to vomit.' She held out her hand. 'How many fingers am I holding up?'

He opened his eyes. 'Three.'

'Good. Can you tell me your name?'

He lifted his arm with the wristband and said, 'Thomas Hannah.'

'That's cheating. Do you have a middle name?'

He lay back and closed his eyes. 'A few. Which one?'

'I'll let you choose.'

'Arthur. My full name is Thomas Arthur Stevenson Hannah.'

'Very good. Open your eyes, please. I don't want you to fall asleep again. Not yet.'

Tom opened his eyes.

'Thank you. Hold my hand and grip it as hard as you can. That's good. Not quite so hard. Do you know what day it is?'

He looked up at the ceiling. That was a good question. He tried to find a thread on which to pull, a point of reference from which to rebuild the time and place, but he couldn't. His mind probed his broken memory as his tongue had probed his broken tooth.

'Monday?' he said.

'Was that a guess?'

Tom rubbed his face with his bandaged hand and nodded. 'I've got that Monday morning kind of feeling.' He tried to laugh but it still hurt too much. 'Ouch.'

Maggie gave him more water. 'Well, you're right. It is Monday. You came in yesterday. You had an accident. Do you remember much about that?'

Tom looked at her, at her neat blue tunic with its white piping, at her fob-watch that told him it was 8.10am, at her badge that said *Ward Manager: Margarida Monroe*, and at her round, clear, bespectacled face. *Margarida, was that Spanish?*

'Nothing,' he said. 'I don't remember anything about yesterday. Have I been run over? Hit by a meteorite?'

'You fell off a multi-storey car park roof.'

That was a surprise.

You fell off a multi-storey car park roof.

There seemed to be too many syllables in that sentence. He tried it out himself. 'I fell off a multi-story car park roof.' It was difficult to say with his swollen lip and bristly moustache and missing tooth.

'Do you remember that?' she said.

'No.'

'Okay.' She looked at him for a little longer as if she were waiting for him to say something more.

'That's not good, is it?' he said.

She smiled again and said, 'It's not surprising. You've just woken up. Can you touch your nose with your finger, please?'

He touched his nose with his finger. The tube that curled under the sheets towards his groin had particles of sediment floating in it. He could feel the bag's weight tugging it. He drank some more water.

'Did you say I fell off a car park roof?' he said.

'That's right.'

'I don't like heights.'

'I can see why.'

'I mean I really don't like heights. And I don't drive.'

Maggie stopped writing in her folder and sat down on the side of his bed and spoke as if she was explaining a great truth. Her eyes were large behind her thick lenses and close up her face was rounder and smoother than it had looked when she was farther away. There was a tiny blemish on her cheek: a mark so small it was hardly visible; a minuscule shallow crater that, were her face a planet, would be apparent only through the most powerful of telescopes.

'I don't know why you were up there. All I know is that yesterday you fell off a car park roof and landed on a market stall and a big pile of bananas, and ended up on a flower-bed full of wet earth. You are very lucky. If you're thinking of buying a lottery ticket, I'd do it now.'

'I landed on a market stall?'

'On the canvas roof.'

Tom thought about that, about his body falling like a stone and hitting the canvas roof. For some reason he imagined himself asleep as he fell, wafting to the ground like a leaf. But perhaps he'd been awake and screaming. 'That was lucky.'

'Very.'

'And then... bananas?'

'Crates of bananas. All piled up.'

Of course, the canvas roof wouldn't have withstood his colossal weight. He was no leaf. He would have smashed through everything between him and the ground.

'How high?'

'I don't know. Six feet?'

'I mean, how high was the car park roof?'

'Oh, much higher. About sixty feet.'

Tom tried to imagine how high 60 feet was. He thought of a tower block and counted six windows up. He pictured nine Toms standing on each other's shoulders leaning against the building, and then he found himself imagining that all those Toms were a circus troupe wearing tights and leotards, each running on with their moustaches bouncing up and down and taking a bow before climbing up and becoming the next rung on the human ladder.

'Sixty feet. Was anyone else hurt?'

'Well, the bananas might need counselling.' Maggie smiled. 'That was a joke. No one was hurt except you. And you got off lightly. Seriously, you're so lucky. You've hurt your hand and lost a tooth. No damage at all to your back. You have a bruise on your head but the neurologist took a look at you and there's no sign of anything to worry about, which is good. You had some pain in your lower back area so we gave you painkillers and something to help you sleep.' She stood up again. 'Follow my finger with your eyes.'

Tom followed her finger with his eyes. She wore no rings.

'My lower back area?' he said.

'The paramedics think you hit the crates with your buttocks but landed face-first in the flower-bed. There was a lot of mud in your mouth.'

He ran his tongue around his gums. Mud in his mouth; mud and blood and a broken tooth.

'Why does my throat hurt so much?'

'It's just dry. The painkillers. I'll get you more water.'

It was a lot to take in. He felt like a witness to a train wreck standing at the mouth of the tunnel. Something had happened in there but there was still too much smoke and debris to see what. He thought about his dry throat and sticky mouth. It was a familiar feeling. This was not the first time he'd woken up with a headache and a large gap where the day before had been.

'Was I... was there alcohol involved?' he said.

Maggie smiled. 'No. Why? Do you feel hung over?'

'I don't know.'

'Well, I don't think there was any alcohol involved. I want you to tell me if you have any headaches or problems with your vision. Or your hearing.'

Tom thought about the barking dog but then remembered: that had been real.

'I feel washed out,' he said.

Maggie stepped back from the bed and surveyed him. 'The consultant will see you soon,' she said. 'No food until then. We took some details from your wallet and I think the police have been to your house. Is there anyone you'd like me to call? Anyone who will be worried about you?'

The police have been to your house.

Is there anyone who will be worried about you?

Is there anyone you'd like me to call?

'Yes,' he said. 'There is. My wife. My wife will be worried about me.'

'I'll call her.'

'Her name is Karen.'

'Okay.'

'Can I call her?'

'Of course. We can set you up with a phone. Would she have been at home when the police called yesterday afternoon?'

'I expect so.'

'Well, don't worry. You can call her soon if you want, or we'll contact her.'

Tom took a deep breath and felt the cool air pass across the serrated edges of his sore throat. 'I don't remember being on a roof at all,' he said.

'What do you remember?'

He closed his eyes.

'Concrete. Shimmering white concrete.'

2

Extracts from a visiting lecture given by Germaine Kiecke at Charles University in Prague, 1 April 2011.

... The thing, the most important thing, to bear in mind when considering the Tash canon of cartoons is his adherence to the art of *ligne claire*. There is no clutter. Life is reduced to as few pen-strokes as possible; a dot, a dash and little more. But within those few pen-strokes an entire universe can be conjured...

... Tash expunges the grimy reality of our world and creates a clean, minimal, sanitised canvas on which his characters can thrive – Plenty the Cat, Billy the Hedgehog, the Pelican, the always-angry restaurant owner and, of course, Scraps himself: the ecologically-motivated fox and hero of all the adventures...

... They are pure, defined, untouchable, immortal. The art lies in what we don't see: in the spaces that surround the characters; in their world beyond the frames. And through this combination of seen and unseen we might catch a glimpse of the mind of the artist, the mind of the creator...

... And as for his creations, it is intriguing to imagine life from their side of the page, how they see the world that has been laid out for them, and what they might say on the subject were they ever to meet their maker... (Kiecke).

3

One of the first things I'd say is that it wasn't shimmering white concrete at all. It was ordinary grey concrete, the warm air rising from a patch of dried oil making it shimmer, the bright morning sun making it look lighter than it actually was.

I walked across the concrete and passed through the warm air and I wondered whether or not I was shimmering too. I hoped so. It would look good for whoever was watching me, as someone certainly was. I could usually tell when hidden eyes were on me.

'I know you're somewhere,' I said.

In front of me was a big brick building. I walked over to it and sat on a low flight of concrete steps and looked around. Opposite, beyond the heat haze, was a grassy slope with a wire perimeter fence running along its top, and a cluster of small industrial units beyond. I didn't know why I'd come to this place or how I'd got there either. But that was all right because that happened a lot of the time. My life wasn't a sequence of events, merely a collection of moments.

I opened a tin of tobacco and started rolling cigarettes, looking around in a furtive manner. I was naturally furtive. I made five cigarettes, put four in the tin and the fifth in my mouth. I lit it with my Zippo and took a long, deep drag, blowing the smoke back into the air in a faint stream.

'Filthy habit,' I said, as I always did.

I sat back and closed my eyes, enjoying the sun and the warm breeze and the peace and quiet of a Sunday morning. No doubt it would become apparent why I was there. It usually did. Meanwhile, I was comfortable simply to be, to let life come to me, to exist.

A shape darkened the light. I opened my eyes and saw that the blockage was Plenty, silhouetted in front of me with the sun behind her head like a solar eclipse. A solar eclipse with wide, pink eyes. How did she get there so silently and so suddenly, I wondered? It bothered me. Everything about her bothered me.

'I knew you were somewhere,' I said. 'I knew you were watching me.'

She stood there, blocking the sun, staring, until she said, 'Where's my ball?'

I blew smoke into the air. 'I don't know.'

'Have you stolen it?'

I studied the end of my cigarette. 'No, I haven't stolen your ball. Have you looked? You know you have to look first.'

She continued to stare at me, no doubt thinking I couldn't see her moving closer, bit by bit, her tail thickening.

'It's your ball,' I said. 'You have to look after it. I don't have it. See?' I spread my arms wide in a gesture of openness and noticed that her claws were out; thin slivers of razor-sharp malice.

'You know the rule,' I said.

'What rule?'

'The no-claws rule.'

She was very close now and she had become still, staring at me. I looked away. I had read somewhere that it's a non-threatening gesture. Cats don't like being stared at. I don't know why I bothered because that sort of stuff never made any difference with Plenty.

'Sometimes,' I said, 'I think about a sack full of rocks and an empty stretch of water.'

'That's not nice.'

She was standing right over me, just a wiggle and a pounce away. And then a voice from above said, 'I've got it. No, I haven't. Yes, I have.'

A large decrepit Pelican dropped out of the sky. It was a rough landing. It hit the ground and bounced, its eyes crossing briefly as its feathers lifted in different directions before it collapsed near the steps in a heap of bones and beak and mottled grey feathers. Its body was moving with fleas and tics and those little rice-like yellow eggs. It was dirty, ragged and diseased, and much bigger and bonier than it looked when it was in the air. It stank of fish – long dead and rotting fish.

'Ouch. That hurt. Did it? It did.'

I opened my tin and offered it a cigarette. 'Even though you're a bird, I don't think you're cut out for flying. Are you all right?' I held out my lighter.

'It's not the flying, it's the landing.'

The Pelican took the light and then spat out a large lump of brown phlegm that hit the ground with a squelch and a muffled tinkle. The Pelican's eyes crossed again as it looked down its own beak and then righted themselves. 'There's your ball,' it said. 'Is it? Well, it's someone's.' It lay on the ground wheezing, looking like a big pile of feathery twigs.

Plenty stared at the phlegm-coated ball and then at me. The heat caused steam to rise from it.

'No way,' I said.

She waited.

'Oh, for God's sake.' I picked up the ball and rubbed the spit on my arm, leaving a patch of slime on my fur that glistened in the sun. 'There.' I tossed it to her. 'There's your ball.' It was pink and had a bell in it. 'Try to keep hold of it. You lose it every day. Don't bat it around so hard.' I relit my cigarette and tried to find my mellow mood again, but Plenty sat down beside me, knees together, head upright.

'Why are you so grumpy?' she said. 'You're no fun anymore. You used to be fun when we had our adventures. Why don't we have our adventures anymore?'

'I am fun. Look at this face. This is a fun face.'

She looked at me, leaned in and wrinkled her nose.

'Very funny,' I said.

That was their joke: that I smelled bad. Sometimes at night when I sat in our alleyway minding my own business, smoking a cigarette and reading a magazine, the others would say to each other that a skunk must be hiding nearby or that somebody was burning rubber. And then they'd look at me and laugh. But what do they know about how a fox should smell? What do they know about anything? Without me they'd starve. Without me they'd have no food, no warmth, no adventures. I let them laugh but sometimes I'd walk over to the wall and piss all over the brickwork just to give them a smell to talk about.

But the thing was, they were right: recently my smell had been getting worse. I knew it because I could smell it too. I was very particular about my scent. And it wasn't only me, the Pelican seemed to be decaying in front of us and even Plenty, not much older than a kitten, even she was looking threadbare.

'I'm hungry,' she said. 'Where's Billy?'

'I don't know. Maybe some kids have gone off with him.'

'Will they eat him?'

'No, they won't eat him. They'll play with him or take him to school or put him in an airing cupboard or something. They won't eat him. Kids don't eat hedgehogs.'

I kept half an eye on her. Her claws were still out. She was looking at the Pelican, which had fallen asleep. Each time it breathed her ears twitched. She watched its narrow, bony ribs rise and fall. Without apparently noticing she kneaded her claws into my leg. I lifted her paw, taking care not to draw blood. She turned and watched my face, neither resisting nor helping.

'Don't do that,' I said.

'Why not?'

'I don't like it.'

Still looking into my face she put her claws back on my leg.

'I like it.'

'Well I don't and it's my leg.'

'I'd like to pull all its feathers off,' she said looking back at the Pelican. The good thing about Plenty was that she quickly lost interest in anything that she was doing. 'Why is it an "it"? Why isn't it a he or a she?'

'It's just the Pelican. It always has been. Why is anything anything?'

'Where did it come from?'

'I don't know. The sky.'

'But where in the sky?'

'A Pelican cloud.'

'It has a big beak.'

'So what?' I flicked my cigarette away and watched it land on the ground, a plume of smoke curling upwards. 'You're bored. Go and play with your ball.'

'I like it here,' she said. 'Why don't you try to bite me and I'll rip out your eyes?'

'Why are you always like this when Billy's not around?'

'Like what? Like this?' She jabbed my leg with her claws again. I showed her my own stubby black nails, chipped and worn.

'Ooh, scary,' she laughed, skipping away.

'Do you mind?' said the Pelican. 'I think I mind. You're treading on my wings. Are you? Yes, you are.'

'Come and sit down,' I said. 'Before the Pelican gets all broken. Or lie in the sun or lick your face or whatever it is that you do.'

'Mister So-What,' she said and laughed. Then her mood changed and she looked sad. 'I should never have left Nanny's. It was nice there. I had my own blanket,' she said, rolling her ball backwards and forwards, 'and my own toys. And my own bowl.' Then she yawned and sat down. 'Give me a cigarette.'

I opened my tin and let her take one. I rolled the Zippo and she put her paw on my wrist – and one by one her needles reappeared from their fleshy sheaths. She looked at me and I looked at her, the flame reflecting in her eyes.

'I will bite,' I said.

She sat back and blew smoke at the Pelican. 'There were little rats at Nanny's. I love little rats. If I see a little rat I'm going to stand on its tail and put its head in my mouth and bite it off. I'm going to shake it until all its insides come out and I'm going to keep it as a pet until it falls apart and then I'm going to watch all the flies eat it and the birds peck it to pieces and then I'm going to watch it dissolve into dust.'

'That's nice.'

I tried to shut her out of my thoughts and return to my peaceful, relaxing, Sunday-morning state of mind. Living in the moment, that was the secret. No past, no future.

But instead a voice said, 'Hey, what's going on?'

Chewing gum and leaning against the wall was Billy the Hedgehog. His bristles were greased back and held in place by a pair of sunglasses which he'd pushed up and onto his forehead.

'Scraps said you were in an airing cupboard,' Plenty said.

'Scraps is confusing me with a bat,' said Billy.

'It was just a scenario,' I said. 'Come and sit down.'

'I like bats,' said Plenty with a dreamy look on her face. 'I knew a bat that landed on a baby's face once and it smothered her to death. The baby wriggled and wriggled but the bat held on with its claws and then the baby died and the bat went to sleep and it was really comfortable.'

Billy looked at her. 'Are you sure it was a bat that did that?'

'Yes. No one saw, anyway.'

Billy squeezed in on the steps. 'Actually,' he said, 'I wish I had been in an airing cupboard. I'm beat. I could do with a few hours tucked up among the towels and linen. I feel like I'm fading away. How come we don't do anything anymore? And what are we doing here?' He looked around. 'I've never seen this place before.'

I didn't have to ask where Billy had been. He wouldn't remember in the same way that he wouldn't know how he'd got from wherever he had been. He had merely shown up as I had; as Plenty had; as we all had. I looked more closely at Billy and saw that there were missing quills on his back and down near the roots some kind of fungus was spreading. That reminded me, I had a question for the Pelican. It was one I'd been meaning to ask for some time now.

'Hey Pelican, I have a question.'

The Pelican shifted its position and pointed its massive beak in my direction.

'What do you see when you're up there?' I said.

'Up where?'

'Up in the air. What do you see?'

'What do I see?'

With its wings outstretched the Pelican was the biggest creature amongst us, but it only had a tiny bit of brain trapped inside its skull.

'He means, when you're flying around doing your pelican-thing, looking for fish or whatever, and you look down, down towards the ground, what do you see?' Billy said. He had always been better at talking to the others than I had.

The Pelican's eyes crossed and uncrossed. 'What do I see?'

'Yes, what do you see?' hissed Plenty.

'Take it easy,' said Billy. 'Breathe deeply. There's no wrong answer. You fly, you look down, what do you see?'

'I see our home. I see the alleyway,' the Pelican said. 'Do I see the alleyway? Yes, I do. I see the alleyway. And the restaurant.'

'Well, that's good,' said Billy.

'But you see other stuff, right?' I said. 'Towns and houses and woods and fields? You saw this place, didn't you?'

There was a long, long pause. We waited.

'I see what's not this,' the Pelican said at last.

'What does that mean?' said Plenty.

'I don't know. Maybe he's going blind,' Billy said. 'Anyway, talking of alleyways and restaurants, where's our buddy, the always-angry restaurant owner? Shouldn't she be here, chasing us with her rolling pin? My day is not complete without some rolling pin action.'

'I'm hungry,' said Plenty. 'Let's go to the restaurant and she can chase us and we'll hide and then slip into her kitchen and eat all her food with napkins tied around our necks, and she can jump up and down outside the window because we've locked her out. And Scraps will say something funny and everything will be funny. Except her.'

'It's early,' I said. 'Let's wait. It's not too bad here.'

'I feel strange,' the Pelican said returning to life, its head rising up from the mess that was its body. 'I feel like we should be doing something. Or nothing. Or something.' It sank back into its feathers, now seemingly perplexed by its own words.

I was going to say that I felt the same way but a shout interrupted me.

'What was that?' said Billy. 'Somebody's calling.'

It was a loud and urgent shout and it seemed to come from nowhere and everywhere. I watched Plenty's whiskers twitch and her ears make minute adjustments as they assessed the sounds and vibrations around them.

'What?' said the Pelican, shifting into a more compact, defined shape. 'What can you hear? What can I hear? Nothing.'

I listened for the sounds that the Pelican couldn't hear; sniffed the air for scents it couldn't smell.

'Something,' I said.

'Running,' Plenty said. 'Over there.'

In the distance a dog was bounding across the concrete.

'It's chasing a ball,' said Billy.

'My ball?'

'No, not your ball.'

The dog was big and sand-coloured. A yellow Labrador. Its tongue was hanging out and its heavy head was lifting up and down as it ran. It looked clumsy and excited. It caught up with the ball, fell over itself and started running back, turning in a wide semi-circle and galloping away from us.

'That is one big dumb dog,' said Billy. 'All meat and muscle. Let's go. Dogs don't play nicely with us urban types.'

'No,' said Plenty. 'I'm not going because of a stupid dog.'

'I don't want the dog to come back,' the Pelican said. 'Do I? No, I don't.'

It released a pungent fishy smell as it stood up and extended its huge wingspan. The Pelican was getting out of there. It pushed with its feet and flapped its wings, and against all probability it lifted into the air like a galleon rising from the waves. Lice and feathers and bits of other birds' shit fell off as it ascended with its legs dangling beneath it.

'I'll see you back at the alleyway. Will I?'

'You will,' I said.

The Pelican continued to rise, the slow flapping of its flea-ridden wings somehow carrying it upwards until it seemed to shrink into a small, distant object that floated away towards the horizon and then disappeared entirely.

'Hey,' I called out after it. 'What can you see?'

I see what's not this.

'Here comes Goofy again,' said Billy. 'Or is it Pluto? I always get those two confused. How can a dog own a dog? Actually, let's talk about that another time.'

The ball bounced past us on the far side of the concrete and landed near the wire fence on the grassy slope. Again the yellow dog came into view, running from somewhere beyond our line of sight. It was closer than before and I could hear its rapid panting and sense the heat of its breath. There was saliva dripping from its teeth.

Plenty stood up and watched it, her tail big, the guide-hairs in her fur fully extended. I saw that her claws were out. I put my finger to my lips and caught her eye.

'Shhh,' I said.

'You shhh,' she said.

The dog caught up with the ball. It paused for a moment, breathing heavily, and then trotted down the slope, waiting for whoever had thrown it to catch up. It was about 20 yards away. It was a very big dog.

'Let's go,' I said.

'I want to stay,' said Plenty.

'Hey,' said Billy, distracting her. 'Forget the dog, where's your ball? We'll play catch in the alleyway.'

'Someone's stolen it.'

'No, it's here, look.' Billy picked it up and handed it to Plenty, who took it and seemed to forget all about the dog. 'What is all that stuff on it?' he said. 'Have you been sick again?'

'It's Pelican juice.'

'The Pelican has juice? You're joking with me. That's disgusting.'

'It's seen us,' I said.

The dog wasn't moving, it was simply looking at us, its legs set wide apart, its tongue hanging from its mouth, its eyes glowing like embers buried deep inside a coal fire.

'I'm going to rip off its face and scoop out the jelly behind its skin and make little balls out of it, and then suck out its brains and eat them and then sick it all up, and then make little balls out of that too,' said Plenty.

'That's a comprehensive itinerary,' Billy said. 'But I suggest we evacuate.'

'It's not like us,' I said. And it wasn't. I could sense it. 'It's not like us at all. Look at it.'

'I'm looking at it. But let's go.'

I walked along the side of the wall and Billy followed, so close that he was inhaling my tail. Behind us I heard Plenty say, 'I'm going to rip its face off.' She had become bored with her ball.

The dog barked. Or perhaps it roared. Whichever, a considerable proportion of my insides turned to water and I had to resist a strong urge to roll over and play dead.

'That's a big bark,' said Billy.

The dog ran at us, head down, ears flying, paws slipping and clattering on the concrete, gathering momentum like a runaway train. I saw in its eyes the desire to chase, catch and destroy. I knew that desire. In our alleyway we lived amongst dustbins overflowing with cardboard boxes and torn plastic bags and the rich smell of rotting food and the sour, bitter smell of personal waste – mostly mine, admittedly. Those smells both excited and repelled me and recently I'd been having a crazy desire to tear the bags and boxes apart, bury my face in the mushy mess and force the slime and grease into my mouth until my belly bloated.

'Time to leave,' Billy said, and he did, streaking along the wall with his quills trailing behind him and his sunglasses bouncing up and down on top of his head.

'I always forget how fast he can run,' Plenty said.

The dog was close.

I looked into my tobacco tin and saw that I had two cigarettes left. In some other place and time, I thought, there was a Scraps who lived a quiet and contented life with his feet up, a newspaper on his lap, pondering life and meeting up with old friends for a meal every now and then. A Scraps with a past to look back on and a future to contemplate.

'You go one way, I'll go another,' I said. 'He can't chase us both.'

The dog chased me.

4

Meadow Ward was for people with head injuries or, as in Tom's case, possible head injuries. Porters and nurses passed by his bay with patients on trolleys and in wheelchairs. Some patients had skulls that were held together by metal vices and others had cables coming out of their heads. Tom didn't want cables coming out of his head. He wanted to go home.

The sweet, seductive, sickliness of the anaesthetic had worn off but Tom was still trying to connect with the knowledge that he had been on a car park roof, fallen off and almost died. The puzzle was, why a multi-storey car park? Apart from the minor detail that he didn't drive, one of Tom's most defining characteristics was his fear of heights. He never went anywhere high. He was acrophobic through and through. Cut him anywhere and you would see the message: low good; high bad.

He looked at his damaged thumb and sucked his broken tooth and shifted his bruised buttocks. What was memory, he wondered – physically what was it? A jump between two neurons? A synaptic connection? An electrical crackle in that slab of meat that was his brain? He tried to imagine switching on the lights in his mind, lighting a crackling fuse that would illuminate the corridors, trying to remember anything about the previous day. But it was like turning on a black light in a black hole.

He remembered once, as a child, he had awoken in the middle of the night and looked up at the ceiling and felt that something was wrong. It was only after several minutes that he realised the bedroom door beside his bedhead was open. The door was right beside his head and slowly he'd sat up and peered around it onto the landing. It had been utterly, utterly dark. An impenetrable blackness so deep that he might have been looking up or down instead of across. A blackness so deep that his retina had sent pictures of itself to his brain. What had happened? He must have been sleepwalking or his parents had looked in or a draught had opened the door. But the sense of darkness, of a chasm beside him, remained.

He shook his head, careful of his dizziness. He could remember a childhood incident but he couldn't picture the previous day. And the more he tried, the more he became aware that there were other large chunks of his life he couldn't remember at all. But that was normal, wasn't it? Who could remember everything? All those minutes and hours since Day One of his life. Were they gone forever, like evaporated dreams, or were they still there, locked away in a place he couldn't find? Somewhere in his brain, was there a memory of being born, a memory of being in the womb?

Sunday had vanished and the days leading up to it were not much better. His recent past was foggy with scattered showers. He would remember one thing and then it would disappear and he would be thinking of something else.

'How are you doing, Tom?' said Maggie. She stood at the foot of his bed with her blue folder. 'Do you feel better than you did earlier, or worse?'

'Better.'

'Good.'

'Although I have a lisp.'

'You need a new tooth. How's the memory? Have you remembered what happened?'

'It's getting better but there's still a black hole where Sunday used to be.'

'You mean a hole or one of those star-things?'

'That's a very good question.' Tom imagined a black bullet hole in his head. 'No, not an actual hole. I suppose I mean one of those star-things. A collapsed star-thing. It's all in there but you can't get to it.'

'Does it come with a headache?'

'No. It doesn't come with anything. It's there but not there.' Tom lay back in his pillows and looked at Maggie. He was surprising himself. He was not someone who normally said very much to anyone, let alone someone who tried to express their thoughts.

'I see,' Maggie said.

Tom sat up again. 'So, now I'm wondering. Imagine, if yesterday is a black hole, then do you think that other nearby memories might disappear too? You know, like the day before and the day before that, and then weeks, months, even years; they will all be sucked into my missing memory until nothing is left?'

'You mean will you lose more memory?'

'Yes.'

'It's possible, but I don't think it would happen in the way you're describing. It's not like a spreading ink blot.'

'I like that.'

'But it's not. Think of it as a gap. A temporary gap. Like a missing jigsaw piece or an advent calendar with a door that needs opening.'

'An advent calendar?'

'Yes.'

'With chocolate?'

'If you like.'

Tom nodded. 'Do you think any more of the cardboard doors will close?'

Maggie laughed. 'I don't know. I hope not.'

After she'd left, Tom lay there thinking about his memory being like chocolate shapes in an advent calendar. Then he thought about a Christmas scene with Maggie wearing a Santa Claus hat and a red Christmas jumper, taking chocolate figures off a Christmas tree. He liked that image.

He investigated his bedside locker. On the shelf was his wallet, a set of keys, some coins and a bag of sticky liquorice sweets. No phone.

I don't want this. I don't need this.

He wondered where those words had come from. They were in his voice but had he said them?

Hanging beneath the shelf were his clothes: a heavy-knit blue cardigan, a white T-shirt with a cartoon on it and a pair of blue cords. A pair of worn brown zip-up boots were underneath on the floor, and folded up on top of those was a woollen overcoat, socks and a pair of boxer shorts.

The cartoon on the front of the T-shirt was a coloured print of the *Scraps* characters that had also been printed on a thousand mugs, posters and keyrings. Tom had drawn it in perspective: animals in the foreground and the always-angry restaurant owner in the background, smaller, running and shouting while shaking her rolling pin. A cloud of dust had been raised by her running feet. The Pelican's wings were open like a protective shield. It looked good: clean and compact, like a picture of superheroes.

Tom held up his bandaged thumb.

'Hi,' he said to the characters on his T-shirt. 'Don't expect too much from me for a while.'

It occurred to him that his brain was damaged. He put his hand against the bandage on his head. It didn't feel too bad; a bit tender; but nothing broken. How did he get that bruise? On the crates? After the bananas? The paramedics said he'd landed bottom first and then fallen onto his face. Did he hit his head on the way down? Did a bird fly into him?

How fast had he been travelling? If he hit a flying insect at speed would it leave a bruise like those tiny fragments of dust in outer space that can rip through a spacecraft? Maybe somewhere there was an insect hospital in which a traumatised bug was struggling to remember what had happened.

I don't know, I was just flying along, buzzing, and then… pow. Some kind of massive cartoonist hit me.

And then he wondered if a blow to the head had caused his fall.

Shortly before lunch a man came to see him who looked as if he'd recently rolled down a hill. His sparse hair stood up in wispy strands and his crumpled shirt was untucked at the front, allowing his heavy stomach to droop below like a billowing tumour.

'I'm the senior consultant, Brian Wiley,' he said. He shook Tom's hand. He sat on the plastic chair beside Tom's bed and slipped into a horizontal position while he leafed through the blue folder. His chin rested on his chest and his glasses rested on the end of his nose. From a distance he might have been asleep if it wasn't for the turning of pages. He looked at Tom over his glasses and said, 'Here, we like to talk about losses, deficits we call them, and you seem to have none other than some localised amnesia. Of course, that may have a psychological cause. You have suffered a trauma, after all. To be honest, we weren't sure whether to bring you here or the Fracture Ward. Physically- and neurologically-speaking, there is very little damage. Your blood pressure is normal. We gave you a CT scan and that was clear. There is nothing to indicate that you have a heart condition or suffered any kind of stroke or aneurism. I don't suppose you can remember if you fainted?'

Tom shook his head.

'No? Well, people faint for all sorts of reasons: anxiety, dehydration, hunger, alcohol. I know people who have sneezed and fainted.'

He sucked his pen and flicked through the remaining pages.

'Physically, you have a broken front tooth, a dislocated thumb, a bump on the head and two tenderised buttocks. Not surprising: dropping through a canvas roof at forty miles an hour is going to leave a mark. And we had to remove some of the flower-bed from your mouth. No sign of the other part of your tooth, I'm afraid.'

'That's a shame.'

'Yes.'

Tom felt sad that there was a bit of him out there somewhere alone. He wondered where it was. He felt sorry for it. Had someone picked it up? Or was it lying in the earth surrounded by puzzled ants who wondered what it meant, in the same way that he had once stared at Stonehenge and scratched his head. Perhaps his missing tooth would become the basis of a religion or be the catalyst for scientific development amongst insects.

'Forty miles an hour. Is that how fast I was going?'

'That or thereabouts. We put the collar on you just in case, but I think that can come off now. Any discomfort around your neck? No? There's no damage to your back, thank goodness. No chipped vertebrae. As for that bump on your head' – he leaned forwards again and lifted up the bandaging, his podgy face near to Tom's – 'it seems to be more surface bruising than anything we need to worry about. No corresponding lesions or bruises on the right hemisphere of your brain, the so-called creative side, or anywhere else for that matter. Have you noticed any changes in your thoughts? In the world around you?'

'Just the slight lack of memory.'

Wiley nodded and looked at his notes again. 'There's nothing we can do for the tooth. It's snapped along the gum-line. You'll have to have the root out. Do you have a good dentist? Mine's a butcher. If you can afford it, go for an implant. If you can't afford it, still go for an implant. Bridges fly out in restaurants and you're too young to have a plate.'

He closed the folder, dropped it onto the end of the bed, heaved himself into an upright position and leaned forwards, his hands on his knees.

'I'd like to keep you here for another day or so. Not too long. Just to see how things work out. I think we may do one more scan too. Any questions?'

'I'm not… there's no damage? To my brain?'

'Not as far as we can tell. We'll keep an eye on you, and if you feel any loss or impairments or changes to your thoughts, your moods, or anything like that, then you tell us.'

He looked at his watch.

'You've been here for twenty-four hours and for most of that time you've been asleep. It's very early days. Don't be surprised if your thoughts are a bit foggy. Things might come back over time, or suddenly, or not at all. Beware false memories, though. There will be a temptation to fill in the gaps. Confabulation. Don't try to force it. If you remember, you remember. If you don't, you don't. To me, you seem to be functioning perfectly normally. You'll meet Doctor Muller later. She'll talk to you about a possible discharge plan and perhaps a visit to the memory clinic. Do you have a family, Mister Hannah?'

'Yes. I have a wife, Karen.'

'Children?'

'Two. Teenagers. Holly and Dan.'

'Well, you may have to lean on them for a little while. Lead a healthy lifestyle and try not to worry about things. Easier said than done, I know, but it works. Keep an eye on your weight too because you're a big fellow. I know I can't talk but I'm not lying in a hospital bed. Physically, I can't see any reason why you shouldn't make a full recovery but don't pretend that this hasn't happened. It has.'

Tom's day continued as if he were the fixed point in a revolving carousel. Nurses made notes and took his blood pressure and temperature; porters collected and deposited patients; cleaners mopped floors and sprayed surfaces with their blue-gloved hands. A magazine trolley went past and then a tea-trolley and then a drugs trolley, followed by the magazine trolley again.

Towards lunchtime a stern, silent doctor stopped by, looked at Tom's notes, peered into his eyes and left without a word. Was she really a doctor? Tom wondered. She could have been a vet or a mortician for all he knew. The sounds of hospital life, the beeps and buzzers and bells, became entwined with Tom's own background hiss that ebbed and flowed between his ears until he couldn't be completely sure if what he was hearing was inside or outside his head.

Bee came by and gave him painkillers, removed the dressing from his head and took away his collar as if he were being unwrapped and prepared for display. And then, not long before lunch, she and Maggie returned with towels and a bowl, and took down his *Nil-By-Mouth* sign.

'Hungry?'

'Starving, but I'll need a straw.' His mouth was still swollen, hidden beneath his monstrous moustache. He looked at the towels. 'You're not going to give me a bed-bath are you?'

'Would you like one?' said Bee.

'No.'

Maggie laughed. 'We're joking, but talking of straws...' She drew the curtains and put on a pair of her own blue gloves. Ten minutes later his catheter had been removed. Together they helped him off his rubber ring and into a chair while they remade the bed and gave him clean hospital pyjamas instead of the thin gown he'd been wearing. The pyjamas were far too small: the trousers flew above his ankles and the jacket stretched across his back and squeezed his stomach into a series of button-bursting bulges.

'They're a bit snug,' said Bee. 'I'll try to get something bigger. Can your wife bring something in?'

'I'll ask her.'

'That reminds me,' said Maggie. 'I still owe you a phone. You can use the bathroom now, if you want. I'll show you where it is. You haven't had anything to eat since yesterday so you'll be a bit wobbly. We'll make sure you get something to eat when the lunch comes round.' She opened the curtains, and Tom stood up and assumed his full height. He towered over Maggie and Bee. He felt like Colossus returning from the grave, his massive head turning this way and that, surveying the landscape.

'How do you feel?' Maggie said. 'Tell me if you are dizzy.'

He felt wobbly but not too bad. 'I'm okay.'

He followed Maggie to the toilet where she left him with a warning: 'The first time you go after the catheter has been removed, it can feel a bit uncomfortable,' she said. 'Call one of us if you have any problems.' Tom entered the toilet and locked the door. On the wall beside him, over the wash-basin, was a mirror. He turned and looked at himself.

Sometimes on medieval tombs the faces of the dead occupants are captured in images cut from stone and pock-marked by years of erosion and neglect. Tom's stone-lidded eyes and wildly curling hair, beard and moustache had the same look. His beard was mostly stubble but the moustache was huge and luxuriant and as wide as his head. It was not a moustache that could be grown over a weekend, or a week, or even a month. It was a commitment; a long-term project; a way of life.

He lifted his head and studied his swollen lip, battered gum and the gap where his tooth had been. He stuck his tongue into it and wiggled it about, then closed his eyes and tried to imagine poking a memory into the gap in his mind and wiggling it about.

He opened his eyes again and looked at the bruise beside his right eye. It was bright purple, about the size of an egg, and it had lifted part of his eyebrow outwards, as if he did indeed have a small egg under his skin. He looked more closely, searching for some indentation or mark that might give a clue as to what had caused it. But he could see nothing.

He turned his attention to urinating. There was a moment of inaction and then agony. It was like passing shards of broken glass. Had he been one of his own cartoon characters, then jagged lightning bolts would have emanated from his groin while he danced a jig of pain. He made a mental note to question Maggie on her use of the phrase 'a bit uncomfortable'.

He washed his hands, left the toilet and walked back towards his bay. The fluorescent lights on the ceiling were heavy on his eyelids and he felt as if he had stood up after half an hour in a very hot bath. He stopped walking and leaned against a wall to keep his balance.

At the far end of the ward, near the entrance to his bay, he saw a stout woman with a lunch trolley. She had stopped to read a newspaper. She seemed engrossed. 'Hi,' he called out. 'What's on the menu today?' His voice sounded over-loud in his ears and he wished he hadn't said anything.

She looked up. She seemed familiar. There were stains on her chef's jacket and he could see strands of hair that had escaped her headband, and wrinkles on her forehead. Her chest rose and fell beneath her over-long apron, and there was something odd about her shoes. They were black, rubbery and formless, with thick laces tied in a large bow.

You were never good at drawing feet.

He bent over and smelled blood in his nose. He felt very sick.

'Can you hear it?' she said.

Her voice was flat. It was a voice to be seen and not heard; a voice unused to creating waves that could tickle his eardrums; a voice used to being heard inside, not out. Tom looked at her again and into her eyes. They were small, red-rimmed and blue. She had small, blue eyes; eyes, not dots. He took a step backwards. She looked angry; very, very angry. She had a rolling pin in her hand.

'You...' he said, and then gave up. His mouth felt clumsy, sticky and dry, and his tongue stuck to the gap in his teeth.

'The dog,' she said. 'Can you hear it?'

Tom looked around. Where were all the nurses? He shook his head. 'No.' But suddenly, in the distance, came the sound of a dog barking, and like the hiss between his ears he thought it had always been there. How had he missed it? He walked with stiff legs back to his bay and climbed into his bed.

'Are you in a dream?' he said to himself. He could have been. It was possible he had fainted in the toilet or keeled over when he had leant against the wall. Or perhaps the anaesthetic was still in his system, filling the black hole in his brain with its sweet, seductive, sickliness again.

Heavy footsteps walked along the corridor towards his bay. Tom closed his eyes. He could smell stale cooking and stale grease and fat from frying and roasting and butchering.

'Don't,' he said in a loud voice that seemed to click and scratch against the air.

'Don't what?' said a friendly voice.

Tom opened his eyes. It was Maggie. She was by his bed with a cup of tea in her hand.

'Are you all right?'

The light behind her seemed brighter than usual, heavier, a weight pushing down on his eyelids, and for an awful moment he couldn't remember who he was or where he was. It was like waking in a room without air. He was suffocating, unable to find the door, unable to get out, unable to breathe.

'Tom, what's the matter?' Now Maggie sounded like a nurse. 'Come on, sit up. Sit up, Tom, and look at me. Look at me.'

Tom looked at her and the panic subsided. He was breathing again. He had always been breathing. Maggie's hands were on his shoulder. She looked at him carefully, searching his face as he'd searched his bruise, searching for a clue. He pushed his moustache upwards and outwards, and ran his tongue around his swollen gum. He felt very weak.

'Wow,' he said and took a deep breath.

'What happened?'

I saw one of my cartoon characters walking down the corridor.

Oh really?

Is that normal?

Sure. That happens all the time. Meet my friend, Harvey.

'Nothing,' Tom said. 'Just a wobbly moment. I think going to the toilet took it out of me. It's not going to hurt that much every time, is it?'

Maggie studied him. 'You look pale,' she said, and then, 'I've brought you some tea. I think you should eat something too. Lunch will be here soon. We've ordered you something already. You can have normal food but mind your tooth.' She stood by his bed with the look of a builder assessing whether or not the concrete had set properly. Tom wondered if it had. 'How are you feeling now?'

'Fine. Really.' He heard the trolley rattling along the top of the ward, coming towards his bay. 'Actually, I'm not that hungry.'

'You should eat.'

'I don't think I could manage anything.'

He looked away, towards the window, and for the first time noticed that the view was onto the hospital car park – a multi-storey car park. That was sensitive.

The trolley stopped.

'Normally you choose in the morning but you were exempt earlier so we ordered for you.'

Tom turned to look. A man was waiting to hand out the food. Maggie passed Tom the plate.

'Chicken pie?'

'Lovely.'

While he ate, Maggie worked at the nurses' station. He was

aware that she glanced up at him now and then, and when he had finished she came over.

'How are you feeling? Better than before?'

'Much better, thank you.'

'Good. What happened? You looked upset.'

Tom shook his head and smiled. 'Really, it was nothing. Just the excitement of going to the toilet. I think I may have been dreaming. I think I got into bed and dropped off. Like a sudden power nap.'

'You think you dropped off? You were asleep?'

'Yes.'

'So you didn't have some kind of... episode.'

'Not at all.'

'You didn't look asleep. You looked distressed.'

'I look like that sometimes.'

'When you're asleep.'

'Yes.'

She looked unimpressed. 'That's unusual. And how's the memory?'

'Getting better, I think. You know those moments when you're falling asleep while you're driving and you don't know it? You see a road and cars in front of you, and then you blink for a second and when you open your eyes the car is closer, and then you doze some more and the car is right in front of you, and if you're not careful you'll crash. You don't see the gaps but you know they're there. That's how I feel.'

Maggie nodded. 'I saw a film like that. Somebody was driving while they were asleep and when they woke up their car was covered in hay and chickens. They drove through a house and came out the other side with a washing line on them.'

'I've seen that film too. That's how it feels. Not like a car with washing on it but like the bit about nodding off. I know there are gaps but most of it hangs together.'

'And you remember yesterday?'

'No. Yesterday is still a hidden chocolate.'

'Pardon?'

'The advent calendar.'

Maggie laughed and sat down in the chair by his bed. 'I remember I was driving home one night and the car in front was going slowly and kept braking, and I thought they had a dog on the back seat, and I don't know why but I started waving, and I poked my tongue out and waggled my fingers and did everything I could to make it do something. And then when we reached a set of lights and I pulled up behind, I saw it wasn't a dog at all, it was an old woman wearing a neck brace – and then I saw the disabled sticker in the window and I knew she was in a wheelchair facing backwards.'

'What did you do?'

'I pretended I was looking for something in my bag and waited for the lights to change.'

Tom laughed. 'Embarrassing.'

'Very. Things aren't always what they seem. Like those optical illusions. One moment it's an old woman's face, and the next it's a young woman looking away. How can an old woman in a neck brace look like a dog? But she did. Sometimes the mind plays tricks like that.'

Tom nodded. 'Noted. So, we're still talking about me looking distressed?'

'Yes.'

'Do you think my mind is playing tricks on me? You don't think I just dropped off and had a dream.'

'I don't know, did you?'

'Do you ever wake up from a dream and wish it was true?'

'All the time.'

They looked at each other in silence and then Tom said, 'Even if my mind is playing tricks then that's normal, don't you think? Have you ever caught sight of your reflection when you're not expecting it? It's like seeing a stranger. That's because you don't expect to see yourself. You're out of context. It takes a moment for the brain to catch up. It's the same when you hear your own voice on a tape. It sounds boxy. You don't sound like you think you sound. I don't mean you specifically, I mean in general.'

'Is that how you feel? Boxy?'

'No, I'm just saying. I'm not used to being in hospital. I don't usually fall off car parks. It's all a bit strange. Normal things are out of context. When I see myself unexpectedly, I look like Herman Munster with a moustache. But that's because I don't expect to see myself, so my mind makes an association. The wrong association.'

'Herman who?'

'Herman Munster. Don't say you've never heard of him. He had bolts in his neck to hold his head on. Played by Fred Gwynne. But do you see what I'm saying?'

'You're saying I don't have to write anything in my blue folder. You just had a bad dream.'

'Exactly. And I felt panicky, that's all. Just for a moment.'

'I don't want you to confuse wanting to go home with getting better. If you don't feel right, then you should tell me or one of the other nurses. Or the doctors.'

'I will.'

Maggie sighed and then laughed. 'Okay. Good. See that you do.' She stood up, smoothing her tunic. 'I'd better get back to work.'

'Thank you.'

'For what?'

'For taking the time to talk.'

'That's all right. I'll look up Herman Munster later.'

'Do. He was a great character. And bolts are a good idea, too. If you have a headache you can take your head off, rinse it out and put it back on. All neat and tidy.'

'Is that what you do in your cartoons?'

Tom looked up. He was surprised.

'Bee recognised you and we looked you up on the internet.'

'I'm flattered. What did you find?'

'Well, lots about *Scraps* but not much about you – mostly interviews.'

'I'm a social media non-combatant. I keep out of sight as much as possible. Difficult when you're six-feet four inches and weigh 18 stone.'

'There is still a lot out there – *Scraps* blogs, forums, books, models. There's even a website devoted to your moustache. I think it's got its own fan-base. I didn't realise how big it is.'

'My moustache?'

Maggie laughed. 'No. Your cartoon. You must be good at it.'

'It's all I can do. I have no other skills.'

'Did you always want to be a cartoonist?'

'Always. Did you always want to be a nurse?'

'I wanted to be a zoologist,' she said. 'When I was little I wanted to wear safari shorts and drive around in a Jeep and have a pet lion. Then one day I walked round to see my friend and a dog chased me all the way home. That was the end of that ambition.'

'That's sad. I always wanted to draw cartoons, I can remember that much. I would like to live my life in a three-frame cartoon strip. Bang, bang, bang. Clean and simple. God should have been a cartoonist. Perhaps He is. If I were God I'd give everyone bolts to hold their heads on.'

He paused. She was watching him.

'I don't think I am God, just in case you're wondering.'

'I wasn't.' She laughed again. 'Now I really must get back to work.'

She walked away and he lay back on the pillows, closed his eyes and after a while, he really did fall asleep and dream.

5

Tom dreamed he was a student again and Karen was wearing shorts and a vest-top and sitting beside him in his car. Tom's car was an old heap that had ripped seats and dodgy brakes and a pre-ignition problem that made it cough and lurch long after the engine had been switched off. The doors didn't shut properly and they were tied together with rope, which they had to sit on in order to keep it taut.

They drove through country lanes and empty roads to the coast, smoking cigarettes and sharing cans of cider. They sang along to songs on the car radio with voices so wildly out of tune that it made them laugh until they couldn't sing anymore.

The windows were open and the breeze was warm and the air smelled of summer and in the dream Tom told her seriously that he was going to be a cartoonist, and that he had an idea for a character, a fox. Karen laughed, a happy, musical laugh, and kissed his face.

They were in a café by a pebble beach. They sat close together at a table on plastic chairs and shouted to make themselves heard over each other's voices and played up to the frowns and stares of other people who were eating quietly.

They were on a beach and sat on the pebbles and Tom kissed her. The salty smell of her skin and the wetness of her lips made his

skin tingle so that every touch was like an electric charge. She held the
back of his head and pulled him down onto the stones, and he took
his weight on his arms so as not to crush her. She had a tiny blemish
on her cheek; a mark so small it was hardly visible.

It was night and they were in his room and in the shadows she
stood by the window and took off her clothes – a silent silhouette
swaying from side to side. She got into bed next to him and pulled
the bedclothes up to her chin and lay for a moment, lit by moonlight,
with her eyes closed. When she opened them again her face was calm
and serene and she looked up at him from behind the bars of her lacquered eyelashes. She was perfectly still, silent, unblinking, scarcely
breathing, and then she laughed and reached out to him.

'Hello, Tom.'

Tom opened his eyes and saw, looking down on him like pale
ghosts gathered around a deathbed, Karen, Holly and Dan. He looked
at them while his mind cleared out the dream of long ago.

'Hi,' he said. 'I was going to call but you're here. How are you
all?' He struggled up the bed until he was in a more upright position and could see them more clearly. 'Oh God, what a time.' He gestured around the bay. 'Look at me. I'm in hospital. Did you find me
all right? Is it visiting time?' He looked at Karen. 'I was just dreaming
about you. Really.'

The Karen beside his bed was older than the Karen in his dream.
She stood tall and aloof and remote, and looked slim buttoned up and
belted in her overcoat. Her face was made-up and her hair was tied
back in a businesslike fashion. She still looked calm and serene, though
impassive, with high cheek bones and cool eyes. She had a smoker's
stance: one arm folded, elbow in hand, hand on chin. She looked
down on Tom as if she were considering him as an interesting speci-
men on display in a bed.

Beside her was Holly, a heavy 15-year-old, looking beefier than
she might with her hands in her pockets and her hips pushed forwards.
Her wide-set eyes had a puffy look as if she'd been crying, although
she hadn't. Holly never cried. You could bruise her but you would
never break her. Half-girl and half-woman, she was raw and incom-
plete; scruffy in her sloppy, sawn-off jeans and over-sized T-shirt.

And on the other side of the bed was Dan, two years younger
than Holly and built like his mother: slim and cat-like; his face partly

hidden by an overhanging thatch of hair as impenetrable as a hedgehog's stare. A cocky, geeky boy, full of himself and the assurance of his age, confident that he would live forever, eat pizza and be cool like all his box-set heroes.

Karen leaned in and kissed Tom on the cheek.

'How are you feeling?' she said.

'Like I've fallen off a roof.'

'You have fallen off a roof, Dad,' said Dan.

It was suddenly very important to Tom that they were there. He hadn't realised how alone he'd been feeling. Shock, or something like it, rolled over him and took his breath away. He had fallen 60 feet; flown through the air and hit the ground – even if a wet flower-bed and a pile of bananas had got in his way. Sometimes too much luck can be as scary as too little. He wiped his eyes.

'What's the matter?' said Holly. 'Don't cry.'

'I'm not. How have you been? Did the police come? How did you know I was here?'

'The police came this morning,' said Karen. 'We wondered where you were.'

'This morning?'

'We weren't there yesterday.'

'They came to the house,' said Holly. 'I thought they were going to tell us you were dead.'

'But there was only one of them,' said Dan. 'So I knew you were all right. They always send two people if someone's dead.'

'They should say that straight away,' said Holly. 'The first thing a policeman should say when he goes to someone's house is "Don't worry, he or she is not dead", or whatever.'

'But it wasn't a policeman, it was a policewoman,' said Dan. 'She asked Mum if it would be all right if she came in. Mum said, "What's it about?" And the police lady said it was about you. And Mum said, "What about you?" And the police person said you'd fallen off a roof.'

Tom looked at Karen. 'What did you say?'

'I said, come in.'

'She sat in the living room,' said Dan. 'She was really sweaty. Holly kept looking at her.'

'No I didn't.'

'Did she say what happened to me? Why I fell off?'

'No.'

'What were you doing up there?' said Holly. 'Why did you fall off?'

'I don't know,' Tom said. 'I can't remember anything about yesterday. Did you see me yesterday? Did you come here?'

'We've come today.'

'It was a great way for a cartoonist to fall,' said Dan. 'Were you running in the air until you realised? Did you leave a cloud of dust and a crater?'

'Who knows? I might have.'

'A bit unlikely, though,' said Karen. 'Don't you think? Falling off a roof onto a crate of bananas.'

'It's not Dad's fault they were there.'

'Do you think we'll have to pay for the bananas? They'll be all covered in blood.'

'Dan.'

'What do you mean, unlikely?' said Tom.

'Well, I mean,' said Karen, 'normally somebody falling that far would die. Wouldn't they?'

'Splat,' said Dan.

Tom looked at them but their voices were diminishing, fading out. He looked beyond his family at the nurses' station where Maggie and her cohort were gathered, laughing and talking. He could hear Maggie's musical laugh. He tried to hold onto the sound but he felt as if he were retreating from the colourful, three-dimensional world around him into some dark place, telescoping back into nothingness, into a chalked outline, into an airless room without a door.

Tom, what's the matter? Come on, sit up. Sit up, Tom, and look at me. Look at me.

'Tom, what's the matter?'

'Here,' he said. 'Give me your hand. Let me hold your hand.'

Karen gave him her hand and he held it tightly and looked up at her.

What do you see when you're up there? What do you see when you're up there and you look down? The Pelican looked down. It saw Karen holding Tom's hand. It saw children shouting and chanting and pushing and pointing in a playground. It saw a big man fall hard against a table and an old woman fall slowly to the ground. And it saw a great well of darkness. And far below, deep within the well, it heard the distant howl of a dog.

The Pelican stretched out its wings and veered from left to right, sweeping and swooping like a child pretending to fly, feeling each individual feather lift and flutter – caked though they were with sticky fat and grease and multiple wriggling larvae. Its eyes were closed and the wind streamed along its beak and over its head and away to places that the Pelican would never visit or ever know existed.

Against the empty blue sky the Pelican was a splotch of oil paint; a grey-brown-yellow-white splotch that suddenly didn't seem to move at all. Against the infinite blue sky nothing would seem to move. Even the Pelican, free to fly wherever it wished, would, against an infinite blue sky, remain in the middle of the frame, caught in its moment of flight. Only if you looked beyond the frame would you see its imperceptible movement. Only if you looked beyond the frame would you feel the wind and smell the day and hear the beat of the Pelican's wings.

6

http://www.tashfanz.com/tash%2911interview.htm

A Belgian television interview with Tom Hannah from January 2012.

On 1 January 2012, Tom Hannah was interviewed by Germaine Kiecke for a New Year's Day edition of her late night arts television show *Kiecke in Conversation*. The following is an extract from that interview.

Germaine Kiecke (to camera): Thomas Arthur Stevenson Hannah – Tash to his public; Tom to his friends – is one of just a handful of British cartoonists whose work is regularly syndicated around the world. His cartoon strips have spun off into books, clothing, homeware, games and cosplay conventions, and are discussed daily across dozens of internet fora, blogs and tweets. Among his peers, he is known as the cartoonists' cartoonist, and for almost 15 years he has been delighting us all with his weekly cartoon strip, *Scraps*, about a smart urban fox who wages war against waste and an always-angry restaurant owner, along with his friends Plenty the Cat, Billy the Hedgehog and the Pelican. Tom, welcome and thank you for coming in. And a happy new year to you.

Tom Hannah: Thank you – and a happy new year to you, too.

Germaine: Let me jump straight in – is Scraps you?

Tom (laughing): He has many traits I admire but I haven't got a tail.

Germaine: You share the same eco-ethics. Are the direct methods of Scraps and his colleagues something you aspire to in real life? I'm thinking, for example, of the so-called Freegan Movement.

Tom: Bin-dipping? I'm too squeamish for that but I admire those that do. It makes a lot of sense to me.

Germaine: Can I take you back to the beginning? You wrote once that cartoonists find their vocation early in life. Was that true for you?

Tom: In terms of a vocation, I think so, yes. I can't imagine doing anything else and if I did, I'd probably still draw whenever I could.

Germaine: You were born to be a cartoonist?

Tom: Well, I didn't come out of the womb rubbing my hands and saying, 'Right, give me a pencil.' But I do think I was hard-wired with all the necessary attributes – and the desire. I just needed to be shown the form.

Germaine: Like a potter being shown clay?

Tom: More like a potter being shown a pot. When I was young, pre-school, I used to look at comics and drive my mother crazy asking what they were saying. So she taught me to read to get some peace. Just the basics, you know, 'Look look, see Spot. See Spot jump.' That sort of thing.

Germaine: So it was the words as much as the pictures?

Tom: Well, yes, I mean there are words in comics, and nowadays I like reading prose and poetry, and I love the way a well-told tale creates images in your mind, your own personal cinema. I like that very much. I think there's a lot of crossover between the mechanics of literature and the mechanics of a cartoon strip. But with comics I just got the whole thing immediately, it was my medium: speech bubbles, movement lines, looking out of the frame and talking to the reader. It all seemed so right to me.

Germaine: I'm interested in that appeal to you, the appeal that you're describing. Was it cartoon drawings specifically?

Tom: Very specifically cartoon drawing. Not illustrations or sketches or pen and ink or anything like that. Cartoons. And comics were my entry point. Characters with blobby noses and crazy hair and knobbly elbows and talking pets, and all the visual, cartoon grammar that goes with it. You know, the physics of a cartoon. But a good cartoon strip is more than that. There's comedy, absolutely, but there's more. Or there can be more.

Germaine: I'd like to come back to the 'more' later on, and also to the grammar. But for the moment, there you are: a pre-school Tom Hannah and already you know what you want to do in life?

Tom: Not quite, but pretty soon after. I went to school and I hated it. On day one I wanted to go home; and on day one-thousand-and-one I still wanted to go home. That's how it's always been for me. I don't like having to be somewhere. I'm a home-bird. Fortunately, a kindly teacher took pity on me and dumped me in the school library.

Germaine: This is your first day at school?

Tom: Maybe not the first day, but probably the first week. I was miserable. Always crying. Anyway, I remember being in a library, a little primary school library – low tables, orange chairs, the smell of crayons, posters all over the walls, that sort of thing – and there, on a book-stand with all the elephant stories and big bear adventures, was a Tintin book. Hard-cover; dog-eared and in French.

Germaine: Ah, Remi. A man consumed by his creation.

Tom: Perhaps. But at five I wasn't thinking about that. I remember picking the book up and looking at it and feeling like I'd met an old friend. Even the feel of it was good. The whole tactile experience of holding a hardback book filled with tightly drawn, colourful cartoons struck a huge chord. I wanted to own it because it seemed so much more permanent than a paper comic. Coming across that book made a big difference. A massive difference. It helped me get through... everything really. I knew then, completely, that I wanted to be part of that creative world. I wanted to be on the pen-side of the page. I couldn't understand a word of it but I was hooked.

Germaine: You mentioned your mother. How important were your parents and your upbringing to your creative development?

Tom: Crucial. My dad was an architect, so there were always plenty of drawing materials in the house, and my mother was a barrister. They were both very left-wing so there were a lot of opinions bouncing about, although Dad was relaxed and easy-going. Mum was much more forthright and competitive. But they were busy so I spent a lot of time on my own reading and watching television. That was also important. I don't believe that television, game-playing or anything like that is a waste of time. It's the opposite. You learn and your mind expands. I read every book in the house and I watched everything on television. Endlessly.

Germaine: Some games and some television can be very...

Tom: Violent?

Germaine: Sexist.

Tom: That's a fair point. There's good and bad.

Germaine: Is it that simple for you?

Tom: Life is complex; messy. I know that. But there's

a term chefs use in the kitchen: 'work clean'. I like that approach. So yes, it's that simple for me.

Germaine: You have a sister.

Tom: Yes. She's ten years older than me so it was a bit like being an only child with three parents.

Germaine: Were you spoiled?

Tom: Horribly.

Germaine: Paint me a picture of this young Tom Hannah. Or rather, draw me a cartoon.

Tom: Okay, well, we're looking at a large, lumpy and shy child; something of a loner. We lived in south London in a big, ramshackle house in the corner of a cul-de-sac. It was tucked away and set back and looked like something the Munsters should live in. You remember the Munsters?

Germaine: I wanted to be Yvonne de Carlo.

Tom: There used to be a local newsagent and inside there was this incredible smell of comics and sweets. There was something about the paper or the ink that they used.

Germaine: I feel the same way about a library I used to visit. The smell of well-thumbed pages on a wet afternoon is very evocative. Those big hardback books in heavy plastic covers.

Tom: That's right. I used to visit our local library every week. The whole experience was a ritual. Kicking along the streets on my way there, not in any rush, the big stone steps, the heavy door, the quiet, and all these over-laden shelves of endless choice and the thump-click of the librarian's stamp – eight books in and eight books out. It's a tyre garage now.

Germaine: You used the term 'loner'. Were you also lonely?

Tom: I don't think so. Maybe solitary is a better word. I've always been good at compartmentalising. So if there is something I don't like, I just stash it away somewhere and don't think about it. That's the great thing about imagination. It's huge and you can lose things there – if you want to. And you can go there whenever you want. I didn't choose to be solitary, I just was, and it didn't bother me. Now I like it. I prefer it.

Germaine: Were you picked on at school? Solitary children are often made the outsiders.

Tom: It's hard for me to say. I think there was some bullying. I remember a beefy girl and her brother were less than friendly, and I was big when I was young so there was always going to be some name-calling, but I think it just washed over me. I was very happy. In those days I used to play out a lot. There was an old root ball that had been dug up, about ten feet across, and I made it my secret fortress until somebody set fire to it. The beefy girl, actually. I can still see her doing it. Imagination played a big part in all of my games. I suppose it does for all children. It's a shame so many people forget how to play. Anyway, to a degree physical things were just props for what was going on inside my mind. They still are.

Germaine: Were you good at art at school?

Tom: I was okay but I don't think I had any defined style at that point. I enjoyed it, though. Our art teacher was a boozy, rugby-playing type but he had an eye for good work. He didn't teach us anything. He sat around, smoking and reading, and just let us do what we wanted. I'm sure nowadays he'd be sacked, but I responded well to that kind of freedom. I liked being left alone to get on with things. I still do.

Germaine: You went to a good sixth form college. Was the atmosphere different there?

Tom: Sixth form was difficult for me. I liked maths and music as well as art but the way the curriculum was designed, I couldn't combine those subjects. It was either the sciences or the humanities. Art was treated as vocational along with metalwork, woodwork and so on. Also, I discovered pubs.

Germaine (laughing): That sounds like classic training for an artist.

Tom: I was lucky. I built up enough of a portfolio to get into the local art college.

Germaine: Let's get on to *Scraps*. How did that come about?

Tom: I was 20 years old and part-way through a BA in illustration and photography. I shared a house with three other students, all sculptors, and the place was a tip, filled with papier-mâché manikins, balls of clay, lumps of stone, half-finished plasticine busts. There was one of me. They'd made me look like a gargoyle.

Germaine: The cruelty of youth.

Tom: To be honest, it was a pretty fair likeness. None of these people ever washed or did their laundry or showed any sign of personal hygiene and so I used to spend a lot of time in the garden.

Germaine: Because of the smell?

Tom: Partly. It was definitely a pungent house. But also because they had all told me at various times that the only reason they wanted to be artists was to get women to pose naked for them. So there were always women coming round, responding to adverts to be an artist's model, and these delinquent no-hopers would spend all day trying to encourage them to pose naked for them. It was very sordid. Anyway, being just a doodler of lines and dots and a long way down the artists' pecking order, I got pushed into the garden most of the time.

Germaine: What did you think of that?

Tom: I didn't mind too much. I liked being outside.

Germaine: I mean, what did you think of their motives? You said it was sordid. Would you say it was a sexist environment? Misogynistic?

Tom: Sordid is the wrong word. Sad might be better. These were students who were scared of women and had to hide behind their paintbrushes. Nothing horrible ever happened. I thought they were all crazy. Why did those rancid hooligans think any woman would want to come to our cesspit?

Germaine: But some did.

Tom: Some did. Yes.

Germaine: Okay. So there you are, in the garden.

Tom: That's right. One evening I was out there, staring at a broken fence, when I realised I was looking directly into the eyes of a fox – a big red fox – and it was staring right back at me.

Germaine: Were you nervous?

Tom: I've thought about that. It seems dramatic now but at the time I thought, here I am, face to face with a wild animal, a carnivore, a dangerous predator, and it's just the two of us. It wasn't a pet or something that had been trained, it was a creature that lived by rules I didn't know anything about. But what I saw was curiosity and intelligence and I saw calmness, too, and I liked that. I didn't feel worried. I said, 'Make yourself at home.' Of course, he didn't say anything.

Germaine: Of course.

Tom: He waited and took his time, sizing me up, and then he stepped into full view.

Germaine: He was a he?

Tom: That's a good point. I don't know. He might have been a she. I've always thought of it as male but perhaps that's wrong. Thinking about it, it could just as well have been a vixen on the hunt for some food for her cubs.

Germaine: I'd like to come back to the gender aspect of your work, but for now, let's say it was a he.

Tom: He had a circular way of moving so wherever he stood he always seemed to be facing me, as if his head were a mask and there were puppeteers behind him.

Germaine: Did he come up to you?

Tom: No, he checked out the various tins and bottles and cartons that were planted in our garden and then he wandered back to the fence and slipped through the gap. When he went his brush flicked upwards and it was like a farewell salute. I ran down to the fence and looked through the gap but there was just another garden on the other side.

There was no sign of the fox, no sign of any other animal, but that encounter changed everything for me. I felt that I had seen something worth seeing, that I had made contact with another world.

Germaine: You seem to recall it vividly. It was a big moment?

Tom: A very big moment. I remember I went indoors and there was a girl in the living room telling one of the sculptors to hand over his camera before she punched his greasy fucking head in...

Germaine: We'll have to edit that, Tom.

Tom: I'm sorry.

Germaine: That's okay.

Tom: So, normally I would have watched her do that but I was so taken with my encounter I completely ignored her. I went upstairs, got my pad and pen and straight away I started drawing. I wanted to capture the fox's skinny, hunched-over body. It reminded me of those chain-smokers who always seem to have a rattling, wheezing cough, so I put a cigarette in his mouth. That's what I liked about him: there was none of the muscular sleekness of a well-fed domestic dog, none of the power of a hunting wolf; just a mangy, scruffy, perfectly wonderful animal urchin on the prowl for scraps.

Germaine: And did you know that was his name even then?

Tom: I think I did. There was still a lot to do, of course, decisions to be made: where he lived and whether or not he could talk, and did he wear clothes or walk upright or drive a car, and did he have hands and elbows and knees, and how about a hat? But I knew all that would work itself out. For the moment it was enough that I could see him on the page of my pad, a skinny cartoon fox with a cigarette sticking out of the side of his mouth.

Germaine: Before we go on to the other characters and the huge success that followed, I'd like to talk about your drawing style. Your work is noted for its symmetry and simplicity. Each frame is very economical. You said your father was an architect who presumably had a healthy regard for straight lines; and your mother was a lawyer who dealt in facts. I think you are a product of exactitude.

Tom (laughing): Well I can't argue with that. I do like precision. I always work a three-part gag sequence; three frames: context, conflict, outcome. People say it's like a three-act story structure but I think of it more as a boxing move: a feint, a draw and then bang – the punchline. There is nothing in any of those three frames that shouldn't be there. And everything is always in the 'now', which is completely opposite to real life.

Germaine: What do you mean?

Tom: Well, in a cartoon strip each frame or panel is a moment, a moment frozen in time. But in life that's not the case, is it? I mean, this moment, this thing we call 'now', has already gone, and so has this – and this.

Germaine: You make that sound sad. Is that your tragedy?

Tom: What do you mean?

Germaine: That there is no 'now' for Tom Hannah.

Tom: There is no 'now' for anybody. There is no time associated with now. It's a point. A dot. It exists between what we remember and what will be, or what we think will be, or hope will be, or expect or whatever. So in that sense, everything exists in our mind – as a memory or an expectation. If not that, then it's a dream. The world is in here, not out there.

Germaine: That sounds like a solipsistic point of view – nothing exists outside of the mind.

Tom: It's not so much that nothing exists... it's... well, if I tell you an anecdote that didn't actually happen, you will still hear it and imagine it, and it will become a record stored in your memory. And a memory of something that actually did happen, that's a record too. They sit side-by-side in your head and are equally imagined. And if you didn't know that my anecdote wasn't true, then to you they'd both be real. Right?

Germaine (laughing): Right – I think. Let's rejoin the interview, which I hope is real. You mentioned earlier a cartoon grammar. What did you mean by that?

Tom: I meant there are rules that I follow. For example, Scraps always faces left-to-right, that's because he is driving the action forwards. Obstacles, such as the always-angry restaurant owner, appear from the right. They are impeding the flow. If Scraps's tail is up it means he's happy, down and he's not, similarly with Plenty's claws – out and she's getting cross. Billy's quills, the Pelican's eyes – they all convey consistent signals.

Germaine: There's a lot of violence in your cartoons. And the violent characters are the females: the always-angry restaurant owner and Plenty the Cat. The male characters are peaceful and put-upon. Why is that?

Tom: I don't know. I don't think it's intentional. It's just how it's become.

Germaine: Are the *Scraps* characters based on real people?

Tom: Partly.

Germaine: But you won't say whom?

Tom: I'd rather not. Besides, mostly they grew out of each other. The Pelican, then the always-angry restaurant owner, then Billy and finally Plenty. Five's a nice number. You can always have an outsider with an odd number.

Germaine: The always-angry restaurant owner – she doesn't have a name. Why is that?

Tom: Because as far as the strip is concerned, she is important only as a foil to Scraps's adventures. She doesn't need a name. In fact, I prefer her not to have a name.

Germaine: Isn't that a bit mean?

Tom: I've never thought of it in those terms.

Germaine: You don't feel obligated?

Tom: To what?

Germaine: To your characters.

Tom: I don't think so... no.

Germaine: Can I turn the conversation towards a more recently painful part of your life for a moment? The death of your father.

Tom: Yes.

Germaine: Your mother struggled, I understand. Emotionally. With your father's death.

Tom: Naturally. We all did. A sudden death is unsatisfactory in many ways. There is no time to say the things you would have liked to say. And he was so healthy-looking: huge and hale and hearty and... well, we didn't know there was anything wrong with his heart. He was a huge man yet so gentle. I can't remember him ever being cross. He didn't really suit the modern world. Mum always said he was a ditherer but he wasn't, not in my eyes, he was just gentle. Gentle and wise. I suppose it was true you could never get a decision out of him, though. He had a lot of self-doubt.

Germaine: He died two years ago?

Tom: Yes. I wasn't ready for it. I suppose no one ever is.

Germaine: Did your art help you in managing the mourning process?

Tom: You would think so but not really. When something like that happens nothing else seems to matter. At least, not to me. The hardest thing was being with other people. I resented their happiness. It became physically difficult to go out.

Germaine: Did your father's death have an effect on your approach to work? To your characters?

Tom: I don't think so. Are you still trying to work out who they are based on?

Germaine: Not at all. Let's return to the early days. How did you first get into print?

Tom: Five years after I saw the fox, about three or four years after I left college. At my final year's showcase I met the editor of a weird little science magazine. She wanted to see more of my work, I didn't have much but she was good enough to take me on as an illustrator.

Germaine: Did you showcase *Scraps?*

Tom: One strip. I didn't feel ready and there was only Scraps and the Pelican. The others came later.

Germaine: And why a pelican?

Tom (laughing): Why not? I love pelicans.

Germaine: So there you are, working on a science magazine and what, cartooning in the evening?

Tom: Pretty much – and sending off to agencies and newspapers – anywhere really. It took those years to develop, to work out the characters. It was a slow burn. I was still working on my style.

Germaine: Let's come to Gerard Borkmann and the Borkmann Creative Agency. That was your breakthrough?

Tom: It was. The science magazine had folded and I had no income. I decided to walk my work around the agents in London. It was a tough assignment. The feeling in those days was that animal cartoons were tired and not saleable in an adult market. Urbanites with angst were taking all the column space. The last agent on my list was Borkmann's.

Germaine: He had a fierce reputation.

Tom: Oh yes, and he still does. He didn't give me any time at all. I didn't get past his receptionist. But I left six strips anyway. A week later he called me, him personally, and spent about half an hour shouting at me about why it wasn't a commercial proposition, why the situation was poorly conceived, why there weren't enough characters – what I didn't realise then, and I do now, is that for him, that was constructive feedback.

Germaine: And he took you on?

Tom: Not quite. He said I could draw but *Scraps* needed work. So, I did some research, staying out and watching the night creatures come out to play – hedgehogs, cats, foxes. Dawn and dusk are the best times. And one night I was walking past an alleyway and I saw a cook chasing a cat away from his dustbins. That was when it all came together. I went back to Borkmann a few weeks later and he still shouted at me, but this time he took me on.

Germaine: Do you have a good creative working relationship?

Tom: We're friends. He is an old-school agent. He talks about percentage-points and break-clauses. 'Points off the top, I want points off the top,' he shouts whenever I visit his office. I have no idea what that means but I love that phrase.

Germaine: Going back to your style, some people have compared you to a draughtsman rather than an artist.

Tom: That's nice of them.

Germaine (laughing): But the order and structure in your work seems at odds with your appearance. You have a very individualistic look, if you don't mind my saying. Is the moustache part of your Tash persona? I'm wondering if Tash is one person and Tom Hannah is another.

Tom: The man behind the moustache? I like that idea but it's not true. We're all one Tom in here. At least I hope we are. But my advice to anyone out there is never grow facial hair, not even a little goatee. Once you've got something like this on your face you can never get rid of it. You look naked if you do; pale and insubstantial.

Germaine: It gets you noticed.

Tom: Only in social situations – not in terms of selling my work.

Germaine: You mentioned earlier that Scraps is a voice you can use to express opinions, and in some respects he must mirror your values. Is the same true of the other characters? Do they represent other facets of your personality?

Tom: I don't think so. I know them, I know their personalities, I know their voices, but I don't always know what they'll say next. In that sense they are distinct from me, they have their own lives. But that's true of any author-character dynamic, isn't it?

Germaine: I sometimes think that Scraps has a fondness for Plenty.

Tom (laughing): Let's not go there. I get parodied enough as it is.

Germaine: I'm sure. But what about the relationship between creators and their characters. You don't feel any obligations, no responsibilities towards them at all? Come on, don't you think the always-angry restaurant owner really should have a name?

Tom: I suppose it's fun to wonder about them. You know, imagine what they do when the lens isn't on them.

Germaine: What do you mean by that?

Tom: Well, let's take the term 'creator'. While I was still at college I did a photography project about borders and what lies beyond them. I took pictures of faces and cropped them and put them in larger frames, and the black border that surrounded them was the bit we couldn't see, the bit that exists outside the photograph. In the end all I had were a lot of crop marks with a thin line of the original photographs joining them up. I called the whole thing *What the Creator Sees*. That's what I mean about the lens, it captures only part of a bigger picture. You know, what's outside the photograph, what's in between the frames?

Germaine: In between the frames?

Tom: Don't you ever wonder what happens in between the frames? What happens in that dark line that separates one frozen moment from the next?

7

On the Tuesday following his admittance to hospital, Tom was taken for another CT scan and again the results showed no damage or abnormalities. When Mister Wiley came to see him afterwards, he had with him the doctor who had wordlessly assessed Tom the previous day. Her name was Doctor Irma Muller and while Wiley again sat horizontally on the chair beside his bed, she stood and stared at Tom.

'So,' said Mister Wiley. 'How do you feel today? Better than yesterday?'

'Much better, thank you.'

'And the memory? Still gaps?'

'Just Sunday. I think.'

'Good.'

Mister Wiley passed the notes he had brought with him to Doctor Muller. She looked through them, taking her time. They asked him to walk up and down the ward, and then they asked him the same questions they'd been asking since he'd arrived – how he felt, what he remembered, what his thoughts were. They asked him cognitive questions and watched him closely. Finally, Wiley shifted in his seat and looked at his watch. 'I would say this patient is medically stable and fit for discharge, Doctor Muller, wouldn't you?'

'We should keep an eye on the short-term amnesia,' she said. She tapped her notes. 'Okay.'

'Good,' said Wiley. 'I think we might have our bed back. Will there be someone at home today?'

'My wife.'

He nodded. 'Try to take things easy. And I want you to contact your doctor if you start to feel agitated again. Any questions?'

'None.'

It seemed that Tom's interlude in hospital was to be nothing more than that: a brief adventure and soon over. A three-act joke that wasn't funny: man falls off roof; man gets patched up; man goes home. Bang, bang, bang.

Rather than wait in bed he put on his clothes, pulled together his meagre possessions and then sat on the side of the bed, awaiting instructions. Just before lunchtime, Bee came along with a woman police officer who was carrying a bicycle helmet. Her hair was sweaty and stuck to her forehead.

'Tom,' Bee said. 'Do you feel up to being asked a few questions? You don't have to if you don't want to.'

'It won't take a moment, sir,' the police officer said and introduced herself as Ann Lasley. She sat on the plastic chair by Tom's bed, balanced her helmet on her knee and took out her notebook. Tom sat on the side of his bed, feeling the familiar soreness spread across his buttocks as he did so. His aches and pains were now old friends. He tried to focus and not look guilty of anything.

'How are you today, Mister Hannah?'

'I'm well, thank you. And looking forward to going home.' He loosened up.

'I see you've got a few injuries.'

'You should see the other guy.'

'Should I?'

Tom had loosened up too much. 'That was a joke. You know – I look bad but you should see the other guy. I haven't been fighting.' Tom's lips were still swollen and he had a missing tooth and a bruised eye. Perhaps he had been fighting. 'That's the second joke of the day that's fallen flat on its face,' he said.

'A bit like you did.' Police Officer Ann Lasley smiled. 'Joke. Shall we start? I'm not going to take a formal statement at this moment in time. It's just a chat. Do you mind if I take notes, though?'

This moment in time.

This moment, this thing we call 'now', has already gone, and so has this, and this. There is no time associated with now. It's a point. A dot.

Tom tried to remember when he had said those words.

'Mister Hannah?'

Tom looked at her. 'Sorry. Of course. Take notes.'

'Okay. Tell me about Sunday. You were on the roof of Hardies Lane multi-storey car park.'

Tom knew that place, it was a short walk from his house. 'I didn't realise that's where I was.' In his mind's eye he could picture it, an ugly, squat brick of a building. 'I wonder why I didn't ask before?'

'Ask what?'

'Where it was that I fell. I didn't know. Why Hardies Lane?'

'I'm hoping you can tell me.'

But of course, what he couldn't remember he couldn't tell her and after half an hour of fruitless questioning she stood up.

'I, or one of my colleagues, will take a formal statement in a week or so,' she said before she went. 'Hopefully you'll remember a bit more by then.'

After she'd gone, he sat on his bed and thought about her cycling back to the police station on her pushbike, pedalling through the London traffic in her high-visibility police jacket, mulling over his implausible story. His mind wandered. Was it a police-issue bicycle? Did she have to take whatever size they gave her or had she been measured for the correct frame size? And was it an enhanced model with certain police features that weren't available on the standard model. What he really wanted to know was did it have a siren?

He also really wanted to go home. He was debating whether to just go and not wait for whatever the discharge process was, and call Karen or phone for a taxi to take him home; when a tall, stringy, bony man with a shiny bald head and a barely visible grey toothbrush moustache walked towards his bay.

He was wrapped tightly in a heavy camel overcoat and he reminded Tom, as he always did, of a praying mantis. He fiddled with his gloves and his long, triangular, insect face turned this way and that until his glaring eyes settled on Tom. He nodded in recognition and walked quickly across to his bay. Tom had known this man for a long time.

'Gerard Borkmann,' Tom said and stood up. 'Well, I never expected to see you.'

'Couldn't you have gone private, Tom?'

Tom laughed and shook his hand. 'Not on the commission you take. Have you forgotten something?'

'What?'

'How am I. That's what visitors ask. But I'm fine, thank you, and you do know that visiting hours are later? How did you know I was here?'

'You're being tweeted about, Tom,' Borkmann said, sitting down next to Tom on the bed and hunching up as if keeping disease at bay. 'Tweeted. Our social media intern found you.'

'That was good of her.'

'Him.' Borkmann looked around. 'Loathsome places,' he said. 'Ill people. Unhealthy people. People die here, Tom.'

'You could have just put that in a card and sent it to me. No need to come in specially. Anyway, isn't it good for you to have your asset in the public eye again?'

Borkmann leaned closer. 'Never mind that. Tom, what happened?'

'That's the question of the week. I don't know. I tried to fly and it didn't work.'

'It was an accident?'

'Yes.'

'You're sure?'

'Well, no, I don't know for sure. Did you sneak up behind and push me off?'

'What?'

'I'm joking.'

Borkmann looked at Tom with his black eyes glittering and then nodded. 'Well, you seem well enough,' he said. He looked at Tom's bandaged thumb. 'Is that your drawing hand?'

'Afraid so, but that's nothing, look at this.' Tom bared his broken tooth.

'Your tooth has gone? Where is it?'

Tom laughed. 'On a chain around my neck. I don't know. The tooth fairies are building a castle with it.'

Borkmann sniffed. 'You look more like a bandit than ever. I thought they might have operated on that moustache.' He gestured at Tom's clothes. 'What are you doing now? You don't look like you're in hospital. Why aren't you lying down?'

'I'm leaving. I've been discharged.'

'So soon?'

'They want the bed.'

Borkmann put on his gloves.

'I'll give you a lift home.'

'You don't have to.'

Borkmann ignored him. 'You know,' he said, 'what I don't understand is what you were doing on the roof of a car park in the first place. How high was it?'

'They said about 60 feet. It was the Hardies Lane car park.'

'It doesn't make sense.'

'I know.'

'I mean, what enticed you up there in the first place. I thought you had a height phobia.'

'I do.'

'It's all I can do to get you to my office on the fourth floor.'

'I know.'

Borkmann stood up. He looked dissatisfied. 'Are you ready, then?'

'I suppose so. I'm not sure what happens next. I just go, presumably.'

'I'll get the car. I'll see you down by the entrance in 15 minutes.'

Tom watched him stalk off as Maggie came into view. 'Is everything all right?'

'That was my agent. He's just reminded me why I drink.'

She held up an envelope. 'Well, if you read this you'll see you have to do less of that. This is your discharge summary. We'll send a copy to your GP. There's a letter from Doctor Muller explaining what's happened to you and what we've done, and all the information about your medication is in there, and also the follow-up appointments that Doctor Muller wants you to attend. There are some leaflets about organisations and support services for people who've been discharged after suffering traumas.'

'Have I suffered a trauma?'

'I think you have,' said Maggie.

'I don't feel that way.'

'That's probably a good thing.' She looked at him and smiled. 'Well, we've got your contact details. How are you getting home?'

'My agent's taking me. And don't think that's a good thing because it's not. He has poor spatial awareness. I may be back in A&E soon.'

'Oh dear. Well, tell him to take care. There are only so many times you can fall off a wall and we can put you back together again.'

'You mean a roof.'

'I mean like Humpty Dumpty.' They looked at each other. 'It was nice to meet you, Tom Hannah.' She held out her hand. 'Good luck. Say hello to Scraps for me.'

'I will.'

They shook hands and she walked away. Tom watched her go. He wanted to say something; to call her back. He wanted to ask her how she had got that little mark on her face and whether or not she had a red Christmas jumper.

Humpty Dumpty. He liked that.

'I can always come back,' he said to no one. 'I can always come back and bring some flowers or something, to say thank you.'

He looked around the bay. The beds were all neatly made and awaiting the next casualties to arrive, casualties who would be medicated, healed and discharged – if they were lucky. He had been lucky. Implausibly lucky, as Karen had said. But then life was implausible. He thought about the always-angry restaurant owner and her stained jacket and red-rimmed blue eyes. Life was imperfect.

Tom, I don't want you to confuse wanting to go home with getting better. If you don't feel right, then you should tell me or one of the other nurses.

He picked up his belongings and left.

Part Two

The Draw

8

A beginning, a middle and an end? Is life actually like that? Perhaps for a cartoonist it is, because there's always a sequence, there's always the first frame and the final frame and whatever bridges the gap. Maybe that's why Tom yearned so much to live in the moment, because the bit in the middle was where all the living was done. Act Two is so often a botched job.

Back when we first saw the big yellow dog and I was trying to work out what was going on, it wasn't like that for me. My life was a collection of moments that could be in any order. It's funny but I pictured those moments as being contained in bin-bags piled up around me. I say funny because I was an eco-fox on a mission to combat waste and rid the world of piles of bin-bags. There was no beginning, middle or end in my world. I seemed to stay still while the moments that made up me, that made up my life, accumulated like black bags outside a charity shop on a Sunday night, stacking up and spreading out for as far as I could see; bags filled with scenes and experiences and apple cores. I kept the good stuff close by – the things I liked to buff up and talk about and embellish and embroider and put on display; the life story I like to promote; the official version of me; the happy-smiley stuff – and the rest I left to rot.

So that's how I saw my life: a giant landfill site. I didn't progress at all; life just happened. Not a particularly inspiring philosophy, I have to say. But looking back, I think the question I should have been asking was, where did all that stuff come from in the first place?

It was some time after being chased by the yellow dog (an experience I was happy to leave in a black bag somewhere and forget), and I was walking along a dark street keeping to the shadows wherever I could, smoking a cigarette and enjoying being alone. I liked the dark. Daytime was good if it was sunny and I could find a quiet spot in which to relax, but I preferred a cool, clear night with stars above and a pavement below. I like streets and houses: quiet and empty and echoing. I could hear sounds that were a long way away on an empty, echoing street. Much better than being in the woods and amongst the trees. I didn't like that at all. Things rustle in the woods at night. Things rustle where nothing should be rustling at all. Creatures scurry, wings flap, and there are other noises: cries and shrieks and whistles; sounds far away and some right up close that would freeze my blood and chill my bones. Outdoor creatures like me can die in the woods at night and be picked clean before dawn. Give me a pavement any day. Who would want tall, looming trees with twisting growths and gnarled claws when you could have a nice lamppost lighting your way, creating dark shadows in which a furtive fox could hide?

I was thinking about that as I walked in the dark, avoiding the pools of lamppost light, when it occurred to me that I had never been in a wood. I searched my mind for a genuine experience – a sight, a touch, a scent – and there were none. My world as far as I could remember had always consisted of the shapes and silhouettes of houses and buildings; of alleyways, gardens, dustbins, pavements and street-lights. These were the familiar contours through which I navigated every day. The landscape of concrete and bricks and metal felt right to me. It felt like I belonged there. Where did all that wood stuff come from?

On that night it seemed there was only me. I lit another cigarette and blew smoke into the air just to see some movement. I walked on and came to a park, quiet and empty, the swings motionless and hanging in the air. I slipped through the railings and made my way across the grass, vaulting the gate at the far side. A little further on, the pavement led down to an underpass, where I paused to assess the sounds inside, the smells and scents, and then when I was sure the exit was clear, I passed through, unloading my own scent against the wall on my way. I loved doing that. I loved painting walls with my legs apart and my hips thrust forwards and my shoulders hunched, look-ing furtively from side to side with a cigarette dangling from my lip. What a look.

It was late when I reached the entrance to our alley. It was an odd thing but whichever route I took, whatever road I crossed, in whichever direction I walked, the alleyway was always at the end of my journey, always there waiting for me. My home, ready to receive me.

Before rejoining the others, I went over to a house on the other side of the road, opened the gate and walked up to the window – I wanted to see my reflection. I looked a ghostly figure in the glass. I lit another cigarette. It felt a long time since I'd been chased by the yellow dog. There was some blood on my face, drying but still sticky, a cut on one ear and another on my lip. I spat on the ground and looked at it – there was blood in my saliva too.

You should see the other guy.

I sighed and blew smoke at the window, inhaling some of it again as it bounced back to me, and loosened up a bit, letting my arms swing backwards and forwards at my sides. I walked around the small garden, pacing one way and then the other, before returning to my reflection.

'What's going on?' I muttered. 'Is this a new adventure?'

My reflection said nothing but I didn't think it was a new adventure. It used to be that every week we had an episode of excitement; a short period of happy purpose. But recently things had been different. Events were ongoing, unresolved, painful, unfunny. Like the yellow dog attacking us. There had been no reason for that, no build-up, no outcome. In fact, it had been horrible. A sordid and painful episode. And the dog had been different too: it didn't talk, it didn't stand up. It had been like an animal.

I touched my ear and stared at my spit and thought about those adventures, those collections of moments that had once rolled around as regular as clockwork, like a horse on a carousel. Plenty and Billy and the Pelican, all of us, we would be minding our own business, sitting in the sun or looking for food, or playing cards, and then there would be… something. The air would change and things would clarify. It was the beginning. I knew it and everyone else knew it. My mood would change. I would feel alive and clever and bright and the yearning to tear the bags and boxes and dustbins to pieces with my teeth would go away.

An adventure usually involved tricking the always-angry restaurant owner in some way, but she would be as excited as we were. She might say something or do something or plan something and life would become vivid; the dirt and grime and clutter would be gone and everything would be clean and simple and perfect. And I would always win. I always won and the always-angry restaurant owner always lost. And we would eat and laugh and be happy and some-times drink champagne in bubble-baths while she fumed and sulked and stamped her feet.

That was how it was meant to be; how it had always been. And then things would calm down and we would go back to minding our own business. The always-angry restaurant owner would join us in the alleyway and we'd pass the time again, playing cards and talking until... until our next adventure. I looked at my reflection. Until our next adventure? What was I talking about? It seems a ridiculous thing to say now.

I stopped enjoying the night and started feeling unwell. I looked down at my threadbare body and saw that I didn't look too good either and, looking around, nor did my surroundings. The whole area was going downhill. I studied the sky – were there less stars than before? Was the sky deteriorating too? And the silhouettes of the houses: so many black shapes – squares, oblongs, triangles – but no lights. Where were all the people? Were they asleep? I looked up at the house that stood before me. Had I ever seen any of the people who lived here?

'Anybody in there?' I said, cupping my mouth with my hands and leaning against the window. 'Anybody in there?'

I wondered if I was going mad.

Out of habit I urinated on the lawn and then cleaned my hands with antibacterial gel. Clean, lean and green is my motto. I peered at my reflection for one last time and plucked a hair out of my nostril. How long had that been waving in the wind? The hair was about an inch long. Once I had been svelte and suave, now I walked around with cables growing out of my nose and mould on my fur and blood in my ear. There was a definite change. I could feel it as if a storm were coming. I was falling apart.

I walked across to the entrance to our alleyway: a narrow passage that connected two parallel roads. Either side buildings rose high into the air, leaving just a strip of sky several floors above. No vehicles ever came down there, and so the dustbins and piles of boxes and crates and cartons remained where they were, like props waiting to be arranged. There were no windows that looked out onto the alleyway from above, just two towering brick walls with pipes and grilles and grates decorating their greasy surfaces.

At one end there was a high street lit with bright lights and busy with cars and people; an area filled with noises and smells. There was too much to see and too much to hear on the high street – and that meant too much danger. I had never walked on that road and nor had any of the others as far as I knew, because such places could fill our minds with confusion, and the feeling inside was always to stop and wait for the confusion to pass. But some instinctive fear warned me that it would never pass and if the bright lights did fill our minds then it would be the last thing we ever knew. Or so I thought. As I said, I had never been there. It was part of the world of which I knew but couldn't remember. At the other end of the alleyway was a quiet road – dark and empty. Here there were houses and gardens: the black silhouettes without lights where I had been standing.

As I walked down it, I thought the alleyway looked a tip. There was litter and rubbish and graffiti on the walls. New graffiti too, a word I didn't recognise – *Tash* – was written over and over again, painted in different colours and in different signature styles. Seeing that word had an extraordinary effect on me: I wanted to urinate all over it, to leave my own mark and spray *Scraps* across the walls instead. Interesting.

About halfway along the alleyway, on the left-hand side, was a metal door with barred windows on either side and a large ventilation duct above it. Bright yellow light spilled out into the darkness from the windows and the gaps around the door. It was the side entrance to the restaurant that led into the kitchen. I had often been in there, but I had never seen who made all of the shouts and clattering. A long time ago, I had glimpsed the shadowy shape of some cook, a dopey-looking youth whose eyes were hidden by his chef's hat – but I hadn't seen him recently. And now that I came to think of it, I hadn't seen any creature other than the five of us for a very long time. Apart from the yellow dog.

I put out my cigarette and squeezed my ear. The bleeding had stopped. I licked my lip and felt the swollen bruise but I didn't taste blood anymore. That was good. I walked down the alleyway towards the restaurant door and as I did so I saw that they were all out there: Plenty, Billy, the Pelican and the always-angry restaurant owner; all sitting outside on the steps lit by the kitchen lights within. Wherever we went and whatever adventures we had, we always ended up outside the restaurant. But at this time they should all be asleep. Plenty, usually the sleepiest of them all, was already standing up as I approached.

'Where have you been?' she said. 'You've been gone days.'

'Days?'

'I thought the dog had eaten you.'

'No, the dog didn't eat me.'

'If it had I would have found it and sliced its skin off with my claws.' Plenty made small, vicious, raking movements and her eyes glowed.

I sat down. 'Why aren't you all asleep?'

'We've been waiting for you,' said Billy.

'For days?'

'Yes.'

'Thanks, but I'm fine. You're fine. Everything is fine.' Now that I'd sat down I felt very tired.

'No,' said the always-angry restaurant owner, and her voice was flat and hard. 'Everything is not fine.'

I sensed an atmosphere. An expectant, we-have-big-news atmosphere. I could see Plenty keeping still, holding her breath, watching each of us in turn. Billy's hands were stuck deep in his pockets and the Pelican shifted uneasily, a few grubs dropping to the ground as it did so.

'What's going on?' I said.

They all looked at the always-angry restaurant owner. She remained sitting on the steps, uncharacteristically quiet after her outburst. She was balancing a rolled-up newspaper between the palms of her hands.

'Tell him,' said Plenty. 'Tell him about the thing.'

'Yes, tell me about the thing,' I said.

'It is very weird shit,' Billy said.

'Tell me about the very weird shit.' As if to emphasise the weird shittiness of it all, more detritus dropped to the ground as the Pelican shivered and shifted position again.

'Well? Is anybody going to tell me?' The fur was beginning to rise on the back of my neck.

'I'll tell you. In fact, I'll show you,' the always-angry restaurant owner said, and I thought she didn't look so good either. She handed me the newspaper and the others watched. A few other newspapers littered the alleyway, lifting in the breeze, but this was one I didn't recognise. It felt different, too: heavier, denser, organic. It was a Sunday tabloid, open and folded over at the horoscope page. I looked at it.

'Don't tell me,' I said. 'I'm going to meet a tall, dark vixen.'

'Not the horoscope, idiot. Look at the bottom.'

The horoscopes took up half the page. Below them were puzzles: a word game, a number game, and some sort of maze game. I looked at the bottom of the page. There was a cartoon strip; three frames; clean lines; economical.

It was called *Scraps*.

9

Borkmann was waiting in his car by the hospital entrance. Tom didn't notice him at first because he was adjusting to being outside. He'd only been in hospital for two days and yet he felt as if he were coming out to a new world, a different world – a world similar but not the same as the one he'd known before. It seemed a brighter, sunnier, noisier place, with clouds moving swiftly across the sky and a light breeze that tugged his moustache, and he imagined the hairs twirling at each end like miniature propellers.

There was a smell of fuel and distant fried food but also the smell of the outdoors, of wind that had travelled long distances journeying to and from places far away, across treetops and tall chimneys and hills and mountains and seas and vast oceans.

He lifted his head and let the air rush past, cool and smooth. It was a soothing feeling but it tickled his memory, like a feather caught inside his skull. He closed his eyes and tried to reach it, to pluck it out and examine it. Had there been a cool wind rushing past and buffeting his face when he fell, he wondered, as if he were passing through a stream of pillow-sized air bubbles? Whatever it was, it remained out of his reach, persistent yet inaccessible. He let it go and closed his eyes, feeling the warmth from above soak into his skin and heat his battered and bruised bones – until a car hooted and Borkmann shouted, 'Come on.'

Borkmann was in a small, two-seater sports car. The passenger door had been pushed open, presumably so that Tom wouldn't have to waste time with the door handle. Tom viewed the silent invitation to get in as if he were assessing a potential trap. It looked a very low vehicle. Tom bent down and peered into the interior.

'Do I sit in this or do I wear it?' he said.

'Get in. I'm not meant to park here.'

Tom eased himself into the passenger seat. It was a tight squeeze. His buttocks were still tender and his thumb caught against the door, sending a bolt of pain and flashing lights into the centre of his head. He knocked the rear-view mirror with his bruised eye and then couldn't reach the seat belt because his coat had caught on the head-rest.

'I don't fit.'

'Stop thrashing about.'

'I'm stuck.'

'Do you want me to help you?'

'Just drive. I'll sort myself out.'

Borkmann drove. Tom put on the seat belt but somehow both he and the seat were now wearing his coat, which had rucked up around his neck. He was not comfortable. He was too big for the car and every bump in the road pushed his head against the canvas roof, sanding his skin.

'Thank you for the lift,' he said.

'You're welcome.'

Tom held on to the dashboard and looked out of the window at the passing streets, at the signposts and traffic lights and lampposts, at the shuttered shops with cardboard boxes piled outside, and at a man sitting on the ground in a doorway, watching a woman walk unhurriedly past him. It was Tom's scenery: the landscape of pavements and parks and railings and pubs, a landscape set to the music of sirens and hooting taxis and rattling buses.

Borkmann opened his window and the car filled with noise and petrol fumes. He drove along the road in a series of sweeping, swooping curves as if he were unable, or unwilling, to maintain a straight line. In doing so he managed to strike every pothole, drain, lump and bump in his path, and each jolt rubbed Tom's head further into the canvas roof. He thought that perhaps it would become a type of Turin

Shroud with the image of his forehead imprinted on it. He should have released the clips and let the roof down so that he could sit high above the windscreen with his moustache and hair streaming behind like a returning god.

'What are you doing?' he shouted. 'Why are you driving like this?'

'I'm looming,' Borkmann said.

'What?'

'I'm looming into view.'

'What are you talking about?'

'I'm increasing my profile. This car is very low and people pulling out from side roads might not see me. So I'm making myself more visible with these controlled and precise changes of direction.'

'You're all over the road.'

'I am all over the road in a controlled and precise way.'

They loomed along roads that Tom had known since childhood, past alleyways that he had used as short cuts to school; past the road where a giant root ball had been turned into a fortress before it had been burned; past streets that led to long-ago friends' houses; past tarmac play areas that brought back cloying memories of cold, damp November mornings and scraped knees.

'I grew up around here,' he said.

'I know,' Borkmann shouted, swerving towards a brick.

Halfway to his house, Tom saw the wishing-well where he had first kissed and been kissed by Sarah Marsden – a girl with velvet skin and hot breath. Where was she now, he wondered, and did she ever think about the moment she had shared with the clumsy, eager, teenage Tom? He could remember the smell of her face, her skin cold from being outside, and the taste of her lips and the touch of her tongue. He could remember opening his eyes while they kissed and seeing that her eyes were closed. He could remember his hand trying to slip between the buttons of her shirt.

'Whoa,' he muttered. He had to stop remembering those things so vividly.

A hundred yards farther on they stopped for a red traffic light by a junction where a boy from his class called Bailey – who had long, floppy hair that concealed his face, and who Tom had never liked – had been thrown into the air by a car, flying from bonnet to boot to road and changing from pedestrian to paraplegic as he did so. A cartoon moment with real-life consequences, his hair spreading outwards like a fan as he turned upside down. Tom had never forgotten his shock at how loud it had been. Who would have thought that such small bones and young skin could offer so much resistance?

Occasionally, at unexpected moments, Tom heard the sound that Bailey's body had made when the car hit him. It came as a sudden explosion behind his inner ear, a definite bang. Perhaps Borkmann was right. Perhaps a looming driver would have saved Bailey's agony. But then, Bailey had been a nasty piece of work, a bully, and secretly Tom had been glad.

'Do you think about the past much?' he shouted at Borkmann. 'You know, about being young? How you used to be, how you used to think?'

'All the time.'

'Seriously?'

Borkmann grinned, exposing his teeth like a rhesus monkey. 'Of course not. Do I look like I was ever young?'

'You should. It's good to keep connected with the past, to see the world in the way we did when we were young.'

It was difficult to talk with all the looming and swerving and the open window and the petrol fumes and the relentless battering of his head against the canvas roof, but Tom persisted.

'We plan too much. We should take each moment as it comes. But a moment is so short. We need longer moments... maybe not longer driving moments, though. Remember summer holidays? They lasted forever. That's because we only thought about that moment, that endless moment. When we get older we have calendars and diaries and the whole year is plotted out. We don't think about the "now" at all. You need to connect to your younger self, Gerard. What do you think Tiny Borkmann would think of Big Borkmann?'

'He would want big Tom Hannah to shut up and let him concentrate on driving.'

Tom's home was at the far right-hand corner of a cul-de-sac. It was a big townhouse protected from the street by black railings with tips like spears. It was where Tom and his sister, Caroline, had lived as children. It was the Hannah family home.

The front garden was taken up entirely by a tall cherry tree which, over the years, had risen upwards, lifting the ground with it, its roots exposed above the surface. On the short driveway was a car that had belonged to Tom's father. Its battery was also dead and the car sagged on its deflating tyres like a mortally wounded animal.

'You ought to put that machine out of its misery,' Borkmann said, double-parking outside the house.

'That was my dad's car. It's a tribute to a fallen hero.'

'It's a wreck.'

'It's not moved for five years. What do you expect?'

They sat in Borkmann's car, both staring through the windscreen, perhaps both enjoying the sudden cessation of noise. Tom said, 'I saw him die. You know? Caroline and I were visiting for Sunday lunch. Dad died halfway through the apple and blackberry crumble. He fell forwards so hard he upended the table. It was very scary.'

Borkmann said nothing. He looked through the windscreen and listened. He had known both Tom and Caroline at the time and had been on hand to help, albeit in his gruff, Borkmannian way.

'Caroline and I were useless. Mum did everything: got him on the floor, cleared his throat of crumble, worked on his chest. He was a big man, bigger than me. He would never have got into this car. The doctor said all that work would have made no difference, as he was probably dead before his face hit his plate.'

'Do you want me to come in?'

'Do you have the time?'

'Not really.'

Tom laughed. 'In that case, no.'

He levered himself from the car and unfolded to his normal size. He seemed to have gained more aches and pains from the short trip in Borkmann's car than he had by falling 60 feet from a car park roof.

'Do you need anything? Prescriptions? Medicine?' Borkmann said.

'Nothing.'

'What about food? Do you have food?'

'We have food.'

A car behind hooted loudly before Borkmann could say any more. He turned in his seat to see who had dared interrupt his flow. 'Who is that bastard? One of your wretched neighbours?'

'Quite possibly.' Tom nodded and waved at the driver. 'Better go, Gerard. I'll catch you soon.' He watched Borkmann drive away and then walked up the path to his door. He unlocked it and went inside. 'I'm home,' he said.

But nobody else was. There was no note and no evidence of where they might be, so Tom presumed that Karen had gone to the hospital not knowing he'd been discharged and Dan and Holly were either with her or still at school and college respectively. He went to his study and waited, thinking about smoking a cigarette. He thought about smoking a cigarette a lot even though he'd given up 20 years previously. He lived in hope that, before he died, someone would discover that smoking was good for him.

His study was in the attic. It was a large, open space, an airy eyrie as he liked to call it, uncarpeted with white floorboards and two high, sloping ceilings. A large skylight in each slope framed the passing of the days and nights like the sun and moon windows on a mantel clock. The walls and ceiling were also white. In the centre of the room was a chair, in which Tom now sat, and a workbench with an adjustable sloping easel and a 200-watt desk-lamp that was so bright it flattened everything into two dimensions whenever Tom switched it on. On a separate, adjacent desk was a laptop, mouse and keyboard. Tom looked at it but left it unopened. Time enough for that later.

The entrance to his eyrie was a square opening in the attic's floor, which was made safe by white, wooden handrails on three sides and a gate on the fourth, like a child's stair-guard. Below that was a retractable ladder, which led down to the landing on the first floor. Against one wall in the attic were three large filing cabinets that contained Tom's drawings, sketches, doodles, business documents and the original *Scraps* cartoons he'd accumulated over the years and kept under lock and key. Pens, ink and paper were stored in a free-standing set of drawers beside the desk.

Tom sat in his chair until it became dark outside. There was still no sign of Karen, Holly or Dan. He switched off the light and climbed down the ladder. A headache was building and his thumb was hurting and his tooth was throbbing. He went to the bathroom looking for painkillers but ended up staring into the bathroom mirror.

He stared for a long time because what was looking back was not his face. It was a male fox. He was smoking a cigarette and it was as if they were separated by a wall and looking at each other through a communal window.

Say hello to Scraps for me.

Tom forgot about his headache and the painkillers, and his thumb and his tooth. He stood motionless, slack-jawed, vacant, scarcely moving, scarcely breathing. Each time the fox took a drag on his cigarette, the glow lit up his face. He blew smoke at the mirror-window, spat on the ground and paced backwards and forwards, clearly troubled by something. After a minute or two he turned back, peered in and said something that Tom couldn't hear.

The fox became agitated. He put both hands to his mouth and shouted as if through a foghorn, the mirror-window steaming up. After a while he gave up and shook his head in disgust. Then he urinated on the ground. He washed his hands with an antibacterial gel and then he leaned right up to the mirror-window and pulled a long hair from his nostril. Tom realised at that point that the fox couldn't see him, and that whatever he had been shouting, he had been shouting to himself.

Tom closed his eyes and took a deep breath. And then another, and another until he felt he had breathed deeply enough times. Then he stopped breathing for as long as he could and listened. At first he heard nothing except the hiss in his ears and the sound of his own blood pumping, but then possibly, just possibly, he thought he could detect... something. A sound that seemed to be sitting in the blue mists of a distant horizon. He shook his head to clear it of such fancies and opened his eyes again.

'Okay,' he said. 'That was odd.'

His words hung in the air and he looked around, wondering if he had said them aloud. There was a hole in the silence that made him think he had, and at the same time wish he hadn't. He put his hand against the mirror. It was solid. He turned around and listened some more. Still there were no sounds other than his own. The house was empty. He looked back at the mirror and at the wall on which it hung, and then at the ceiling and the floor and the sink and the taps, and at all the things that ought to be in a bathroom and were.

What are you supposed to do when you're alone in a house and you look in a mirror and see a fox standing on two legs urinating onto the floor and shaking off the drips? What do you do when that fox is a three-dimensional, living, breathing, large-as-life incarnation of your best-selling cartoon character? And what do you do after all the deep breathing and listening, when afterwards the fox is not there anymore and the mirror is just a mirror and time ticks by and it doesn't happen again and cars drive past and birds tweet and everything is perfectly normal everywhere else in the whole world?

'You go to bed,' Tom said to his reflection. 'That's what you do. You go to bed and get some sleep. Because it didn't happen.'

He turned off the light and went to bed, leaving the bathroom and the rest of the house in darkness.

The Pelican looked up and saw that the day was done and that the sky was as dark as the ground. Above and below, it thought, if thinking was indeed what it did, above and below. It extended its massive wings as if they were a cape beneath which smaller creatures could shelter. It looked around at the rooftops and through instinct assessed the shapes and substance of each brick component, comparing and contrasting and weighing the worth of each as a place to perch, a place in which it might blend in and pass a peaceful night.

Below, it could see the others in the restaurant settling down for the night, bickering and teasing, taunting and planning and plotting and preparing for whatever was to come. And elsewhere it saw Tom, his head on the pillow, a shaft of light from outside illuminating his face, his wide moustache lying like a short, rough cord across his face, his eyes open and staring at the ceiling. The Pelican shifted its wings slightly and their shadow fell across Tom's face, and soon he was asleep.

10

The following morning Tom woke up and didn't know where he was. It was as if somebody had scooped out the middle of his brain. He stared at the ceiling and groped in his mind for a thread on which to pull, for a nugget of knowledge from which he could rebuild his world.

He thought he might be in the hospital and looked to his right where a window with a view of a multi-storey car park might be, and to his left where the nurses' station could be located. Neither were there. The walls and ceiling were white – not grey – and blue curtains – not blinds – covered a window that was on his left, with a bedroom door beyond the foot of his bed instead of another hospital bed.

His mind was adrift and he held on to the bedclothes tightly, wondering whether he would have to call out for help. And then he remembered. He was in his bedroom, in his house. It was morning and he was at home. He was Tom Hannah, he was a cartoonist, he was married with children, he had fallen off a roof.

He sat up and saw that he was alone in his bed. On the pillow next to him there was a note. It read: *Didn't want to disturb you. Staying at my sister's. Back tomorrow afternoon. See you then. K.* He read the note several times and then lay back on his pillow. Was tomorrow today?

'Come on, Thomas. Engage.'

He threw back the bedcovers. He was naked. His clothes from the day before were piled up on the floor – next to an empty bottle of wine. He looked at them and he looked down at himself and he couldn't remember going to bed. Oops. The doctors had recommended no alcohol.

'Idiot.'

He picked up the clothes, folded them, and put them neatly on a chair. He went into the spare bedroom and found that the bed was made and there was no sign of Karen. He walked up and down on the carpeted floor and then opened and closed the door several times – he supposed it was possible she had got up and left the house without him hearing.

He went to the bathroom and looked into the mirror. No sign of any fox. It was his face and his face alone looking back. The same cold-lidded eyes, wide-spread nose, stubbled chin and outrageous moustache that he had expected to see. He grinned. He had good teeth. It was a shame one was now missing. He cleaned them but couldn't floss the broken gum and when he spat the mouthwash into the sink it left a reddish stain.

He showered and – taking care of his thumb – he raked his fingers through his hair, which was long and hung like a thick, greying flannel against his neck. He pushed it back from his forehead and then let it drop again – there were too many lines on his forehead, too many shadows under his eyes. He tried a smile and then pulled back his lips into a grimace. He thought his nose looked bent. He looked more closely at his damaged mouth and could see a thin line of jagged tooth poking out from the gum.

'Grrr.'

He towelled his face vigorously, which left his moustache carrying a static charge. It was thicker than the brush on a broom. He stroked it and it felt bushier than he'd ever known it. How big could it grow, he wondered?

Back in the bedroom he pulled out some clothes: jeans and a shirt and a ruined pair of leather boots, and then caught sight of himself in the mirror. Again there was no sign of any fox, just Tom and his amazing electrified moustache. He decided that there was no point in getting dressed and put on his fluffy blue dressing gown instead.

He went downstairs and immediately felt that something was missing. There was a muscle-memory that wanted him to do something but he couldn't remember what. It was another tickle in the back of his mind. He looked around seeking inspiration but found none. Dan would be at school, Holly at college and Karen somewhere, at work now or still at her sister's. He was alone in the house. What else was there to do? Have a drink? But that wasn't allowed.

'Trust yourself,' he said. 'Always trust yourself.'

It was a large kitchen with work-surfaces on all sides and a pedestal in the middle. There was a cooker with six hobs and two ovens, a giant American refrigerator and a long, marble-effect counter with stools that separated the cooking part of the kitchen from the sitting-around-and-eating part. There were three doors: one led to the hallway, one led to the garden and one led to the outhouse attached to the kitchen.

Tom looked at the outhouse door. There was something about that door. He got up and tried it but it wouldn't open. It was old and solid, the type that came with a big key. He looked around for the key but he couldn't find it.

'Why are you locked?' he said.

The door didn't answer and Tom leaned with his head against its wood, picturing what lay beyond. It was a musty-smelling room with white-washed brick walls hung with long strands of thick cobwebs like threads of candy-floss that had escaped their stick. There were shelves filled with cleaning equipment, dusters and mopheads, aerosol sprays long-forgotten and never used, and drawers full of nails and screws and bulbs. There was a rusting, sit-up-and-beg bicycle that once belonged to his mother and was now used for its large wicker basket as a place to store potatoes and carrots and onions. Nothing to keep under lock and key. And where was the key? Tom made a mental note to ask Karen about it.

He made coffee and sat at the kitchen table and looked out through the window and thought about nothing except a leafy branch on a nearby tree that swayed backwards and forwards in the wind.

When the house phone rang, Tom was still lost in thoughts of nothing. He picked it up and said, 'Hello?'

It was Borkmann.

'Tom.'

Tom thought about hanging up and returning to his leaf but Borkmann's voice was like a blade stabbing out from the receiver.

'Tom. Are you there? Tom, it's Gerard.'

'Hello, Gerard.'

'Tom. How are you today?'

'I'm well.'

'The thumb.'

'It's well too. Still bandaged. It says hello.'

'Have you tried drawing with it?'

'Not yet.'

'Don't leave it too long.'

'I won't.'

'Do you need anything?'

'I don't think so.'

'Good. Right then.'

'Right then.'

'I'll call again tomorrow.'

'Okay. Thank you.'

Borkmann's voice had been like a gunshot on a sunny day and the house seemed quieter after his call. The tree and its branch and its leaves no longer held Tom's attention and instead he looked at his reflection in the window.

'Crazy man,' he said.

He finished his coffee and noticed that when he drank there were muscles in his cheeks that pulled his face forwards as if he were whistling a tune. He found a notebook in a kitchen drawer and a black felt-tipped pen, and tried to draw a picture of a man with his face pulled forwards. It wasn't a bad effort given his damaged thumb.

'Crazy man,' he said again, but this time it sounded genuinely odd, so he stopped saying it. The silence inside the house seemed even louder now. His ears hissed and whined, and outside cars drove by and the wind rustled through trees, shushing the cars.

Tom put his drawing to one side. He thought about going up to his study and logging on to his laptop, but the call of the internet and contact with the outside world didn't interest him. Instead he wrote *Tash* on the notebook. He sat back and studied the word. He had heard that people's expressions changed when they wrote their own names. He wondered if a dog's face would change when it marked its territory. Or a fox's face when it pissed on the other side of a mirror.

He wrote *Tash* on every page in the notebook using different styles of writing. He stood up and walked around the kitchen and found a bottle of gin in a cupboard and poured some of it into a plastic tumbler. It was ten o'clock in the morning.

'What?' he said, looking at his reflection in the kitchen window. 'What? I'm trusting myself.'

He added some tonic and drank the gin and poured another, collected a packet of crisps and sat back in his chair at the kitchen table. He thought about the past few days: about being in hospital and about not being able to remember things, about Maggie's laugh. And about Maggie. Then he thought about the note that Karen had left on his pillow and the uneven writing as if she'd written it in a rush or at an angle or on some flexible surface such as her hand. Then he tried to remember what he'd been doing on the car park roof and why he'd been up there in the first place. He wondered what it had felt like to fall. He imagined he was falling backwards into his mind, creating a big splash and displacing his subconscious, letting all the detritus in his head float to the surface.

He closed his eyes and imagined he was his own metropolis, buzzing with activity, teeming with thoughts and memories and feelings, with new sounds and sensations arriving at the borders of his body every second. Blood circulated, nerves tingled, warmth was generated, internal units switched on and off like central heating systems. Then he imagined that he was floating upwards until the ground beneath him was a mosaic of greens and browns and the horizon curved and the sky turned to night. He imagined rising until the world was a tiny revolving disc far below and he was floating in space.

At some point during all this thinking and imagining he fell asleep, and when he awoke it was two o'clock in the afternoon.

You know those moments when you're falling asleep while you're driving and you don't know it?

Everything ached and his mouth tasted odd. Something was hanging down from inside his broken tooth. It felt like a red tadpole and he wondered if it was the nerve. He sucked on it and it popped back into the tooth again.

'You need to see a dentist,' he said, and then heard sounds in the hallway and realised he had been awoken by the front door banging – not a dog barking this time, or a cough, but a door closing. His front door. The daylight coming in through the kitchen windows seemed heavy and over-bright and he rubbed his eyes, not feeling good at all. He sat up just as Karen came into the kitchen.

'Oh,' she said. 'Hello.' She was with a man.

It made for an uncomfortable tableau. Tom, huge and dishevelled, sat at the kitchen table in his fluffy blue dressing gown, staring at them with bleary eyes above his wide, sticky moustache, a half-empty bottle of gin, a plastic tumbler and an empty packet of crisps scattered across the table in front of him. Karen, still belted, buttoned and buckled up in her coat, hovered midway between the kitchen door and the table. And the man, a man who appeared older than both Tom and Karen, the interloper, with sandy hair and almost white eyelashes, slim and skinny-hipped and wearing a narrow grey suit, hung back looking with amused eyes from Tom to Karen as if he were watching actors on a stage.

'That's good. I hoped you'd be up,' Karen said. 'How are you feeling?'

'Tired,' Tom said. He looked at the sandy-haired man. 'Hello.'

The man nodded and looked at Karen with raised eyebrows, as if making the point that it was her turn to speak.

'You remember Lawrence?' she said to Tom.

Tom took a closer look. 'I don't think so.'

Lawrence and Karen exchanged glances, which irritated Tom.

'Okay. Well, this is Lawrence from work,' she said. 'Lawrence, this is Tom. Lawrence, why don't you wait in the living room?' She spoke each word as if it was unconnected to the others, like laying down a trail of stepping stones on which to walk.

Lawrence smiled and said, 'Of course,' and went to the living room without asking where it was. Karen turned back to Tom.

'So,' she said. 'You're home.'

'Indeed.'

'You weren't in hospital for long. That's good.'

'Yes.'

'Very good. It could have been worse.'

'Gerard brought me home. So I was all right.'

She nodded as if imagining the scene. 'That was nice of him.'

'Weren't you going to visit me?'

'Of course.'

'But you didn't.'

Karen frowned. 'Don't get funny. I was at work. I had to work late. I phoned the ward and they said you'd been discharged and that you'd gone home. So I phoned the house phone but there was no answer.'

'I didn't hear you come in last night.'

'I just popped in. You were asleep. I thought it better if you rested.'

'You could have woken me. I wouldn't have minded. Where were you?'

'When?'

'After you just popped in.'

'Tom, we stayed at my sister's. I left you a note.' She looked at the bottle. 'You've been drinking?'

'No.'

'There's an open bottle in front of you.'

Tom looked at it. 'I meant not just now. I had a drink at lunchtime. Yes.' He wondered if it mattered that he could lie so easily, or if Karen could tell, or if she cared. Her expression remained calm and she spoke in a quiet, measured tone as if not wanting to excite any emotion.

'You've just got out of hospital,' she said. 'You're not meant to drink at all.'

Behind her was a large, stainless steel coffee pot. In it, Tom saw his reflection bending round the sides, making his nose extend towards him. His hair was stiff and rising upwards like the grey-black smoke from a forest fire, flat on one side where he had lain on his arms for almost four hours.

'I know.'

'What about medication?' she said. 'They can't just let you out without any... I don't know, supervision, can they?'

'I am being supervised. You're here. And I've got painkillers and a prescription and an out-patient's appointment in a couple of weeks. That's ample supervision.'

Karen stared at him and shook her head. 'You shouldn't drink,' she said. 'And we should go and see Lawrence.' She continued to stare and when Tom said nothing she said, 'He's come out of work to see you. We can't stay too long. Then you should get some rest.'

'Why?'

'Because you've just come out of hospital after falling off a roof.'

'I mean why has Lawrence come to see me?'

She sat down on the other side of the kitchen table and rested her chin on her hands. Tom was reminded of the moment Maggie had sat down on his hospital bed and told him that he had fallen off a roof. He wondered how many times he had seen Karen sit in that very spot: brush in hand, applying the final touches to her make-up, putting up the barriers, locking in her thoughts. Each small, careful, delicate upward movement of the tiny brush creating another layer of control between the Karen inside and the world outside. He wished it was Maggie sitting there instead of Karen.

'I don't understand this memory business,' she said. 'Is it just the Sunday you fell that you can't remember or other times as well? Is it all going to come back?'

Tom leaned forwards until their heads were level across the table, face to face. 'I don't know,' he said. 'The Sunday has definitely gone. There might be other gaps but how would I know? It's only when somebody says something that I ought to know, that I know.'

'But it could all come back, or some of it? At any time?'

'I suppose so.'

'You definitely don't remember Lawrence? You don't remember him at all?'

Tom rubbed his face. Why, he wondered, was life so hard? He looked at the bottle.

'I definitely do not remember Lawrence. No.'

'You asked him to come here. Or rather, you asked me to ask him.' She nodded as if agreeing with herself, affirming what she'd just said.

'Did I? And who or what is Lawrence?'

'He's the one who goes rock climbing.'

Tom hadn't expected that. 'If you tell me that I said I wanted to go rock climbing, amnesia or no amnesia, I will absolutely not believe you.'

'It wasn't that,' she said slowly. 'It was about your fear of heights. You asked him to come and talk to you about your fear of heights.'

Tom stared at her. 'Really?' he said.

11

Lawrence was in the living room, sitting at the far end of the sofa. It was a big room: all carpets and curtains and cream-coloured walls. Tom sat carefully in the armchair opposite, mindful of his still-tender buttocks. He stretched out and sunk low, balancing his chin on his hands and assuming the same horizontal position that Wiley had used in the hospital.

'So you're Lawrence... ?'

Lawrence took his time in replying. 'Lawrence Cob,' he said finally.

'Larry or Laurie?'

'Oh, just Lawrence.'

'I'll make a cup of tea,' Karen said, and she went back to the kitchen.

Lawrence looked at Tom as if he were waiting for him to say something specific. It was an amused, watchful look. Tom wasn't aware of anything he was meant to say. Being sociable was not something he was usually good at and he was already bored with being there. His head felt heavy as he viewed Lawrence. He seldom noticed the details of a person until he'd met them several times. What he usually registered was their basic geometry: were they round or oblong, sharp or blunt, tall or short; and what animal they looked like. Lawrence was tubular in body with sharp joints and a pointed face like a willowy weasel.

Lawrence turned and looked at a framed picture on the wall. It was the same coloured drawing of the *Scraps* characters that Tom had on his T-shirt, except the one on the wall was the original, about four feet high, professionally framed and covered with glass.

'Do you like cartoons?' Tom said.

'Not really,' said Lawrence.

'I'm a cartoonist.'

'I know. You do that dog-thing.'

'Fox-thing.' Tom's head was starting to throb and he wished he had brought the gin with him. 'Karen says you climb rocks. Do you find a lot of rocks to climb in south London?'

Lawrence made a noise that might have been a laugh or a shout. It was a single exhalation: a thigh-slapping 'Ha'. Later, Tom would render Lawrence as a willowy, weaselly gunslinger, dressed in black with sandy fur; a wide, thin moustache and whiskers; and a six-gun revolver hanging from each hip, slapping his thigh and dancing a jig.

'I'm a weekender. I get away when I can. I've got my own kit, though: ropes, shoes, helmet. You should try it. Great fun.'

Tom hoped Karen would hurry up. He had already run out of small talk. 'What do you do the rest of the time? Do you work with Karen?'

Lawrence waved away the question as if it were a fly. Tom marvelled at that gesture. He wanted to use it. It was so confident and dismissive; so wonderfully ill-mannered.

'She's in Finance; I'm in Marketing,' he said. 'You know how these companies like to create their little labels. We are but passing ships in the night.'

In his mind's eye, Tom saw the misty straits of Gibraltar with silent ships passing each other hundreds of yards apart; Karen on the deck of one, Lawrence on the deck of the other, their shadows huge and elongated, cast by fog-lights, crossing each other like unearthly giants on the illuminated waves.

'Or rather ships in the day. We work in different offices.' Lawrence stretched out his legs until his feet were almost touching Tom's and looked around. 'I do like an open fire,' he said.

Tom looked at the empty grate and said, 'They're a devil to clean.' He wondered why he'd said that because it clearly didn't take much to dust out the hearth each morning. He had a sense that he was separated from his own babble and he wondered with a curious detachment what he might say next. 'But worth it.'

'Really,' said Lawrence.

A long silence followed. Lawrence seemed at ease but Tom found it unbearable. He began humming. Karen returned with a tray on which were two cups of tea and a coffee for Tom. She hadn't asked Lawrence whether he preferred tea or coffee, milk or sugar. Perhaps they made tea for each other at work, as ships in the day do. She perched on the arm of Tom's chair and said, 'Why are you humming?' Even though she was a tall woman, she seemed half his size, like a puppet or a ventriloquist's doll. Tom looked up at her and thought she looked different to how he had always seen her. Was it that her nose was longer or her chin rounder or her eyes smaller? He couldn't be sure but it was unsettling. She reminded him of a fruit, a plum perhaps, that has once been firm but now was soft.

She looked like she was ripening – but ripening in a bad way; bloating and opening up.

'I don't know,' he said. 'I didn't realise I was. How rude.'

Karen looked at Lawrence. 'Things have moved on since we last talked about you coming here. Tom has had an accident.'

Lawrence nodded. 'You said. Fell off a roof. How exciting for you.'

Tom sipped his coffee. It was nice to think he was being talked about. Karen turned to him and said, 'We were talking at work and I happened to mention that you had a height phobia and how you can't walk across a bridge or drink in a rooftop bar, and how we can't stay in high-rise hotels or sit on balconies. Do you remember I told you that I had talked to Lawrence about that?'

'No.'

Again Tom thought it was nice to have his private details discussed with strangers.

'Lawrence told me about the different techniques he's learned in dealing with panic attacks when he's climbing.'

Lawrence looked at Tom as if Tom were an exhibit in a cage, a feathered cartoonist who couldn't fly. 'A fear of heights is a very common thing. It's easy to worry about what might happen but who says it's going to happen? Nobody. Nothing is written down. There are no rules. You have to keep your thoughts in the moment and don't think about things – just do them. Let your body take over. It's liberating.'

Tom nodded. 'I know what you mean. My sixty-foot drop off a multi-storey car park was quite liberating. It liberated my front tooth.'

'Yes, I thought you were lisping. Difficult to see beneath all that... hair.'

'Tom can't remember Sunday at all, can you Tom?'

'No, I can't. It's called a moustache.'

'Nothing?' said Lawrence. 'That's inconvenient. So you don't know why you were up there? Or anything? Nothing at all?'

'Correct.'

'So anything might have happened?'

'I'm ruling out flying,' said Tom.

He heard footsteps on the front path outside the window. A key rattled in the lock and then the front door slammed, leaving it shaking in its frame. Something large and aggressive had entered the house.

'Holly's home.'

Karen looked at her watch and then at Lawrence. 'I have a meeting at four. Tell Tom what you told me today.'

'Well,' said Lawrence. 'I was going to suggest I help you with your fear of heights, but after Karen told me about your amnesia...'

Is there any part of my private life you don't discuss?

'... I wondered if I could help you in a different way. I told Karen that there are techniques, you know, for improving your memory. There are exercises you can do. I could come round, if you like. Do a couple of sessions? I wouldn't mind. What do you think?'

'Well, you know. I wouldn't want to put you out.'

'Not a problem. It would be nice to try them out. What's the point of learning something if you can't use it?'

Karen nodded. 'So... ?' she said.

Tom was struggling to maintain focus on the conversation. He was tired. He closed his eyes for a moment and imagined that he was alone in the room; a peaceful, quiet, un-tormented moment. 'So what?' he said.

'Lawrence's idea.'

They were both looking at him. 'The thing is, I already have a discharge plan,' Tom said. 'I should probably do all of that first. And then think about the other stuff.'

'It wouldn't hurt, though, would it?' said Karen. 'To do a bit of both. You said your appointment is three weeks away.'

Tom ran a hand through his hair. He caught a glimpse of his reflection in the window and thought that with his vertical hair, monstrous moustache, missing tooth and fluffy blue dressing gown, he looked insane. He wished that Lawrence didn't look so composed, so knowing.

'It could be like a supplement to your hospital plan,' Lawrence said. 'An augmentation.'

'I don't know.'

'He's offering,' said Karen.

Lawrence straightened up and leaned forwards. 'It really is no problem, Tom. Don't think you're putting me out. How about Saturday morning?'

'This weekend?'

'Why not? Strike while the iron is hot.'

'You've nothing to lose,' said Karen. 'And it might really help.' Again, she spoke each word as if it occupied its own sentence.

'Come on, Tom, it will be fun,' said Lawrence, slapping his own knee. 'We'll all get on like a house on fire. Won't we, Karen?'

'Of course we will.'

'All right,' said Tom. At least Lawrence would go now. Or would he?

'Good man,' Lawrence said, and Karen patted Tom's arm.

'I think it's a good idea,' she said.

They stood up and for a moment Tom thought he was telescoping towards the ceiling, like Alice in *Alice in Wonderland*. They shook hands and walked out to the hallway, the business concluded. Tom held open the front door.

'I'll be late tonight,' Karen said as she passed him. 'It's month-end and they want all the numbers in. Will you be all right to get yourself something to eat?'

Tom wanted to tell her about the fox he'd seen in the mirror but instead he said, 'Of course. Shall I leave something out for you?'

'No. I'll eat on the way home. Holly and Dan can see to themselves.'

'I don't mind, I'll feed the beasts. Dan should be home soon and Holly's already in her cage.' He nodded at Lawrence, who was waiting by the gate. 'He's very something, isn't he?'

'Intense?'

'Old.'

'Be nice. He's doing you a favour. He doesn't have to.'

Tom waved away her words as if they were flies. 'I know.'

Tom remained in the hallway after Karen and Lawrence had left. He felt switched off, empty, vacant, as if he were a machine awaiting instructions. From Holly's room he could hear the deep thump-thump of music and from Dan's room no sound came at all. No sound ever came from Dan's room. The feeling that something was missing came upon him again. He rubbed his chin and pushed his moustache upwards and outwards, finding its thickness and texture soothing. It felt very real.

'Fresh air,' he said, and went back to the kitchen and out into the garden. Like the house, the garden was large, and like the house, there were parts of it that were well-tended and parts of it that were left to spiders and insects and other creatures.

A path divided the garden into two halves. On one side was a lawn and on the other side was a small greenhouse filled with unused pots and sacks of dried-up fertiliser. The greenhouse was surrounded by an untended vegetable garden that Tom liked to call his wild patch. All plants and creatures were welcome in the wild patch and, although it was mostly weeds and cats that took up the offer, sometimes strange and enormous multi-coloured plants grew there, swaying in the wind and sending their seeds into the air until the relentless accumulation of cat urine shrivelled them up and they returned to the earth.

Tom liked to lie on the grass and gaze at these plants, imagining they were travellers from outer space come to his garden to conduct their mysterious tasks. Karen said they were merely big weeds, but Tom didn't care. Weeds and flowers, plants and shrubs and trees were all the same to him. He sketched their shapes and contours, breathed in their scent and rolled their parchment-like leaves between his fingers. He wished he knew more about their alien world. He wished he were part of it.

He walked down to the far end of the garden where there was a wooden summer house that his father had built, calling it his Gin Palace. Tom sat on the bench, put his hands on his knees and rested his head on the back of the bench. Above, in the timber eaves, a spider completed the last stages of embalming a small, broken insect. Tom watched it work and admired the precision of the spider's movements as one artist to another.

He glanced up at the house and saw Holly watching him from her bedroom window. He waved and she disappeared, reappearing moments later at the kitchen door, where she leaned against the frame, half in and half out of the house, her jaw set to its full extent of truculence.

'No one told me you were coming home from hospital,' she said.

'Nobody told me you were coming home from school,' Tom said.

'You're not funny. And it's called a college, not school.'

She walked across the grass, huffing and puffing and avoiding looking in his direction. Tom made way for her, and she sat down with a great explosion of sighing.

'When did you get home?' she said.

'Yesterday afternoon. Where were you?'

'Mum made us stay at Auntie Sylvia's.'

'Why?'

'I don't know. We're staying there tonight, too. Who was Mum with just now? Where's she gone?'

'She's gone back to work with Lawrence. Lawrence works in Marketing and he's going to help me with my memory.'

'I didn't like him.'

'You didn't meet him.'

'I saw him out the window. Why is Mum always working?'

'I don't know. She's a ship in the night.'

'Who is?'

'Mum is. And Lawrence.'

'I don't know what you're talking about. Why are you wearing a dressing gown? Only weird people wear dressing gowns outdoors.'

'I am a weird person.'

'No you're not.'

They sat in silence until Dan came home from school. He walked down the garden path and threw his school bag onto the lawn and squeezed in between Holly and Tom.

'God, Dad, you look a wreck. What's happening? Have you escaped from hospital?'

'He's come home,' Holly said.

Tom thought he could hear a dog barking in the distance. It had a raw tone, like a dog locked in a kennel that had barked all day and all night, for weeks on end, for years. Had it been barking all the time, Tom wondered, and he hadn't noticed? It had a relentless quality; a desperation; a madness in its endless, hoarse repetition.

'Can you hear that?' He stood up and walked to where Dan's bag lay abandoned on the lawn. He wanted a cigarette very much. He wanted to hold one in his lips, strike a match and cup the flame in his hands. He turned round and stared at Holly and Dan, who sat together like clockwork toys left on a shelf. 'The dog barking. Can you hear that?'

They cocked their heads to one side and listened, and the symmetry of their movement disturbed Tom. It was as if they truly were clockwork toys. He squinted at them through the diminishing afternoon light. His eyelids felt heavy. He was tired again.

'Hear what?' Holly said.

'He means the dog,' said Dan.

'Are you all right, Dad?' They said it in unison and laughed.

'It's just a dog,' Holly said.

'A poor dog all alone in the night.'

'Coming to eat you.'

Tom wanted to go in. He didn't like the garden anymore. The sky was darkening and it was cold. He picked up Dan's bag and tossed it to him. It felt empty. 'I'm going to have a bath while you two do your homework, and then I'm going to order pizza for three, and after that I'm going to relax with a glass of wine.'

'Or two,' said Holly.

'Or three,' laughed Dan.

'Or a thousand.'

'Or ten thousand.'

'Hey, Tommy,' Holly said in a different voice. 'I can smell something burning. Can you?'

Tom walked back to the house. His hands were shaking and he felt unwell. In the kitchen he poured himself another drink and took it upstairs. In the bathroom he let his dressing gown fall onto the floor and he stared at his reflection in the mirror. He looked haggard, hollow and drawn; baggy around the eyes and mouth. His shoulders slumped, his chest sagged and his stomach bulged.

'Not coming out today?' he said to the mirror. But only his reflection was there to answer. And it said nothing.

While he was in the bath he heard the front door slam. Rising from the soapy water, he stood up and peered through the open window onto the street below. He saw Holly and Dan walking away with backpacks on their backs. Back to Auntie Sylvia's, then, with no goodbyes. No pizza for three, either. Tom sat down, careless of the waves he created and the surge of water that overflowed the bath and splashed onto the floor.

He felt as if everything he did required a conscious effort: breathing, blinking, talking, moving; as if he were a separate creature inside himself, driving himself along like a human vehicle. He got out of the bath. The bandage on his thumb was soaked.

'That's coming off,' he said, and then added for his own comic effect, 'The bandage, not the thumb.' He laughed and listened to his laugh bounce off the walls. 'Tomorrow you draw. Tomorrow and tomorrow and tomorrow.'

He sat on the toilet seat and dripped water onto the carpet until he was dry. He wondered what he'd see if he looked in the mirror. He wondered what was happening to him and he wondered if he cared. He went downstairs and opened another bottle of wine.

Later, sprawled on the sofa, half-drunk, feet up, headphones on, Tom opened his eyes and saw that it was eleven o'clock at night. The headphones were hurting his ears and his neck ached. A pain stabbed the back of his head. The bottle of red wine, now empty, was on the floor. He switched on the lamp beside him and the sound of the clicking switch felt like something snapping inside his head.

Karen was standing in the doorway looking down at him. She still wore her coat and it was still belted and buttoned up. How long had she been standing there? A long time, perhaps, because she didn't move when he looked at her, as if she too had fallen into a trance.

'Hello,' Tom said, squinting up at her.

'Hello.'

'You're back. I wasn't sure if you were staying at Sylvia's or not.'

'I can if you want.'

'I wasn't saying that. How was it?'

'What?'

'Work.'

'The same as usual. I'm tired. I'm going to bed.'

'Have you eaten?'

'I had a sandwich. How are you feeling?'

'I'm tired, too.'

'I'll sleep in the spare room.'

'You don't have to.'

But she had already gone.

Tom switched off the lights and went to the front door to lock up, but instead he stepped into the night. It was cool and still, and the street lights gave the pavements and hedges and parked cars an artificial effect, as if they were all props on a film set.

When he heard the barking again he wondered if it had ever stopped. He wondered if the dog had been barking ever since he had first awoken in the hospital. He wondered if it was outside or if it were in his head, nestled deep within his ear like a parasite laying its eggs; a plaintive howling that was becoming louder, becoming bigger; a sound that might one day fill up his brain and send him into madness.

12

'Read it,' the always-angry restaurant owner said. 'Read the cartoon.'

I read it.

In the first frame a fox, a cat and a hedgehog were hiding behind a dustbin while an angry-looking woman in a chef's jacket and an apron approached carrying a large cake on a tray. Behind her was an open door with the sign *Restaurant Kitchen* above it. I glanced up at the sign above our door. It read the same but whereas the words in the cartoon were single lines, our sign had neon lighting and cast a shadow.

In the second frame, the animals seemed intent on snatching the cake, but the angry-looking woman had pressed a button and the tray elevated high above her on an extendible device. She looked happy as the three animals clutched at thin air instead of the cake.

In the final frame, a pelican flew over the angry-looking woman and took the cake from the extendible device and hid it in its beak, apparently without her noticing as she seemed to be unconcerned and was whistling, as shown by a tiny quaver hanging in the air by her pursed lips.

I put the newspaper on the ground. The others waited while I lit a cigarette. For once I didn't offer any around. I took several deep drags before saying, 'I'm hungry. Is there any food around?'

'Hungry?' said the always-angry restaurant owner.

'Starving. Have you guys eaten?'

'Are you being serious? What about the newspaper? What about the cartoon strip?'

'What do you want me to say about it?'

'I'm going to hit you,' she shouted. 'It's us. We're in the newspaper.'

'Why are we in a newspaper?' said Plenty. 'Am I famous?'

I blew a long stream of smoke into the air. 'You're right: it is very weird shit. But I'm still hungry.' I knew I was being dumb but I was tired and I wanted to think about it.

'Is that all you can say?'

I leaned back and looked at them all hovering above me, waiting for instructions, for some wisdom, an action plan, an explanation of our depiction as a cartoon strip in a national newspaper.

'Well, I like the title,' I said. 'I think that should stay. That's about all I can think of.'

'Well, that's not good enough,' said the always-angry restaurant owner. 'You're meant to be the one with all the ideas. What are we going to do about it?'

'I'd like to eat before I do anything.'

Some inner heat seemed to pulse behind the always-angry restaurant owner's face. 'You know that actually happened,' she said. 'That thing in the cartoon actually happened. I had that extendible whatsit. Remember? I was making a big cake for some reason and I needed some fruit, some cherries or something, and I promised you all some of the cake if you got me the fruit and then when you did, I laughed and said you couldn't have any? And then when I was delivering it somewhere, the Pelican snatched it and I chased you and it ended like it always ends, with me jumping up and down and you having all the fun. Don't you remember? It's got everything right.' She pursed her lips and blew a long whistle. 'See? It even got my whistle.' She looked as if she might be sick. 'Don't you get it? Somebody's been watching us.'

'I did do that, didn't I? I did. I took the cake.' The Pelican clapped its enormous wings, showering us with fishy offal.

I picked up the newspaper again. What was the correct procedure on discovering that someone had been drawing you in a cartoon strip; that your life had been recorded by an unknown hand? Call the police? Burn the newspaper?

'Do we know any cartoonists?' I said.

'Come off it. We don't know anybody,' said Billy. 'Seriously. We don't know anybody, do we? Outside of us?'

I put my cigarette end against my cartoon face in the newspaper and watched it smoulder. I took the cigarette away and there was my charred head on top of my body running across the frame from left to right. I felt my own face. It was fine.

'What are you doing?' said the always-angry restaurant owner.

'I just wondered... you know.'

'What? If you burn the paper you burn your face? Don't be stupid. It's not black magic. Somebody's drawing us and I think we should find out who that person is and tell them to stop.'

'And then kill them,' said Plenty.

Tell them to stop?

And then the always-angry restaurant owner covered her face with her massive beefy hands and her shoulders began to shake. She was crying. Such a thing had never happened before. I had never seen the always-angry restaurant owner be anything other than always-angry. I stood up, unsure of what to do, acutely aware that any attempt to console her might result in me getting hurt. Billy danced an agitated jig as he too looked on helplessly, and the Pelican opened and closed its beak foolishly. Such was our conditioning to her anger.

It was Plenty, the fearless cat, who stepped in.

'Are you crying?' she said, walking up to the always-angry restaurant owner and pulling her hands away from her face so that she could see more clearly. 'Did you hurt yourself?'

'No, I didn't hurt myself. Get off.'

But Plenty put her furry forehead against the always-angry restaurant owner's teary face and held on to her hands.

'If anybody has hurt you,' she whispered, 'I will hunt them down and rip out their throats and climb inside them and eat their bodies from the inside until only their skin is left, and then I will put them on a stick and leave them out all night for the ants to eat and to take back to their anthill in lots of little, tiny pieces.'

The always-angry restaurant owner sniffed and wiped her eyes. I saw that they were blue and she had make-up on, which was now smeared down her face. I had never noticed that before. It was as if I were looking at her for the first time and seeing her as completely different to how I had imagined. Not only because she had been crying but also because she looked like she was ripening – but ripening in a bad way; bloating and opening up. They all did. I did. We all looked like we were stuffed toys with our stitching coming loose.

'That's very kind of you,' she said to Plenty. 'But no one has hurt me and if they did then, well, you know.' She patted her rolling pin, which was in her apron pocket. 'They would only do it once.'

Plenty seemed to have lost interest in being kind. 'I think I am the most famous,' she murmured, picking up the newspaper.

'If you were,' Billy said, 'then the cartoon strip would be called *Plenty*, wouldn't it?'

The always-angry restaurant owner stared at Billy and I knew that he'd added to her distress and I didn't know why. She sat down on the steps and shook her head, staring at the ground.

'I have a question,' Billy said. 'Are there more of these? More cartoons? I mean different ones. Like every week? Or every day? Going back in time? Or even some, you know, already drawn but not...'

'I don't know,' I said. 'But I suppose somebody must be drawing this stuff and it would be nice to know who.' I looked around as if I would see an artist in the corner with an easel, painstakingly capturing the moment, an artist wearing a smock and a beret.

'It was drawn by someone called *Tash*,' the always-angry restaurant owner muttered.

'Who is Tash?' said Billy.

'The person who drew the cartoon,' said Plenty patiently.

'I mean, who *is* Tash?'

'Look at the walls,' I said. 'It's sprayed everywhere.'

I closed my eyes and tried to think. I felt that something very big and very important was in the vicinity. I felt that behind the air that we were breathing, something was pressing towards us, like a face pressing into a balloon, stretching the atmosphere so thin that it might tear and rip, and everything around us would dissolve.

I was ill-equipped for this sort of thinking. I was a creature that lived in an alleyway. I was an eco-fox who was meant to lead my compatriots in a crusade against waste, the waste created by the always-angry restaurant owner in her pursuit of profit. Except it wasn't like that. Nothing ever changed. The waste kept coming and in the end all I wanted was a clean corner somewhere that I could call my own. We were grubbing a living, that was all, scoring points off something we didn't understand. My intellectual capacity extended only to imagining my life as a pile of bin-bags. I was the sum of my experiences and any question I might conceive to ask would be similarly rooted. I knew I could never breach the bubble in which I lived. I was like a plant that knew only sun, soil and rain and would never be able to imagine that a plastic pot bought from a garden centre might be constraining its growth.

'Where did you get the newspaper?' I said. 'Was it here, in the alleyway?'

The always-angry restaurant owner looked up at me and said, 'I found it in the hospital.'

'What hospital?'

'I don't know. A hospital.'

'What were you doing in a hospital? Why were you there?'

'I don't know why I was there, but I was. I just found myself there – while you were away and these idiots were out looking for you.'

'I'm not an idiot,' Plenty said. She was sitting on a wheelie bin swinging her legs, rolling her ball backwards and forwards on the lid, irritating us all with its tinkling sound. Which I'm sure was her aim.

'You were out looking for me?'

'Of course,' said Billy.

'It wasn't like our alleyway,' the always-angry restaurant owner continued, her voice less emotional now. 'There was so much detail. So many little things. So much sound and different colours and smells and touches. Even the air felt like it was made of things.'

'So what happened?'

'I was pushing a trolley. A food trolley. I was like a mobile always-angry restaurant owner.' She glanced at me and again I was conscious of a hurt I couldn't name. 'Then I found this newspaper and I started reading it and then... then I saw the cartoon. There we all were. I couldn't believe it. And then a dog started barking.'

'A dog?'

'A dog.'

'Not the dog that attacked us?'

'I don't know. I didn't see the dog that attacked you. But this one was loud. I couldn't see it and I didn't know if it was in my mind or what. It sounded so... all around. And then there was a man. A huge man with a horrible, hairy face. And he shouted at me and his voice was loud too. It wasn't like our voices. It moved all the air around me. I couldn't bear it. I had my rolling pin...'

'Did you hit him?' said Plenty, her eyes glowing again.

'No, I asked him if he could hear the dog too but he walked away. And then I was back here and I thought perhaps I had been dreaming but I still had the newspaper in my hand.'

'I don't understand it. Do you understand it? No, I don't,' said the Pelican helpfully.

'This man,' I said. 'What sort of hairy face? Hairy like mine?'

'Not like yours. Like a man's hairy face.'

'A beard? Eyebrows?'

'A moustache. A huge moustache like a broom.'

'A moustache.'

I looked again at the graffiti on the walls.

Tash.

I knew this man.

I took the newspaper from Plenty and looked at the strip again. An oblong box divided into three frames; three panels. Buildings in the background drawn merely as an uneven line of roof tops. The characters were all in silhouette. Clean, uncluttered, minimalist. I looked around at the three-dimensional disorder in which I stood and then back at the cartoon. On the right-hand side of the final frame I could see the far end of the alleyway – the dangerous place with cars and buses and motorbikes and people and shops and hustle and bustle. It had been drawn simply as a vertical line, a half-formed outline of a woman and the back of a car, its wheels off the ground and a cloud of smoke shooting from its exhaust pipe.

Things aren't always what they seem. Like those optical illusions. One moment it's an old woman's face, and the next it's a young woman looking away.

'Hang on, I want to try something.'

It was still dark. I walked towards the busy high street.

'Where are you going?'

'Nowhere.' And I think I meant that.

I walked to the end of the alleyway and it was as if a long piece of elastic was attached to my back and was now at full stretch. I looked into the bright light beyond and braced myself to walk into the city street. But I didn't. The light was too bright for my eyes, so bright that it might as well have been a physical barrier, and one that I simply could not pass. I stood there, trying to feel my way into the main road, and then when I couldn't, I walked briskly back to the restaurant's side-entrance.

'Well?' said the always-angry restaurant owner. 'What was that all about?'

'I don't know. But the noises from that busy street are no louder at the end of the alleyway than they are here.'

'Fascinating. So what?'

'Let's go inside,' I said. 'And talk.'

'Inside?'

We normally only went inside when we had somehow tricked the always-angry restaurant owner and ate her food at a table by the window while she fumed outside. We never went inside just on a whim. There always had to be a reason for it. We didn't even sleep inside. We slept outside amongst the crates and cartons. Only the always-angry restaurant owner slept inside.

'Why don't we talk out here,' she said.

Not for the first time my answer was drowned out by a bark,

although that little word doesn't do justice to the sound that erupted from the dark end of the alleyway. If the earth opened up and an enormous hole that stretched all the way to the planet's superheated iron core appeared, and it barked, it would have made a similar sound. It echoed around the alleyway, bouncing from wall to wall and back again.

'That is a big bark,' said Billy.

'That's like the barking I heard in the hospital,' said the always-angry restaurant owner, standing up and peering into the darkness.

'It's a dog,' said Plenty.

'You don't say.'

It was a dog, although it seemed to be mostly head, jaw and teeth. And it was hurtling towards us, emerging as if from the wrong end of a telescope, with huge gobs of saliva streaming from its mouth and steam blowing from its nostrils.

'Is that the dog from the other day?'

'I don't think so,' I said. 'The dog that chased us was, well, it was like a dog; a real dog. But that thing, that thing is –'

'Like us,' said Plenty.

'Yes.'

'It looks familiar.'

It was difficult to tell in the dark and we were also being showered by oily feather-ends and dollops of evil-smelling gristly jelly which hampered our vision. The Pelican was ascending. 'I'm going to the window,' it said. 'No, the roof. No, the chimney.'

'Let's go inside,' Billy said. 'Before the dog eats us or the Pelican poisons us.'

Adrenalin is a wonderful thing. We moved from one spot to another without any discernible motion. We were inside the restaurant following the always-angry restaurant owner through the kitchen and up the stairs. We stopped on a gloomy landing that was poorly lit by a low-watt bulb. The banister rail was old and scratched, and the carpet – as far as I could see in the dim light – was covered with a thick layer of dust that obscured a fading pattern of intertwined flowers. There was another staircase at the far side of the landing leading upwards, and two doors. I opened one door, thinking that we could hide in there in case the dog followed us, but it was an empty room; floorboards and plain walls and one window. It made me shiver and I closed the door. I felt as if I had looked in on some terribly sad and private scene.

'Tell me you closed the kitchen door,' I said, looking over the banister.

'I shut it,' said the always-angry restaurant owner. She seemed uneasy.

A voice came from above. 'Hello. Hello? Hello.' The Pelican had found its way to the roof.

We went up the second set of stairs and found a wooden door at the top. I opened it and we stepped out onto a small square area set amongst the tiles and chimney pots of other roofs. Below us on one side was a sheer drop to the alleyway. Above, laid out like a vast black blanket, was the night sky, lit on one horizon by the glow of the light I had seen at the bad end of the alleyway. From our new vantage point it looked more like the light from a fire. The Pelican was perched on a chimney pot, the fleshy sack below its beak hanging loose and blowing in the wind, its eyes crossing and uncrossing as it focused on each of us in turn.

'I see the dark,' it said.

Billy leaned over the parapet and looked down. 'And I see the dog,' he said. 'It's still down there.'

The dog, which still seemed to consist mostly of a head with a small, barrel-like body attached, was ripping the alleyway apart. Boxes, cartons, dustbins, litter, restaurant rubbish, it was all being strewn across the ground.

Plenty said to the always-angry restaurant owner, 'Can I see your bedroom?'

'No.'

'Can I see another room, then? Can I see your little sitting room or your bathroom or your –'

'No.'

'Why not?'

'Because you can't.'

'That's not a reason.'

'It is when you're in my restaurant. Tell her, Scraps, tell her to shut up.'

I looked at them both, one tired and careworn in her stained chef's jacket; the other small and torn. I looked at Billy, composed and yet fading, quills dropping, worry lines around his eyes; and at the Pelican, a loosely coupled collection of bone, beak and feathers held together by maggots and decay. And what, I wondered, did they see when they looked at me? A scrawny, skinny and wasted animal with the glow of desperation lighting his eyes? Or merely another fox?

'You can't look in them because there's nothing to look at,' I said to Plenty while watching the always-angry restaurant owner. 'There's nothing in the rooms because she never leaves the restaurant. She never goes upstairs.'

'Don't be so stupid.'

'It's true and it doesn't matter. We're all the same. We all use the same bits of this' – I gestured around – 'this place. It's half-formed, like we are. We know stuff but we can't remember how we came to know it.' I looked at Plenty. 'Tell me, what did Nanny actually look like?'

Plenty shrugged. 'Like a nanny.'

'Yes, but what exactly?'

'I don't know. Stop asking me questions.'

'I see the dark,' the Pelican said again.

'Stop saying that,' said the always-angry restaurant owner. 'Of course it's dark. It's night-time.'

I looked at the Pelican more closely. When its eyes were crossing and uncrossing like knitting needles, it usually meant it was thinking, or it had swallowed something large and acidic.

'You asked me,' it said. 'You asked me, "What do I see when I'm up there and you're down here?" That's what you asked me. Didn't you? I'm sure you did.'

'That was ages ago,' said Plenty.

'Okay,' I said. 'So you see the dark. But what do you see during the day?'

'Dark. I see the dark. I see the nothing. Although sometimes I see other things.'

'The nothing? During the day? What do you mean? Where?'

'Down there.'

The Pelican pointed its beak at the silhouetted horizon and its words hung in the air like the smoke from a firework, until the always-angry restaurant owner said, 'Do we have time for this? Of course there's something there. The Pelican doesn't know what it's talking about.'

I took a deep breath. The Pelican had subsided back into whatever passed for thought. 'I think we have to leave the alleyway,' I said.

They looked at me. I waited. Braced. I expected dissent. I expected argument, refusals, huffs, and a long and painful process of talking them round. But it had to be done. I didn't know why but I felt that it was imperative to our well-being that we left as soon as possible. And no matter what they said, or how stubborn and intractable they were...

'Okay,' said Billy.

'Beg pardon?'

'If we have to go, we have to go.'

The always-angry restaurant owner nodded too. 'It won't be forever, though, will it?' she said.

'Can I take my ball?' said Plenty.

'I'll pack. No, I won't. I haven't got anything to pack,' said the Pelican, fluttering its feathers up and down, releasing waves of noxious, opaque gas that drifted up into the air and changed the colour of the stars.

I was shocked. 'Really? No argument?'

Billy came over to me. 'Look at this.' He plucked a quill from his back and then snapped it in half like a dry twig. 'Do you know what happens when a hedgehog loses its quills?'

'No.'

'Neither do I, but it can't be good. We are dying here. The Pelican would look better if it was inside out, Plenty's got more patches then fur, you look like shit and the almost-angry restaurant owner smells worse than one of her fish stews.'

'Hey.'

'I think we have to find the hairy man,' I said. 'I don't know why, but I do.'

'Fair enough. I don't know why we do either, but if you think we do, then that's good enough for me. You're Scraps, right? Our fearless leader. What happens when we find him?'

I looked at Billy and at the others, at the night sky and the silhouettes of the buildings and at the dog down below trying to eat through the walls. I thought about the blood in my saliva and the bright light at the end of the alleyway and the dark that the Pelican saw when it flew in the sky. I remembered my smouldering face in the newspaper and the word *Tash* that now seemed to swirl around and around inside my head. I tried hard to think beyond those things because I knew that it was all important. But all I could do was shake my head and say, 'I don't know.'

13

weekendingnews.com/lifestyle/jean_hannah/111009/
Dancing on Tables: An Interview with Barbara Hannah
By Germaine Kiecke – 8 May 2013

As part of our series of occasional interviews with parents of creative artists, our Arts Editor Germaine Kiecke was lucky enough to catch up with Barbara Hannah QC, widow of Joseph Hannah, the award-winning architect, and mother of cartoonist Tom Hannah. How did these two indomitable females hit it off? Read on...

The Regency Palace Retirement Village has all the trappings of a first-class hotel. It's large, friendly and, I suspect, very discreet. The taxi-driver confides, in the way that taxi-drivers do, that more than one A-List celebrity from the 1960s is a resident, as well as a number of notables from the worlds of art, commerce and science.

I'm met in reception by an efficient young lady who assures me that I am expected and shows me to the communal lounge: a large and sunny area that leads onto a terrace and the rolling lawns beyond. This is a place to take tea, read the papers and reminisce, but the people I see around me look too busy to dwell on the past. Most are talking on their mobile phones or bustling past on their way to meet friends, relatives and, for one resident at least, a journalist.

There is a tangible aura of accomplishment in the air and I suspect that behind the sensible cardigans and floral dresses, the smart ties and polished shoes, there are people who know exactly what to do in an emergency, and would do so with an understated efficiency.

While I wait I run through my notes on my intended interviewee, Barbara Hannah: human rights barrister, eco-campaigner and now, since her retirement from public affairs, a self-confessed thorn in the side of all things unfair, unjust or plain daft.

I can't wait to meet her.

Exactly on the hour, the door on the far side of the lounge opens and a tall, rangy woman appears. She is dressed in fur-lined slippers, a tartan skirt, a blue cardigan and a white shirt buttoned up to her neck. She walks slowly and with the aid of a stick.

'It's the inconvenience of old age,' she tells me as she sits down. 'But better than falling down all the time. My husband used to say that the secret of a long life is to stay vertical for as long as possible.'

She is concerned that I may have found it difficult to park – apparently, the visitors' car park is being used for a fête which may account for the profusion of the floral dresses – but the fact that I came by train and taxi meets with approval. Railways, it seems, are a fond memory.

'We always used to travel by train to visit my parents who retired to the coast. Joseph and I would cycle to the railway station, catch two trains, and walk a mile. This was before the children were born, of course. It was the rituals of the journeys that we loved – buying a coffee at the same café while we waited for our connection, sitting on the bench at the furthest end of the station, choosing a forward-facing seat at the front of the first carriage. It was all part of the fun. Fun is so important, don't you think?'

I nod and wonder if I am having enough fun in my life. I can see why Barbara was such a formidable lawyer. Her certainties make others doubt their own.

We go back to her apartment, which is neat and tidy, light and airy. There are flowers in vases and the walls are covered with family photographs, framed newspaper articles, *Scraps* cartoons and postcards from abroad. In the centre is an aerial photograph of the so-called Peanut Building, the construction that won her husband the RIBA Stirling Award in the late nineties. Barbara has her own terrace that overlooks the side of the house, and her table is laid with plates, cutlery and a bottle of white wine with glasses.

'I thought we might have fish and chips,' she tells me. 'They do a delivery. It's very good. And I've got some nice bread. Do you like wine?' I say I do, which meets with more approval.

Barbara Hannah is 80 years old and going strong. Born in London in 1933, she was an only child and evacuated during the Second World War to Dorset, where she fell in love with the sea.

'It was wonderful. We weren't allowed on the beach because of the mines being washed ashore, but of course we used to sneak down there anyway. And then a patrol caught us. Goodness, one of the soldiers gave us such a dressing down. All I can remember are his boots – great, shiny lumps of leather. I didn't dare look at his face. I was scared stiff because I thought he was going to arrest us and tell my mother. I don't think we went within a mile of the sea after that, but I still loved being beside the seaside. Such a change to London. Although I adore London, too.'

She was relocated to an arable farm, growing vegetables for the war effort.

'And they were all cricket-mad. Grandfather, mother, father, aunt, uncle and four little boys – all built like Shire-horses. We'd play cricket in the lanes in the evenings with an old swede that was rock-hard and a hockey stick. I could throw the swede further than any of them and it stung like a wasp if it caught you.'

I sense that if given the chance she would still like to throw the odd vegetable around.

'I would love to but I don't think my eyesight is up to it. It's all part of becoming old. They gave me glasses that turn dark when I go outside and light when I come inside. I told them I didn't need glasses at all, I mean I can see, but she told me to go outside with her and I did see the difference. Mind you, I caught sight of myself in a window: an old, grey-haired woman with a stick and dark glasses. I told her I didn't want glasses if that's what I'm going to see.'

I ask her how she met her husband.

'My parents wanted me to settle down and marry a "nice young man". A nice young man? I didn't want a nice young man. I wanted to have some fun. Joseph was fun and he made me laugh. We met at a charity function. Joseph tripped over me when I was demonstrating a wicket-keeper's crouch. He burst through a door and he was so tall he didn't see me down there. We both ended up on the floor talking about the quality of waxing on the floorboards. He was a very funny man, but different to me in every way. He was a ditherer and would take forever to come to a decision. I'd say, what do you want to do, Joseph? And he'd say, I want to do this, no I don't, I want to do that. Goodness knows how he ever got his buildings built. Not like me. I'm straight to the point.'

They had two children, Tom and Caroline. Caroline is the eldest by almost ten years and I ask if Barbara felt that such an age difference meant she had had two only children.

'I suppose so. But we were always a close family emotionally. Joseph was away on building projects a lot of the time, and I travelled too, but we were close. I suppose we weren't a stereotypical family unit but, well, they turned out all right.'

The fish and chips arrive and we squeeze into tight, old-fashioned and solid dining chairs. Barbara cuts the bread and arranges the slices in a circle on a plate while I open the wine.

Barbara is a forthright person and she freely admits that her directness can come across as abrasive, but she makes no apology for that and her zest for life remains undiminished, and she is clearly at ease with herself and her surroundings. She seems to prize having fun over most things.

'It's an attitude,' she says. 'It brings out the best in people: generosity, kindness, laughter. It's not about having fun for the sake of it, or having fun at the expense of others, it's about a willingness to do new things and enjoy them, to be with people, to not be so solemn about life.'

After her legal career ended, Barbara chose to campaign on behalf of No Waste No Want – an environmental pressure group for which she became its most vociferous spokesperson.

'I spent a year at home while Joseph worked and then I thought, right, enough loafing. Time to get out there and do something. I saw a homeless man taking food from a bin at the back of a restaurant. I went and had a look and there were piles and piles of discarded food – perfectly edible. And the same is true in countless other alleyways in countless other towns and cities. Yet elsewhere people are going without. It's wrong.'

Barbara retired from public campaigning when Joseph died of a heart attack in 2010. They had been married for 52 years.

'It was simply the most dreadful thing. He died at the dining table. One minute he was alive, the next he wasn't. It's impossible to describe the effect that the sudden absence of someone you love can have. Nothing else matters. Whatever other issues or concerns you may have, they simply vanish in the face of death. Joseph was a big man and he left a big gap in life – for me and for Tom and Caroline.

It's the finality as much as anything. We live our lives planning ahead, dreaming of tomorrow and when there is no tomorrow it's... well, it's difficult to reconcile. We lay them in a coffin and there it is: the beginning, middle and end of their story, of their life. It's terribly sad.'

Finding herself suddenly living alone, Barbara took the remarkable step of selling everything and moving into the Regency Palace. Was it an escape from reality, I wonder, or simply a pragmatic decision made by a practical woman?

'I had a friend who lived here and I always thought she was having the most marvellous time. I wasn't going to get any younger and the children had their own lives, so why not? I didn't want to rattle around in that big old house on my own. Besides, I'd rather make the decision myself than be put away when I'm too old to argue.'

I can't imagine Barbara ever being too old to argue. She devotes her time now to letter-writing and emailing people and institutions that annoy her. An innocuous occupation for most but a potent pastime in her hands.

'I am unashamedly left-wing. It is the absolute duty of the strong to look after the weak – economically, militarily, socially, domestically. I can't bear this jingoistic nationalism that people call patriotism. It's not patriotism, it's xenophobia, plain and simple. I can't abide bigots.'

After lunch, we clear the table and Barbara folds the tablecloth neatly along the seams. She is, I notice, very precise. We go for a walk around the gardens and Barbara's glasses do indeed turn dark when exposed to light. I ask her about her children's success and how that has informed her own life.

'I learn from them all the time. It's always a wrench when you realise that you are not the only influence in their lives, and that they listen to other people: teachers, friends and so on, and start forming their own opinions. But it's thrilling at the same time. It's the essence of life, I suppose, the accession to one's own individuality, to one's own liberation. At least it is for me.'

Caroline is an aid worker based in the Gambia.

'She has a wonderful and fulfilling life. She lives in a compound and keeps dogs – lots of dogs. We had a family Labrador years ago. Joseph bought him from a rescue centre and Caroline went mad for the thing. She learned to walk by dragging herself up on his ears.

But he was completely untrainable. We'd take him for a walk and he would zoom off into the distance until he was just a dot, and then zoom off in another direction. There was never any fetching of sticks; he was just a ball of yellow fur zooming backwards and forwards in the distance. Whenever we had visitors he got excited and urinated all over them. Have you ever been extensively urinated on by a large dog?'

I confess that I haven't.

'It's not something you readily forget. But the poor thing got tetchy as he got older. We had to have him put down after he turned on Tom and bit him.'

For a time, Barbara had travelled to Banjul each year to visit Caroline, but has been unable to do so since her balance has deteriorated. Does she miss the travel?

'When Caroline used to collect me from the airport we'd drive back to her compound, bouncing wildly up and down in her car, and I'd stay for two weeks each year. I'd sleep under a mosquito net at night and sit on the verandah during the day, sipping gin and tonics and watching toucans in the trees. Of course I miss the travel. Wouldn't you?'

We sit on a bench beneath an apple tree and look back at the house. It seems so calm and serene. There's not a cloud in the sky and it's still warm. I can imagine that these comfortable and capable people create their own world of endless summer days. I mention this and Barbara laughs. She is no stranger to surreal imaginings.

'Tom was an imaginative little boy, a real daydreamer. Of course, he was Tommy then. I still call him that sometimes. He hates it. I used to worry that he was spending too much time on his own but I suppose it was his choice. We weren't the sort of parents to set any rules in that respect. He was quite a large child and one always assumes that big equals strong.'

Did he share his mother's love of fun, I wonder? Did he have fun as a child?

'He loved his comics and books and going to the library, and playing with his soldiers in the garden. He had names for them all. I don't think it mattered that he didn't play with other children. He had the whole world in his head. He was very inventive. He wanted to invent a pill that would keep us all alive forever. I suppose all children want to protect their parents. You don't often think of that, do you? Children protecting their parents. He used to imagine that he had a communication device and if he pressed the button he would see his future self. See how he turned out. Isn't that a good idea?'

I wasn't so sure that I would like to be judged by my younger self.

'It has helped him a lot in later life, being self-reliant. Tom took his father's death very hard. A pity he never managed to invent that pill. Apart from the obvious emotional devastation, I think it was the sheer messiness of it that upset him. No one would want to see their father face down in crumble and custard. Tom is an *orderly* person.'

An inherited trait?

'From me, you mean? I suppose so. Joseph was less neat but, of course, his drawings were precise. He was an architect, after all. We were a defined family. Each of us in our own little compartment. And I think that sense of fitting in together was very important to Tom. It was his base. His anchor. Caroline has always been a free spirit. Tom needs a family.'

Had Joseph wanted Tom to follow him into architecture?

'He was a better draughtsman than his father, Joseph always said that. He has an engineer's hand and an artist's heart, he used to say. Joseph could never have drawn something like *Scraps*, although I think he may have liked to. But Tom was always more creative than technical. I can picture him now, sitting at the dining table drawing imaginary worlds. We used to say he spent more time inside his head than out.'

I ask her if she feels that through *Scraps* Tom is continuing her eco-campaigning, her war on waste.

'Tom feels the inequity of it all and he takes his social responsibilities seriously, but he's more satirical than I am. I am very matter-of-fact, but Tom sees things that I don't. He's more imaginative. I feel sorry for the always-angry restaurant owner. She never seems to win and, after all, she's only trying to run a business. But I suppose she's the symbol of waste so she can't really triumph, can she?'

We return to the communal lounge where, in the far corner, there is a film on the television. It's a musical in which people frequently jump on tables and sing and dance.

'Don't you wish that real life were like that?' Barbara asks me. 'Imagine how much fun it would be.'

I wonder if, even if real life were like that, I would jump on a table and start dancing. I conclude that I am simply not as much fun as I ought to be.

All too soon the time has come for me to leave. The wine, the conversation and the company have been wonderful and I feel sad that I have to go. I would like to stay longer. I ask Barbara if she is happy.

'Of course, and I'm not done yet,' she tells me.

I am reminded of the time that I interviewed Tom, when he told me that the 'now' doesn't exist, it is merely a moment between what was and what will be. I think Barbara lives very much in the here and now. I make this point and she says to me, 'For some people there are only ever tomorrows and yesterdays. Poor Tom, no matter how much he wants to hide in the moment he can never relax. I wish he could.'

On my way back to the station, the taxi-driver confides, in the way that taxi-drivers do, that in his opinion the Regency Palace must have its fair share of gossip, given all 'those ex-celebrities and what-nots living there'.

I'm tempted to tell him that he doesn't know the half of it. And why shouldn't there be gossip and intrigue? After all, what is life without a little fun?

Editor's note: Sadly, two weeks after this interview Barbara Hannah passed away. She was 80 years young. Our deepest condolences go out to her family, her daughter, Caroline, and her son, Tom.

14

Two weeks after leaving hospital, a weekday routine had developed in Tom's home that accommodated but didn't include him, much as a tide ebbs and flows around a pebble. Monday to Friday he seldom saw Karen or the children. She said he needed time and space to recover and their presence would disturb him. So she worked all day, came home late and slept in the spare room while Dan and Holly stayed with her sister.

Tom disagreed. He missed them all. He missed waking up with

Karen, their legs tangled up, her face close to his on the pillow, her breath mingling with his. He missed Dan's hair-obscured face, his casual disregard for everything, his slouch, his directness. He missed Holly and her heavy movements from room to room, her personal micro-climate of resentment, the way she slammed doors hard enough to loosen plaster and vibrate the dying nerve in his broken tooth.

He spent the weekdays in long periods of silence, during which he sat in his chair in his airy eyrie and seldom moved, seldom blinked, seldom did anything except watch the rise and fall of his chest, and listen to the passage of blood in his ears and the internal hissing and humming and growling that accompanied it.

Sometimes he looked up at the twin skylights in the roof and watched rain fall against the windows and roll downwards, droplets that criss-crossed each other's tracks when the wind blew and raced each other to reach the woodwork. And when he shut his eyes he could still see the window imprinted on his retina, with the black dots running downwards like insects. He listened to the hollow sound of the house's central heating and wondered how long it would be before a pipe burst or an element failed or the ceiling caved in and the house fell in on him.

Occasionally he checked his email, but seldom got beyond looking at his in-box with its pages of unread messages. He was tempted to delete them all. He had no social media accounts other than those administered by Borkmann's creative team and so, after a few minutes of aimless clicking, he logged out and returned to his quiet contemplation of the passing weather.

He wanted the chaos of family life: the loud voices and bruising movements, the kicking off of shoes and throwing down of bags, the thundering up and down stairs, the talking and shouting and eating and clattering of dishes. The only human contact he had, if you could call it that, was with Borkmann during their daily telephone calls; oases of terse information exchange.

How are you?

I'm fine.

Drawing yet?

Not yet.

Don't leave it too long.

The weekends were different. At least the house was populated at the weekends and, as promised, Lawrence had shown up on the first Saturday, inflicting his willowy, weaselly presence on Tom with Karen's apparent endorsement.

'Hello, Tom,' he had said, standing in the kitchen and making tea, as if Tom were the guest. 'Sit yourself down.' He wore trainers and jeans and a T-shirt that was tucked in. His legs were longer than his body and the jeans rode curiously high. Tom was wearing baggy shorts and a pyjama top. He smelled like he was fresh from his bed. Which he was.

'How's the old memory box today?' Lawrence boomed.

'The old memory box is fine.'

'But is it, Tom?'

Escape was impossible.

'You don't have to do this, you know,' Tom told him. 'Seriously. You don't.'

But Karen had tutted and hissed that Lawrence had given up his day for Tom, and Lawrence had simply smiled. 'It's my pleasure, Tom. Anything to help the husband of a work colleague.'

The techniques that Lawrence claimed to have learned seemed to Tom to have come from Christmas crackers. First, they played *Word Association*, which was a game in which Lawrence sat across the kitchen table from Tom and used what he called trigger words and phrases, such as 'car park', 'falling' and 'aaahh', and Tom had to say the first thing that came into his mind – such as 'car', 'banana' or 'ouch'. When that failed to yield any results, Lawrence shook his head sadly and smiled, and looked at Karen and said, 'Never mind, it's early days yet.' He sat at the head of the table as if conducting a family get-together.

'Are you married?' said Tom.

'Once. Not anymore.' He held Tom's gaze and Tom wondered what had happened to this man's wife.

'Divorced,' said Lawrence after a long pause. 'All very amicable.'

They played *Picture Association*. This was the same as *Word Association* except Lawrence drew trigger diagrams such as a car park, a man falling and a man lying on the pavement. After *Picture Association* came *Movement Association*, in which Tom had to adopt trigger poses, such as looking down, looking up and lying on the carpet.

Karen stood to one side throughout those memory-recovery sessions, as Lawrence liked to call them, watching carefully as if she were waiting for a sudden breakthrough. But the only association Tom managed to have during all of these games was the recurring image of Lawrence as a weaselly weasel, dressed in black with a revolver hanging from each hip. He wanted to capture that image very much. Perhaps even draw himself into the picture, firing bullets at the ground while Lawrence danced a jig to his tune. His thumb was more mobile now and he thought he might be able to manage it.

'How did he get in? Has he got a key?' Tom said to Karen after Lawrence had gone.

'Of course not,' she said. 'Why would he?'

'I don't know.'

'Why are you being like this?'

'Like what.'

'You know like what.'

On the second Sunday, two weeks after Tom's fall, Lawrence arrived with a new game. Tom was lying on the sofa and staring out of the front window, stroking his moustache. Since returning from hospital he hadn't trimmed it, in fact he seldom shaved at all, and it was now so bushy it extended beyond his face on either side and outwards to the tip of his nose. Lawrence came in and sat on the chair opposite him. He wore a tan leather jacket and hiking boots.

'I'm quite tired today, Lawrence. I should have phoned. Do I have your number? Where do you live?'

But all Lawrence said was, 'Location Association.'

Karen had come into the room too and stood by the door in her smoker's stance, arms folded, hunched forwards as if she were huddled against the cold, wearing her usual watching and waiting expression. Tom shook his head. Had he died and gone to hell?

'Let me guess,' he said. 'You say a location and I tell you what comes into my mind?'

'Wrong. We *go* to a location. We get up and we go out, and we go to a location. *The* location. Why not? It's better than sitting around here all day.' Lawrence looked up at Karen.

'It's a great idea,' she said.

Tom thought about it. He lay on the sofa and stroked his moustache while Karen and Lawrence seemed to float on either side. It hadn't occurred to him to go back to the car park and he felt unexpectedly excited by the thought. He might see the market stall and the crates of bananas, or new ones at least. He might find his missing tooth.

'I do like that idea,' he said.

Karen was peering at him closely. 'Will you go to the top?' she said.

'We could,' said Lawrence. 'Why not?' He looked down at Tom with his amused eyes. 'Up for a stroll down Memory Lane?'

They set off almost immediately. Lawrence and Tom together. It was a 20-minute walk to the car park. Lawrence had no car, at least no car that Tom could see.

'Where did you say you lived?' he said as they walked.

'Over there.' Lawrence pointed towards the horizon beyond the houses. 'East.'

They left the cul-de-sac and walked along cracked and uneven pavements that had been punished over the years by tree roots and frosts and wind and rain, and cars driven by people such as Borkmann. They walked through an underpass that magnified their footsteps and stank of urine, and cut through an empty children's park with motionless swings.

Tom said, 'Do you know, today is exactly two weeks since I fell off the roof. Perhaps I was walking along this path then, doing what I'm doing now, unaware of what was to come. Doing the exact same thing at this exact same moment.'

Lawrence glanced at him. 'What do you mean, the exact same thing?'

'I mean this.'

'Do you mean walking along with me?'

'Well no, not walking along with you. But perhaps walking along here at about this time.'

Away from Karen, Lawrence seemed a little less affable. His urbane and amused expression had altered slightly, much as a ringmaster's gaze might narrow when a lion-tamer brings on his lions. He kept his head down as he walked, watching the ground rather than his surroundings. The wind was lifting his dry, sandy hair backwards, revealing more scalp that he probably would have liked. He was a good six inches shorter than Tom, probably two stone lighter, too.

And ten years older if he was a day. Too old for Karen, Tom found himself thinking.

'I have an outpatient appointment tomorrow,' he said.

'Are you going?'

'I think so.'

For once Tom found himself in a talkative mood with Lawrence and, 'I went to the top of Vesuvius once, on holiday. This is going back a few years, before it became a national park. We walked up. It was quite a climb. When you get to the top you can walk around the rim. It's pretty steep when you look down into the crater. There's a shallow slope on the inside and then a steeper drop into the crater.

'I felt all right and then I saw a boy sliding down the slope and skidding to a stop just before the drop. It looked so dangerous and I think it did something to my mind. I think in some way my mind was traumatised by what I was seeing. There was nothing to stop him falling and I was suddenly aware of how precarious it was up there. I imagined myself doing the same thing, sliding down the slope but this time not stopping.

'I thought to myself, I've got to get out of here before I panic and do something stupid. And thinking about panicking made me start to panic and I thought I might actually do it. I might actually run down that slope and not stop and fall over the edge – deliberately, because my mind wouldn't be able to stop me.

'To get down I had to walk all the way around the rim because there was an official entrance to the pathway, and I felt trapped. I thought at any minute I'd do something stupid and die. I think that's the essence of my height phobia: it's about being trapped up high and having no fast way of being safe, and then panicking and doing something stupid.'

Lawrence said nothing.

'What do you think of that?'

Lawrence shrugged. 'I've been abroad hundreds of times,' he said. They walked on.

Tom thought about Lawrence. He was conscious of himself striding along with his hair and moustache and jacket flying in the wind, unshaven, a missing tooth, which he was growing to like, presenting himself to the world as a huge, unconventional and extravagant creature. The artist Tom Hannah. While Lawrence, slim and effete, had to lope alongside to keep up.

Knock him up in the air.

Tom frowned. That was a thought that hadn't entered his head for many years, not since his student days. About the time he had seen his first red fox in the student-artists' garden, he had known a group of animators whose approach to life was to do everything with the safety-catch off, or so it seemed to Tom. One of their favourite sayings was 'knock him up in the air', which referred to a cartoon uppercut that sent victims sailing towards the ceiling. Anyone they didn't like or who made a crass statement or overstepped the mark, warranted being knocked up in the air. For three years the pubs and bars around the college reverberated to the hooting of 'knock him up in the air'. How would they have treated Lawrence? Tom wondered. Would they have shouted 'knock him up in the air' as soon as they saw him? Imagining that made Tom feel guilty because, after all, Lawrence was giving up his Sunday morning to help him.

Hardies Lane car park was attached to a shopping mall behind the high street. The first thing Tom saw was the market. He walked along it looking for the greengrocer's stall that had saved his life, but it wasn't there. That week's market seemed to be devoted to household items, gardening tools and car parts.

'They're not here,' Tom said.

'Who?'

'The banana people. The fruit and vegetable stall. I must have scared them off.' He laughed and a shopper looked at him carefully before walking away. Tom was used to that and took no notice.

'Do you know people here?' Lawrence said.

'No – why?'

'I just wondered. That man's looking at you.'

Across the road, Tom saw a council worker with a hoe along the edge of a patch of grass that bordered the pavement. He was young and scruffy and wore grey coveralls with high-visibility stripes on the trouser-cuffs. He'd stopped his work and was staring at Tom.

'You don't remember me, do you?' he called out.

'Who is that?' said Lawrence.

'I don't know.'

The man put down his hoe, looked quickly up and down the

road and ran across to where Tom was standing. 'You're the one that fell off the roof, aren't you? I was there.' He held out his hand. 'Peter Hobbes. I waited with you until the ambulance came. I'd recognise you anywhere. How you doing?'

'You saw me fall?'

'Absolutely. You scared the life out of me. Seriously. Pow!' He punched his hand with his fist. 'I thought the stall had blown up. Stuff everywhere. I didn't actually see you come off the top but I saw you land. Right through everything – tarpaulin, crates, the lot. You were like a bomb. It's lucky I'd turned the earth the day before or you would have been dead.'

Tom stared at him. 'Did you see me before I fell?'

'What, up top? No.'

Lawrence tugged Tom's sleeve. 'No point in dawdling, let's get to where we're going,' he said.

'I mean before, anywhere, did you see me walking along? With anyone?'

Hobbes shook his head. 'I didn't. First time I really saw you was when you were lying face down in the mud. How fast do you think you were going? A hundred miles an hour?'

'They think about 40. But that's fast enough. Look.' Tom showed Hobbes his missing tooth and he looked impressed. 'I don't suppose you saw it lying around anywhere, did you? My tooth?'

'Sorry mate, no. I'll have a look if you like.'

'Would you? It's stupid, isn't it, but it's a part of me and I don't like to think of it, you know, out in the cold. On its own.'

'That is weird but I know what you mean. I'll have a look but I wouldn't hold out any hopes. What are you going to do? Leave it or get a new one? No one can see it underneath that moustache, anyway. That is a corker of a mouser. I could use something like that to pull in all the leaves.'

'Tom.' Lawrence was beckoning in the background.

'I have to go – but look, thank you. I can't remember a single thing about what happened, so I don't know exactly what you did, but whatever it was, thank you.'

'No worries, mate. Just don't do it again.' He laughed and trotted across the road, back to his work.

'Come on,' said Lawrence. 'No procrastinating.'

'I wasn't. Do you think there are other people around here who saw me, who saw me before I went up? They could help me remember what I was doing, who I was with.'

'Let's stick to the programme and take a look at the car park.'

'I want to look around here first.'

'Let's do it afterwards.'

Knock him up in the air.

'Okay, but I am going to look around here once I've seen the car park.'

'Of course.' Lawrence smiled and Tom noticed that his teeth weren't good. He'd not seen that before. Not that Tom felt he was in much of a position to pass judgement given his new gappy look. But even so. He looked away. 'Let's get on with it, then.'

They walked down a side road, turned a corner into Hardies Lane, and there it was: the multi-storey car park that Tom had no memory of climbing or falling from. He looked up at the roof and wondered if his father had ever designed a car park.

'I feel strongly that tall buildings should be equipped with safety nets, ropes, cages and harnesses,' he said.

They carried on walking and turned into an access road where a wide patch of grey concrete greeted them, beyond which, on the far side, was a grassy slope topped with a wire fence and, on the other side of that, a grouping of industrial units.

'This rings a bell,' Tom said. 'This definitely rings a bell.'

'That's the beauty of Location Association,' said Lawrence, slapping Tom on the shoulder.

Along the car park wall there was a ramp with a low wall running alongside it. At the end was a narrow opening with steps leading up to a yellow access door.

'Fancy looking inside?' Lawrence said.

'Okay.'

Inside was a flight of concrete steps. Tom shivered and looked up. The stairs rose in a zigzag pattern to the top, to a tiny square high above them.

'How high is this?'

'Six floors one end; five the other,' said Lawrence. 'It's on a slope.'

'I fell off the front, onto the market.'

'Yes, you did. Sixty feet give or take a few inches. How do you feel about walking up?'

'Walking?'

'The lift's not working.'

'Really?'

'Come on. Give it a go.'

They began the slow trudge upwards, past pitted walls cut with crude graffiti, up narrow, echoing, concrete steps, two flights for every floor, 13 steps each, with their heads down and their bodies bent forwards like mountaineers; Lawrence in the lead and Tom behind, breathing heavily. His head was starting to throb again and he realised he had forgotten to bring any water.

As they walked, Tom imagined the builders constructing this car park, whistling and calling to each other, sitting on scaffolding and eating their sandwiches, looking out at the view with their legs dangling over the edge, ropes and buckets swaying in the wind, bags of sand and cement left where someone might trip or stumble.

After five flights Tom said, 'Let's take a rest.'

'There's only one more floor to go.'

Tom waved him on. 'Go ahead if you want.' Lawrence shrugged again and stopped. He leaned against the far corner with his hands in his pockets, gazing at Tom in the same way that Karen had done earlier, and as Dan and Holly had done in the garden when he'd come home from the hospital – with a watchful, ready-to-react expression.

'Look.' Tom nodded towards the only two cars he could see, which were parked side by side. 'All this space and they park next to each other.'

'Drug deal, I expect,' Lawrence said. 'Or sex.'

'But the cars are empty.'

'Maybe they're on the back seat.' Lawrence's voice echoed around the stairwell like a bullet bouncing off the walls. 'Maybe it's a suicide pact. A lot of people jump off car park roofs these days. Come on.' Lawrence peeled away from the wall. 'One more floor.'

He started walking and Tom looked through the window at the two isolated cars parked next to each other. They reminded him of his father's car, sagging on his driveway. Tom wished, for a moment, that his father was there with him. It was a wish that lacked the power of his younger grief but it saddened him nonetheless. It would be nice to be in the company of giants. Nice to feel his shadow fall across him.

They walked up the remaining steps and stopped at the top of the stairwell. Another access door faced them but this time a breeze blew beneath it and Tom was aware of the brightness beyond the window. It was the brightness of the outside.

'Well, I think this is it,' said Lawrence.

Tom put his arm against the door and rested his face against the window. It was cool against his hot skin. His mouth was dry.

'Are you all right? Not getting twitchy?'

'I'm fine,' Tom said. 'Just catching my breath.'

He was becoming aware of himself, of his posture, his position in relation to the outside and to the ground far below. He recognised those feelings as the first gentle touches of panic, as gentle as a cobweb touching his face.

'Did I tell you about a friend of mine who fell off a mountain?' Lawrence said. 'His boot caught on a tree branch that was growing out the side of the mountain. Saved his life.'

'I don't think there are any trees growing out the side of this car park.'

'Very true, but that's not my point. My point is, he didn't keep thinking about what might happen, and so when it did happen, it wasn't what he thought would happen.'

'I see.'

Lawrence held on to Tom's gaze, smiling. 'Let's go out onto the roof,' he said.

'I'm not sure yet.'

'Yet? There is no yet. We're here now and this is where it happened. This is real Location Association. You are right in the centre of the location and now it's time to start associating.'

'Just give me a moment.'

'What are you thinking?'

'I was thinking, can an intangible thought be stronger than a physical movement?'

'Oh dear. That really is too much thinking even for you. A little less brain, a little more body – that's what I always say.'

'Do you? Well, I'm wondering if I can trust myself not to panic. What would happen if I pushed open the door and something went wrong in my mind, some rogue synaptic connection occurred, and I ran across the roof and jumped off the edge? It's like that Vesuvius thing I was telling you about.'

'You'd fall,' said Lawrence. 'But you're not going to do that, are you? Why would you?'

'I don't know.'

'You are over-thinking everything. Seriously, I'll hold on to you.'

Tom briefly imagined Lawrence trying to restrain his 18 stone bulk. 'I'm not sure that would work.' He could feel his thoughts becoming lumpy, becoming less to do with thinking and more to do with thinking about thinking, of simulating thinking, as if each thought were a single, shaky snapshot rather than a smooth, continuous film. 'I think I want to go down now.'

Lawrence laughed and pushed his hair back, revealing a shiny area of dry, freckled scalp. 'But we've only just walked up. You know, there's no difference between standing up here and standing on a three-foot high wall.'

If Lawrence had said anything other than that, then Tom might have remained. He might have walked out onto the roof, conquered his fear of heights, remembered why he had been up there and how he came to drop off the edge, and the trip would have been a complete success. But because Lawrence said that Tom said, 'I'll see you down there.'

'Really? You're giving up? Just like that?'

'Just like that.'

'How about just one minute? We walk out, walk round, and then go back down. One minute. Thirty seconds, even.'

But Tom had already started his descent, putting the door behind him and returning to the gloom, taking one careful step at a time, holding on to the handrail, focusing on the moment when he would be on terra firma again, looking up instead of looking down. 'Do you know what G.K. Chesterton used to say?' he said.

Lawrence was clumping down the stairs above Tom. 'I don't really follow cricket.'

'He wrote a bit, too. G.K. Chesterton used to say he'd rather live in the valleys where everything looked grand and magnificent, than in the mountains where everything looked small and distant.' Tom stopped and looked back up at Lawrence. 'Shall I tell you the difference between standing on the multi-storey car park roof and standing on a three-foot wall?'

'I'm all ears.'

'One is very high, and one isn't.'

Back on the street, Tom told Lawrence to go on without him, saying that he wanted to speak to the market stallholders in case any of them had been there on the day he fell, although in truth, he was tired of Lawrence's company and wanted to be alone to stand amongst the market stalls and look up. He wanted to imagine his descent, imagine himself as the turning, twisting, tumbling meteorite that had struck the earth. He also wanted to search for his tooth, to at least try to find it. He owed it that much.

But Lawrence said, 'No problem. I'll come with you. We walked out together; we'll walk home together.'

So Tom resolved to return another day and they walked home in silence and Tom reflected on the trip and wondered how Lawrence had known that the lift in the car park wasn't working.

He fully expected Lawrence to come into the house with him, assuming that he was now a weekend fixture, but Lawrence stopped at the gate and said, 'I have to go now. See you soon. And don't feel embarrassed about today. It happens to the best of us.'

'I don't feel embarrassed.'

'Really?'

He walked away and again Tom wondered if he had a car and, if so, where it was parked, and exactly where on the horizon he lived. He was glad he wasn't staying for lunch, but when he went inside he found that there was no lunch for which to stay, and no Karen either. No Karen, no children, no food. Only Tom.

'Knock her up in the air. Knock him up in the air. Knock them all up in the air,' he said.

He hung his jacket in the hallway and went into the kitchen. In the fridge he found four cans of beer. He checked his watch.

'Excellent. Oh-wine-hundred hours.'

He took out two cans, opened one, drank it all, opened the other and poured it into a glass. He took a third can, back-heeled the fridge door and went upstairs. He paused for a moment outside Dan's door, then tapped lightly and looked in. There was a desk with a laptop on it, clothes on the bed, a rucksack on the floor. Books and posters on the wall. No Dan, though. He withdrew and closed the door and crossed the landing. Ignoring the sign that said *Warning: Girl Zone – Keep Out*, he looked into Holly's room.

In here there was a dressing table overflowing with make-up, and bottles and cards and magazines all over the bed and the floor. Clothes were piled high – dumped, strewn, discarded – and photographs of Holly and her friends were stuck across the wall-mirror and every other free surface. The bed was unmade and the curtains drawn. And no Holly. It looked like she had simply woken up and walked out, after which a cyclone had struck.

Tom went downstairs and made himself a sandwich and drank another beer. All the time, the presence of the door to the outhouse bothered him. He turned the knob and pulled. Nothing. He leaned his head against the wood and listened. Again, nothing. He stood there for a long time, leaning against the door, listening to nothing.

'Get the key off Karen,' he said at last.

He went into the living room, sat down and ate the sandwich. He was sleepy now. For a while he lay there looking at the clouds crossing the sky and then he became aware of a distant barking, and again he wondered if it had always been there. It seemed to carry on the wind, on the rhythm of his pulse, a mournful hooting of a distant dog singing to him.

He stood up and went to the window. He stared at the garden and at the car on the drive and thought of his mother and his father and it made his skin tingle; an acute, precious feeling that was quickly gone. He was about to sit down again when he saw Police Officer Ann Lasley cycle up to his gate. She propped her bicycle against the wall, unbuckled her helmet and walked up the path. Tom stepped to one side of the window and didn't move when the doorbell rang.

He waited.

He could imagine the silhouette against the window in the front door, an all-seeing eye peering through the frosted glass. The doorbell rang again. It seemed louder. Tom scarcely breathed. He thought he heard her walking back down the path but he couldn't be sure, and so for the next half an hour Tom sat on the floor, concealed from the window by the side of the sofa.

While he sat there, he wondered what the purpose of her visit was. Perhaps the police thought he knew more than he did. Perhaps they thought he was unstable, a jumper, a danger to passers-by and fresh fruit produce. Or did they suspect foul-play, that he was the victim of an assault?

Tom allowed that idea to wander around the inside of his mind. It was unpleasant to think that he might have been fighting for his life and had no memory of it. He felt sorry for himself and wished he'd been there to help himself. And why? Why would he have been fighting on a car park roof? A random mugging? Car park rage? Why had he even been in a car park? And on the roof of all places?

'But you were up there today, weren't you? Like a little lamb trotting up the stairs.'

Tom got to his feet, dragging himself upwards on the sofa arm as if he were hauling on heavy ropes, a man battling the tide and bringing a ship in to its moorings. He peered through the net curtains. Ann Lasley had gone but now it looked as if Lawrence was lurking at the end of the cul-de-sac, leaning against the lamppost. Tom couldn't be sure, but if it was, then what was he doing there, skulking like a willowy weasel? What was he up to? Was he waiting for Karen? Was he watching Tom?

Tom had no intention of letting him in again. He had had enough Lawrence for one day. He bolted the front door and went to his study. Karen and Dan and Holly would have to ring on the doorbell when they came home. He sat down at his desk and flexed his fingers, including his healing thumb. There was a drawing pad on the desk and he picked up a pencil and wrote at the top, as neatly as he could, the word *Facts*, and underlined it. Then he wrote:

She works late.

He knew where the living room was.

She knew he drank tea instead of coffee.

She knew he took sugar.

He knew the car park lift didn't work.

He put down the pencil and found that he was picturing Karen as she had been when they were young and starting out, doing new things together and having fun. He could see her happy, laughing her musical laugh, her smooth, round face looking up at him... Tom stopped. He wasn't imagining Karen; he was imagining Maggie.

He put the list to one side and read the discharge letter, which he had left in its envelope. It included the outpatient appointment for the following day with Doctor Muller. Tom had planned not to go but now he thought, why not? He returned to the list.

He must have a key.

He looked at that and then wrote:

He's done it once; he'll do it again.

Like today?

Tom looked at the words. Is that what he thought or was he letting his imagination get the better of him? He tore the paper from the pad and threw it into the bin. His mind felt stale and used and worn out. Enough thinking.

Enough imagining.

He climbed down the ladder, went into his bedroom, lay down on the bed and fell asleep within a few minutes. When he awoke again it was dark. He listened. He could tell without checking that he was alone in the house. He got up, unsteady on his feet, his mouth sticky from beer, and went to the bedroom window and looked out. There was no sign of Holly or Dan or Karen. No sign of Karen's car. They, like the barking dog, were out there somewhere, but unlike the barking dog, they weren't getting any closer.

15

It was a disturbed night for Tom. He woke many times, turning from side to side, finding comfort and then losing it again; the covers too hot and then too heavy; unfocused worries snaring his muddled thoughts and keeping him from reaching a deep, dreamless, peaceful sleep.

He dreamed vividly, each vignette a richly textured experience. In one, a granite boulder rolled around his cul-de-sac on the pavement, its knobbly protrusions crushing the kerbstones to powder, each splintering contact bringing an exquisite sensation of sadness, the anticipation of the rock arriving outside his house too much to bear and waking him up for a moment, lifting him to the surface of sleep before letting him fall to the bottom again.

In another, Tom was trapped in a glass aquarium. A large dog that looked like a hyena had its nose against the glass, snuffling and sniffing, following Tom with blind relentlessness as he ran from one end of the glass to the other. And in a third, Tom had given up smoking and his temper was immense, a huge, joyful release of rage that consumed him and exhilarated him. He was arguing with Karen on a bridge overlooking a motorway, and as he stared into the headlights below, he flew into the windscreen of an oncoming car.

He woke in the morning wearier than when he had gone to sleep. He looked to see if Karen was on her pillow but she wasn't. He was alone in his bed and in the house. He went downstairs to the kitchen, opened another bottle of vodka and poured himself a large glass. He took it back upstairs and into the bathroom, where he ran a hot bath.

The almost boiling water further depleted any remaining energy he might have had and when at last he stood up, the glass empty, he felt the same dizziness he had experienced in the hospital. He looked fearfully at the mirror, but it had been coated by the steam and no reflection, man, animal or otherwise, was visible.

Still wet beneath his dressing gown, he went downstairs, made coffee from ground beans and ate croissants with butter and jam. Then he went upstairs, let the dressing gown fall and assessed his naked body. It didn't please him. He'd lost muscle in his arms and shoulders and gained a roll of fat around his waist. He looked flabby, tall, lopsided and pale; a lumpy torso on gangling legs. His oversized head hung forwards from his neck, his huge moustache and uneven beard the only items on display with any vestige of virility. He frowned. He went to his wardrobe and put on a white shirt and a blue suit. He raked his hair back into a ponytail and waxed the ends of his moustache into pointed tips.

Then he ordered a taxi. He was going to the hospital.

It was the Borkmann journey in reverse, although this time he was neither squashed nor flayed against the roof. He sat in the back, content to let the passing scenery fill up his mind.

At the hospital Tom went to the main reception and showed them the discharge letter. They found his records on their computer and then directed him to the outpatient department's reception on the next floor, where they found his records again and told him to take a seat until Doctor Muller was ready.

Someone had written on a whiteboard that Doctor Muller was running 20 minutes behind schedule. When, Tom wondered, had that been written? And how often was it updated? He sat down and surveyed his fellow outpatients. In the far corner, a large, elderly man, wrapped up in multiple layers of jumpers, jackets and overcoats, studied a puzzle magazine. His face was red and purple like a farmer's face that had spent hours in windy fields and local pubs.

Opposite Tom, a teenage boy in a tracksuit was lounging next to his mother, who sat neatly in her light raincoat and whispered constantly to the boy, which seemed to irritate him. A thin woman sat beside him. A man in a cap dozed across the room in a chair next to a table piled with magazines, and two receptionists clicked and tutted behind their desk while they looked at their screens.

Tom stretched out his legs and folded his arms. How would he draw these people? The big, old fellow was clearly a badger, or maybe a bulldog, or possibly an old and aggressive goldfish. The mother was attractive, a swan or a deer, but her son was one of those tall, leggy pups, not grown into its body yet. The receptionists could be two newborn chicks tweeting in their nest. The rest of the outpatients were merely foliage to Tom.

He got up and poured water from a machine into a plastic cup. A harassed nurse appeared from somewhere beyond the reception desk and called, 'David Miller? David Miller?'

The dozing man in a cap looked up, startled, and then stood up. He followed the nurse quickly with his head down and without looking at the rest of the cohort who were left behind, as if he were ashamed of his condition. Something vile, Tom thought, something vile and sore and dripping. He stood up and went over to Miller's seat and looked through the magazines – fishing, fishing, knitting, fishing, fishing, knitting and a candle magazine. The blotchy farmer had done well to find the puzzle magazine.

It had become quiet. The mother had stopped whispering, the chicks had stopped twittering and then amongst the silence Tom heard a happy, musical laugh. He would know that laugh anywhere: Ward Manager Margarida Monroe.

Tom sat up and looked over his shoulder. Maggie was coming down the corridor with Bee. She looked younger, rounder and happier than he remembered. Her glasses were thicker. Her hair was longer. She was shorter and taller and wider and slimmer and bigger and smaller than he remembered. She looked more Maggier. Had he ever seen her before?

He stood up, suddenly self-conscious in his suit, and the image of his deficient body beneath his clothes, of his ludicrous moustache and unnatural height, made him wish that he was somebody else, anybody else, somebody suave and svelte and confident. She walked towards him, eyebrows raised, a wide smile on her face. This was why he had come. The hell with Doctor Muller and Karen and Lawrence and the whole lot of them. Prepare to be knocked up in the air.

'Mister Hannah,' Maggie said. 'Come back to see us?'

Bee smiled too. 'You look very smart,' she said. 'Been somewhere nice? Or going?'

'Hello,' said Tom. 'No, I'm just here. Visiting. It's my outpatient appointment.' He could think of absolutely nothing else to say and was finding that speaking aloud felt strange. It was as if he were unused to the language, a savage brought to civilisation, dressed up in a suit and sent out to mingle with polite society. He stood there grinning and then stopped, conscious now of his broken tooth. Why had he not yet visited a dentist? He cursed himself. Bee and Maggie, however, continued to smile at him. Tom was unused to meeting people who were genuinely pleased to see him. Borkmann had said it was Darwinian, that people were genetically predisposed to avoid people who looked like Tom.

'So, how have you been?' said Bee.

'Good,' said Tom. 'Very good. Very good indeed.' He stopped himself before he added any more goods to the sentence.

'Well, that is very good indeed,' Maggie laughed. 'Is this your first time back?'

'Yes.'

'You haven't had your tooth fixed yet?'

'No, not yet.'

'How are you coping at home? Are you getting all the help you need?'

'Not bad. You know... not bad. Could be better.' He hoped that he was conveying the message that things were not good between him and Karen, that the children were like strangers and that he had a lot of time on his hands should Maggie ever wish to pop round.

'I'm sure you're doing fine,' Maggie said.

Bee was beginning to edge away. 'Well, good luck with your outpatient appointment,' she said.

Tom wondered if they could smell vodka on his breath. Or perhaps it was the coffee and croissants that they didn't like.

'Wait...' he said.

Maggie waited. Bee waited. Tom waited too, because like everyone else in the waiting room, or so it felt, he wondered what he was going to say next. But Maggie's eyes were greener and larger and darker than he remembered and they were interrupting his thoughts. He had a sudden vision of looking into those eyes while she lay on a pebble beach, taking his weight on his arms so as not to crush her.

There he is.

Tom heard the words and jumped. They were like rifle shots. It felt as if the world moved beneath him, giving him a genuine sense that he was about to lose his balance because the planet was spinning too fast. He looked up. At the far end of the corridor, from where Maggie and Bianca had come, stood a fox, a cat and a hedgehog. They stood on two legs, as large as humans, clustered in the same pose as on his T-shirt, as on the picture in his house, except that instead of the Pelican, it was the always-angry restaurant owner who stood with them. She was pointing at Tom and the others were looking at him with a hungry curiosity in their eyes.

Bee said, 'Are you all right, Tom?'

He looked down at her and then raised his head again and looked along the corridor. They were still there and Scraps was lighting a cigarette, leaning forwards and cupping the flame with his hands.

'That's not allowed,' Tom said, although he was unaware he had spoken. He could smell the cigarette smoke. He could smell them all. He could even hear Billy chewing his gum.

Maggie turned to where Tom was looking and then back to him. 'Tom?'

'Thomas Hannah? Is Thomas Hannah here?'

He was being called by the nurse. Doctor Muller was ready to see him.

'Tom? Do you want to sit down?' said Maggie.

Tom didn't want to sit down. He wanted to stand and to continue staring. They were not fading out of view. They weren't vanishing when he blinked. No one was saying, 'Wake up, Tom. It's time to get up.' He looked at his own wrist and pinched it as hard as he could. It was such a comical thing to do but it was all he could think of.

'Tom, what are you doing?'

He pinched himself and it hurt and that was all that happened. The creatures remained. They were solid and they were there and they were casting shadows and leaving marks on the world. His world.

As if to prove the point, Plenty batted her pink ball into the air. She looked muscular and aggressive, and seeing her as big as a human frightened Tom – in the same way that seeing a lion prowling the corridors of the hospital would have frightened him. He was as much physically afraid of her, of the violence that emanated from her, as he was of her sheer impossibility.

The ball fell on the floor and rolled up to where Maggie was standing.

'Is Thomas Hannah here?' said the nurse again, looking at him now. 'Are you Thomas Hannah?'

He felt Maggie's hand on his. Her hand was smaller and softer than he remembered.

'Tom, come and sit down.'

'Look at this,' he said. He stooped and picked up Plenty's ball, and stood slowly and stiffly as if he were wearing a heavy backpack. The ball was wet and sticky. He shook it and the bell tinkled. He held it up to Maggie's face. 'Look.'

He's got my ball.

'Tom.'

Tom released the ball and let it drop onto the ground. Drips of liquid splashed the floor. He looked at his hand and saw that it glistened.

'That's odd,' he said. 'I didn't think she put the ball in her mouth.'

Maggie looked at his hand and he felt Bee's touch on his arm. He was being guided towards the chairs. He looked along the corridor. They were watching him. Scraps threw down his cigarette. They were going to come to him.

Tom looked at Maggie and took in every detail of her face, of her hair, of the way she moved and looked and smelled and spoke. 'I have to go now,' he said. He stepped back, turned and walked away from

Maggie and the reception area and the nurses and the outpatients and his cartoon characters who couldn't possibly be there but were.

'Tom.'

He picked up speed and, by the time he reached the glass fire door that led to the stairs, he was running. He barged through and ran down the steps and then walked briskly through the main reception. Outside he saw a bus about to leave and, risking cars and curses, he crossed the road and stepped on, giving the driver more money than the fare cost. He looked back at the hospital only once as the bus pulled away. There was nothing out of the ordinary to see. Nothing whatsoever.

'Come on,' he said. 'Let's go home.'

He felt as if he were emerging from a stupor. Slowly colour and sound and movement returned to the world: traffic, people, hustle and bustle, shouts and conversations, the jolting of the bus, people getting on and getting off. After half an hour or so, Tom stood up and, lurching from side to side with the bus's movements, made his way to the doors and stepped onto the street at the next stop. He walked randomly from street to street, changing direction suddenly and keeping to open areas. He knew he was a long way from normal but he felt in control.

He found an empty pub down a side street, went in and ordered a pint and a whisky. He sat at the bar and watched the door, his heavy-lidded eyes seldom blinking. The barman kept looking at him and at first Tom wondered why, because he wasn't drunk, he had paid, he was being quiet, keeping himself to himself. But in the mirror behind the bar, he saw an enormous man bursting out of his suit, dishevelled, pale, sweating and wildly hairy, his hair loose from the pony-tail, his moustache colossal. Who wouldn't be looking at him?

He ordered another two drinks.

In the far corner was a table with two tired-looking street people sitting at it: an old man and a young girl. They were nursing an almost-finished bottle of lager between them. Tom watched the barman go over to their table. He was a fat man with heavy forearms. His stomach overhung his trousers. His shirt was stained.

'Out,' Tom heard him say to the girl. 'This isn't a refuge.'

'I'm with him,' she said.

'Not in here you're not.'

The barman pulled the girl and she stumbled and almost fell over. The old man tried to get up and Tom thought he might be coming to her rescue, but he got his words mixed up and the barman couldn't understand him. 'You can get out too,' he said.

Tom watched them leave, huddled together like two monkeys who'd had a fright. The barman came back to the bar and started loading glasses into a washer. Tom looked at him and then around at the empty pub. He felt the thin line of anger extending upwards from his stomach to his brain, an anger he knew could expand and thicken until... what? Until he erupted? Was he capable of the sudden, savage assault that he was imagining, that would end only when he ran out of breath? He could already picture himself walking calmly from the empty pub, leaving his bloodied victim on the floor amongst the smashed remnants of his trade.

Nothing like that happened. He drank his beer and whisky and left quietly and peaceably. But as he stepped outside, something made him pause. It was a half-revealed memory, a light attempting to escape the black hole. It related to the moment the barman pulled the girl and she almost fell over.

A struggle.

Stumbling.

Not for the first time that day, Tom felt disconnected from his surroundings, as if he were watching his life from another place. Across the road he saw the girl and the man who had been evicted from the pub sitting on the kerb. They were simply sitting there, not talking, not doing anything. He went over, dug into his pockets and gave them all the change he had. The girl took it and looked at him and said, 'Thanks. Are you all right?'

Careless of his suit, Tom sat down on the kerb. He stared at his outsize feet. His hair hung down, partially obscuring his face. He ran his hands through it and sighed. His moustache smelled of beer.

'Probably not,' he said.

The girl nodded. 'Got a cigarette?'

Tom shook his head. 'I gave up.' He ran his tongue along his uneven teeth and added, 'Weird day.' What was he doing there, sitting on a kerb? He heaved himself back onto his feet and looked down at them and then back along the road that had led to the pub. It had been a weird day indeed. He nodded at the odd couple, who were watching him, and walked off. He was several steps away when the girl said, 'Are you the one that fell off the roof?'

Tom stopped and turned back. 'Pardon?'

'Are you the one that fell off the roof?'

'Why do you ask?' he said.

'In order to find out.'

'Did you see it?'

'It was on the news. *Cartoonist Falls Off Car Park Roof.*'

'And you recognised me?'

She peered at him through narrowed eyes. 'Yes.'

Tom pushed his fingers against his moustache, thinking. 'Where did you see it on the news?'

'On the internet.'

'Really?'

'Don't you believe me?'

'Of course.'

'Do you think people like me don't have the internet?'

'I don't think that at all.'

The girl tut-tutted. 'That's not nice,' she said. 'Not to believe me.'

'I do believe you.'

Tom looked around. How had he ended up arguing? The street was deserted, the pub was quiet and it was getting dark. How long had he been in the pub? It all felt surreal and again he felt disconnected from events.

The old man stirred. He looked up at Tom. 'She didn't even know her own name,' he said.

Tom looked at the girl.

'Not me,' she said. 'The other one.'

'What other one?'

'You know the one,' the old man said. 'The one with those animals.'

Tom frowned. His mouth felt dry and sticky. 'What do you mean? What animals? Can you see the animals?'

The girl ran her tongue around her lips and laughed. 'Course we can. I'll tell you something else, too. You might be the one that fell off the roof but there were two of you up there.'

Tom backed farther away. She and the old man cocked their heads to one side as Holly and Dan had done.

'How do you know that?'

'Listen,' she said. 'Can't you hear him calling you?'

'Who?'

'Give me a cigarette and I'll tell you.'

Tom turned and walked away. Who said there was no problem too big it couldn't be run away from? Compartmentalise. Deny. Dismiss. He kept walking, putting distance between himself and whatever-they-were sitting on the kerb. He didn't know what would be worse: if he looked back and they were still there, or if he looked back and they weren't.

He walked until his throat stopped throbbing and his hands stopped shaking and then he searched for a familiar street, all the time expecting to hear Plenty's ball rolling along behind him, or feel the beat of the Pelican's wings above his head, or see Scraps and Billy leaning on a wall in front of him, or feel the heavy hand of the always-angry restaurant owner fall on his shoulder.

You might be the one that fell off the roof but there were two of you up there.

It was evening when Tom arrived home. Where had the day gone? A purple gloom had settled on the cul-de-sac and the light from the houses and street-lamps appeared diffused, as if covered by a damp mist. He unlocked the front door and pushed in, kicking off his shoes and throwing his jacket on the banister, thinking only of loading up with alcohol and slumping in an armchair. But he heard voices in the living room. He was so used to living in an empty house that he was unprepared to find Karen, Holly and Dan at home. He looked in on what appeared to be a perfectly normal domestic scene.

'Hi Dad,' said Dan. He was sprawled on the floor, absorbed with his phone. Holly was lying on the sofa eating garlic bread. Tom could see the crumbs falling from her mouth when she spoke, like hailstones bouncing off her clothes and onto the floor. On the coffee table were boxes and cartons of food, bottles of soft drinks and bottles of wine. The curtains were closed and the room was hot and filled with the smell of food and warm packaging, and the noise and flickering lights from the television.

'We've got a takeaway,' Holly said.

'Come and watch some television,' said Karen. She was curled up in an armchair. 'We've got curries and pizza.'

'We've put cushions out and everything,' said Dan. 'Look at all the food Mum's ordered. That will sort you out.'

Tom sat in the armchair opposite Karen's.

'Do I need sorting out?' he said.

'Everyone needs sorting out, Dad. We're watching a blooper show. You'll love it. Even Holly likes it, although she's pretending she doesn't. Wouldn't it be good if they had a video of you falling off the roof? Have you checked the internet? Maybe someone filmed you.'

'Dad doesn't do the internet, do you, Tom?' said Karen. 'Too social.'

'I bet Dad's got some secret stalking accounts, though. Probably calls himself "The Masked Cartoonist".'

'Mum's got you some wine,' said Holly. 'You like wine, don't you?'

Tom felt lost amongst the hot fumes of family life. The television was too loud and the floor was littered with empty boxes and trays. Everywhere seemed cluttered and chaotic. Karen handed him a glass of wine. 'That will sort you out,' she said, and smiled. She had dirty teeth too, Tom noticed, like Lawrence's. 'A Monday night treat.'

'Is that like a Friday night special?' said Dan. 'Wink wink.'

'Shut up,' said Holly. 'Gross.'

Tom looked at the glass in his hand and wondered what had happened to the time between him walking home and arriving at the house. It seemed like a moment. Perhaps that was all it had been. A moment between a full stop and a capital letter. A moment between frames.

'You're not eating much,' said Karen.

Tom looked at his plate. It was true. The tiny portion he'd selected was untouched.

'What's the matter, Dad?' said Dan. 'Are you missing *Scraps*?'

'Who do you like best,' said Holly. '*Scraps* or us?'

'Maggie or Mum?' said Dan.

'What?' said Tom. 'What did you say?' His voice sounded unnaturally loud and large against the electronic voices coming from the television.

'I remember when there was just Scraps,' said Karen. 'No other characters... no wait, there was the Pelican. Just Scraps and the Pelican.'

'No Billy the Hedgehog? Impossible,' said Dan. 'He's me, isn't he? Billy's me. And Plenty is Holly, and the horrible, always-angry restaurant owner is Mum. Because you hate Mum, don't you Dad? And you're Scraps. Right?'

'I don't hate Mum.'

'Idiot,' said Holly to Dan. 'Who's the Pelican, then?'

'The Pelican's nobody,' Dan said. 'He's just the butt of everybody's joke. He's a big useless nothing.'

They all laughed and Tom could see them as if they were in a picture on a page in a book.

'No,' he said. 'You've got that all wrong. You're not Billy and Plenty is not Holly. And Mum isn't the –' He found it difficult to talk. 'You should think who you are,' he managed before his voice tightened.

'How did the roof trip go?' Holly said.

'He didn't go through with it,' said Karen.

'You should have gone onto the roof. Mustn't be a chicken,' said Dan.

'You have to do it. It's the law. Police Officer Ann Lasley will come and arrest you.'

'Lawrence said you acted weirdly and wanted to come down.'

'Dad's always acting weirdly.'

'Dad's a bit odd.'

'It must be all the drinking.'

'You shouldn't drink so much, Dad. Not if you don't want to be odd.'

'How's the old memory box today?'

Tom looked at his hands and they seemed too large. Dan was wrong. The Pelican and the always-angry restaurant owner mattered. They mattered a lot. He picked up his glass of wine but his fingers felt lumpy and unresponsive, and the glass fell and rolled across the floor, spilling red wine onto the carpet. Tom saw Holly rock backwards and forwards, her hands locked together, her face laughing with glee. He couldn't hear any sounds at all. Karen stood up and walked towards him and her leg knocked against a tray of food and it all fell slowly onto the floor. Everyone looked very tall but that was probably because Tom was lying on the floor. And then the sound came back and he heard Dan saying, 'What are you doing down there, Dad?'

He tried to get up. 'I'm okay, Bailey,' he said. 'It's hot, isn't it?' He looked at Holly. 'You set my root ball on fire.'

'What?'

'Who?'

'Have you gone cuckoo, Dad?'

Tom hauled himself onto his knees and then stood up, swaying from side to side as he tried to maintain his balance.

'You off?' said Karen.

'I have to do some work.'

His head hurt. The lights were too bright. He didn't want to be in that room anymore. Bouncing off the door frame, he left the room, and feeling sick, he went upstairs to the landing and climbed the ladder to his study.

In the clean, clear, quiet air of his eyrie, against the backdrop of white walls, white floor and white ceiling, Tom sat quietly and allowed his thoughts to reorganise themselves. Looking up at the skylights, he could see that it was dark outside. Night-time. He wondered if Karen, Holly and Dan would stay in the house. He hoped not.

He turned to his filing cabinets and the drawers that contained his old *Scraps* cartoons – almost a thousand A3 pages, each one layered in tissue paper. He opened a drawer at random and leafed through them, letting each page fall forwards, making the tissue paper waft in a puff of air. They were all in date order, most published, a few still work-in-progress, kept back until he could re-work them and make them perfect. The life and times of Scraps, Plenty, Billy, the Pelican and the always-angry restaurant owner immortalised in pen and ink. Scraps had hardly changed since the beginning but Tom could see how he'd developed the others, using less lines over time, yet creating more personality.

He thought he knew them as intimately as he knew his own family. He thought he would be able to hold them up to the light and recognise each facet and flaw of their construction as if he were a diamond-merchant inspecting his hoard of jewels. But now he was beginning to wonder if he knew them at all, if he knew anyone at all. He leafed through them one by one and then, abruptly, he sat up and took notice.

It was a drawing of a dog.

He pulled out the drawing and laid it on his desk. Part of his working method was to draw his cartoon strips four times as large as they would appear in the newspapers, and in front of him lay three clean frames precisely drawn in black ink.

It was a continuation strip: it had its own punchline but it was part of a longer story line. Not all the characters were present, only Scraps, Plenty, the always-angry restaurant owner and...

Bullet.

Bullet was a savage-looking dog, all jaws and teeth and crazy eyes with a small muscular body. A proper cartoon dog. And she was a she.

And the violent characters are the females: the always-angry restaurant owner and Plenty the Cat... Why is that?

Tom remembered her now. She had appeared in only a few strips. Tom had drawn her for the always-angry restaurant owner to help her keep order outside the restaurant. He had thought it might be fun to have an animal on her side of the storyline. But it didn't work. Bullet had unbalanced the strip.

Five's a nice number. You can always have an outsider with an odd number.

In the end, Tom had cut Bullet loose and had drawn her slipping her lead and running away.

'Are you coming back?' Tom said, his voice sounding flat against the white silence in the attic. 'Are you coming back because I abandoned you?' He put the drawing back in the drawer and closed it. Then something caught his eye and he looked up. It looked like a large bird flying past the skylight.

He thought he heard a stair creak. He got up quietly and closed the trapdoor that led down to the landing. He felt sure he could smell cigarette smoke. Although he had no mobile phone, he had a landline extension. He picked it up, listened and then dialled. He waited until a familiar gruff voice said, 'Borkmann.'

'Gerard. It's Tom. I'm in trouble.'

Part Three

Bang

16

The Pelican tucked its scabby head into the crook of its neck and let the weight of its beak press its face into the oily comfort of its chest. It shifted position slightly and then with the slightest of sighs, it fell asleep.

Below, the dog had stopped barking and ceased trying to eat the alleyway. It lay amongst the dustbins, its head on its paws, and it too slept, its heavy, laboured breathing sounding like an idlfing engine, only a snort and an occasional grunt punctuating the rumbling rhythmic rise and fall of breath.

Nothing happened while they slept…

… until the night sky began to lighten, as if a greater consciousness was awakening, and the Pelican, high above the alleyway, perched on the top of the wall with its webbed feet gripping the white concrete cap that ran its length, became visible as a dark silhouette against the horizon, a gargoyle guarding its friends who slept in the restaurant below.

It had dreamed of shapes: strange, geometric shapes that appeared and disappeared. Blue circles and lines like unformed faces drifted through the Pelican's tiny mind. Triangles and squares, corners and edges were drawn and rubbed out, recast and abandoned.

The Pelican realised that it was no longer asleep, that it had awoken without knowing. A light breeze ruffled its feathers and it sensed that dawn had arrived. It could feel the newness, the freshness, the light in the air.

Slowly the Pelican lifted its head. Its neck cracked and sent a bolt of lightning across its eyes, making them cross momentarily behind its lids. It opened its beak and inhaled cool air and released by way of trade a cloud of musty, stagnant gas. It stretched its wings and felt the breeze rise beneath them, the hint of upward movement, the light sensation of burgeoning flight. Then it opened its eyes and looked around.

All the other buildings had gone.

Bacon drives me wild. It's as simple as that. Don't get me wrong, insects, earthworms, rotting fruit and rancid meat are all fine foods, and if I see them on the menu then I'm the first to pull up my chair and tie on a napkin. Nor am I discounting the distinct attraction of pouncing on a clucking hen rooting for feed amongst its wood chips. That will certainly bring out the animal in me. But pound for pound, ten times out of ten, and here I apologise to any pig friends, the food that's going to draw me into your kitchen and risk a beating with a broomstick is a pan of frying, popping, smoking bacon.

I mention this because that's what I awoke to – not a beating with a broomstick, but the smell of bacon and the sizzling sounds of food being fried. A slight fine-tuning of my nostrils further revealed the preparation of sausages, fried bread, egg, mushrooms, tomatoes and, I was fairly certain, baked beans. I scented toast, too, and coffee. What's a hungry fox meant to do when taunted with such smells other than curl up into a ball and whimper and gaze hungrily at the closed kitchen door?

Daylight was coming in through the front windows. I was lying on the floor beneath a tablecloth. I stopped whimpering, stood up, stretched and yawned, and scratched my belly, which made a loud rasping sound where my stubby claws massaged the dry fur. It was morning and I was in the always-angry restaurant owner's restaurant.

Apart from the Pelican, we had spent the night downstairs. None of us had felt confident enough to stay upstairs in one of those vague, dusty, neglected rooms that lined the landing corridor. It was strange, although the essentials were there – walls, ceiling, floor, a window and a door – they lacked substance. When I had looked at the carpets in those rooms, I couldn't clearly see the patterns. They seemed to drift and change in front of my eyes. I didn't like it. Even the always-angry restaurant owner was uneasy.

'I'll sleep down here with you,' she had said.

'Don't you want to be in your bedroom?'

'I need to keep an eye on you lot. A pack of mangy gutter animals in a restaurant isn't healthy. I need to make sure you don't raid the kitchen.' But no one had believed her. 'And don't think you can slip into my bedroom when my back's turned,' she had said to Plenty.

'I'll do what I want.'

But Plenty had stayed downstairs too.

So we had settled down in front of the fire at the back of the restaurant and slept amongst the tables and chairs, using tablecloths as covers to keep ourselves warm with cushions and seat-backs to lie on. I took stock of the room. Billy was still asleep, curled up in a ball of quills, but Plenty was awake. She sat neatly by the fire watching me.

'You sleep with your mouth open,' she said.

'Do I?'

'And you snore.'

'Good morning to you, too.'

I wandered amongst the tables, picking up knives and forks, cups and plates, examining them and putting them down again. I licked the salt, sniffed the pepper, sneezed, and blew my nose on a napkin. I was a classy act.

The restaurant seemed smaller in daylight than it had the previous night. I went over to the window to look out but it was too bright. I shielded my eyes and thought about the light I had seen at the end of the alleyway the previous night. Now I should have been looking onto the busy high street, but clearly the time of day or night made no difference. It would always be an impenetrable white wall. Why hadn't I noticed that before? I felt as if I were seeing the world for the first time and finding that it wasn't as I'd assumed it to be. Still scratching, I poked my head into the kitchen where the always-angry restaurant owner was cooking. 'Good morning,' I said. 'That smells good. Is that bacon? I'll just take—'

'Get out.'

I went back into the restaurant and pulled a chair to the fireplace.

'And you were dribbling,' Plenty said. 'While you were asleep you were dribbling.'

I looked at her. 'Aren't there some mice you can chase?'

'I've looked.'

We sat in silence. Plenty watched me with her ears twitching, trying to hear my thoughts. 'Are you thinking about the dog?' she said at last.

I rolled a cigarette, tapped it on my knee and then lit it. I sucked down the smoke. The first puff of the day was always the best. Even more so if I was outside and it was a cold, bright morning. Cold air and grey smoke hitting my lungs like a stone: I loved that. And after a meal was good, too. I kept my eye on the kitchen door. I was beginning to tremble with the thought of food.

'Well? Are you?'

'Yes, Plenty. I am.'

'Are you thinking that you recognised her?'

'Her?'

'Bullet.'

I stroked my muzzle as if I were a professor with a beard.

'You know it's her,' said Plenty.

'I couldn't get a proper look.'

'It is her. Who else would it be?'

Who else indeed? Now that I thought about it, there weren't that many individuals in our world that I could identify as being... individual. There had always been an impression of other people, of crowds, but I'd never actually taken notice of their specific components. Why should I? A crowd was a crowd; a collection of heads and faces. Who cared about the detail?

'If it is her, why has she come back?' I said.

Plenty yawned. 'I don't know.' She looked at the closed kitchen door. 'I'm bored talking about it. Is she cooking for us?'

On cue, the kitchen doors slapped open and the always-angry restaurant owner appeared balancing four plates. She dropped them onto the nearest table, sat down and started eating. In mid-chew she looked up and said, 'Well? What are you waiting for?'

Cautiously, Plenty and I joined her at the table and Billy, sensing food, uncurled from his place on the floor and looked up with sleepy eyes. 'I'm dreaming,' he said. 'I'm dreaming that the always-angry restaurant owner has just cooked us breakfast. Nobody wake me up.'

'Very funny,' she said. 'If you don't want it, I'll give it away.'

Still wrapped in his tablecloth, Billy quickly pulled up a chair. 'What about the Pelican?' he said.

'I'm not having that bag of lice in here.'

'But even so...'

The always-angry restaurant owner glared. 'Even so what?'

'Well, it must be hungry too...'

'Oh, for God's sake.'

She jumped up and slammed into the kitchen. We heard rattling, crashing, muttering, and then she reappeared with a plate of bread and cold meat. She pushed through the tables and thumped up the stairs.

'This is a restaurant,' we heard her shout. 'Not a home for flea-bags.'

'She loves us really,' Billy whispered as the ceiling shook.

We listened. Doors slammed and then we heard the thumping footsteps returning. The always-angry restaurant owner came into the restaurant and sat down again.

'The bird is not there,' she said. 'Satisfied? Now eat.'

We ate.

The Pelican was airborne. Below, the restaurant building and the strip of alleyway that ran along one side of it were the only recognisable features. It swooped and glided and flapped and criss-crossed the alien terrain. There was above and below; over there and over here; in front and behind. There was the Pelican and there were other things. There was dark and there was light.

I mopped up the last of the egg with some bread, and while I was wondering whether I could get away with using my tongue to clean the plate, I said, 'Does anyone have any thoughts on recent events?' I glanced up. The others were looking at me, waiting. 'I mean, we've agreed to leave here and find the hairy man but other things are unusual too. Don't you think?'

'You mean the dog and the decay and the general sense of utter weirdness?' said Billy.

'Yes.' I stared at my plate and picked it up.

'Don't lick it,' snarled the always-angry restaurant owner.

I put it down again. I said, 'I mean, I feel like our lives are changing. I feel like I'm being stretched out, as if someone's squeezed into my head and what they see is different to what I see, and because they're wearing my eyes I see their things too. And they're too big; too big for my thoughts.'

The always-angry restaurant owner said, 'Are you talking the same language as me? I have no idea what anything you just said means.'

I didn't either. I had another go. 'Everything seems to be changing. Nothing looks like it used to and I wonder how can that be? Things are so different but we're not reacting in the way that perhaps we should. We're just accepting it. We're curious but we're not... I don't know, we're not appalled. We're not up in arms staring at each other and running around, saying, "Hey, what the hell is happening?" We're accepting it because we're always okay with everything that ever happens, no matter how crazy. Whatever happens to us we accept.'

'That's because we're cool,' said Billy.

'Is it? You're sure it's not because we're… stupid? I mean, too stupid to even know we're stupid? We don't learn or grow. We have a little adventure and then we hang around and then we have another little adventure. What is all that about? Nothing ever changes. No matter what happens to us, we end up back where we are. There's no cause and effect, no *then*. It's always *now*. If we have an adventure and the restaurant burns down, the next time we look, it's there again. How does that happen?'

'But that's normal,' said Plenty. 'That's natural. Why are you talking so much? I don't like all these words. Let's just do things. There are too many words in the air.'

'I have to admit I feel uncomfortable these days,' said Billy. 'I feel heavy and I think about things.'

'What sort of things?'

'Things that have happened, as if there are lots of me behind me, and it's the things that have happened to them that I think about.' He pulled another dry, dead quill from his side. 'I don't know what I mean either. But yeah, I think you're right. Things are changing.'

The always-angry restaurant owner had been watching us, saying nothing, her eyes following our words. Now she said, 'Thanks for sharing, but shall we keep it real? I don't want to talk about wearing other people's eyes or feeling heavy or how everything is changing. We have a dog situation and we have a somebody-is-spying-on-us-and-drawing-us situation. That's it and all about it. Let's fix on those two things and worry about the multiple Billy effect later.'

She was right, but I had felt that we had been getting close to something. We weren't expressing it particularly well but it was something worth pursuing.

'I think the dog is Bullet,' I said. 'So does Plenty. I mean the dog that came last night, not the one that chased us the other day.' I saw the look of distress in the always-angry restaurant owner's eyes. Bullet had been, for a short time at least, and a long time ago, her dog.

Billy nodded. 'I was thinking about that, too. I wasn't sure but now you say it, I think it has to be her. But where has she been?'

'She slipped her lead and ran away,' said the always-angry restaurant owner. 'It wasn't my fault.'

'Sure. It was for the best,' said Billy. 'She didn't fit in. But...'

'But what?'

'It must have been difficult for her out there, all alone. That's all.'

'She kept chasing us,' said Plenty. 'I'm glad she went.'

'But now she's back,' I said.

'Bad and mad,' said Billy.

We looked at our empty plates and I thought about the dog we had seen the previous night – her massive head and jaws, the rows and rows of teeth, her insane, blood-red eyes. What had it been like for her, wherever she had been? And where had she been? Where do we go when we're not here?

'Is she still out there?' said Billy.

'I've looked,' said the always-angry restaurant owner. 'She's gone and so have all the bins and rubbish and everything. The alleyway is empty.'

'Where has it all gone?'

'How would I know?'

Plenty got up, stretched and went back to the fire. She settled lazily into the warmth, stretching out on the floor, her eyes dark and glittering. 'You know the cartoon,' she said. 'Is that us?'

'I think we've established that,' the always-angry restaurant owner said.

'I mean, is that *us*? Am I a cartoon cat?' she purred. 'That would be nice, wouldn't it? Then nothing I do is my fault. I can do whatever I want because I'm not real.'

'How can you not be real? You're here.'

'Am I?' she said without apparent interest in the answer.

Out of the mouths of babes.

'Of course you are,' I said. 'The cartoon is just a drawing of us. Not the other way round.'

I picked up the newspaper, which had been left in the middle of the table, now scruffy and torn and singed, and turned to the puzzle page where the *Scraps* cartoon strip was. I looked at it for a long time and then at my scrawny, threadbare arms on the white tablecloth next to the newspaper, at the reddish-brown fur that showed skin and tendons beneath it. That's when I began to think about all the bin-bag stuff and where it came from. I sat back and took out my tin of tobacco. I laid a pinch of tobacco in the paper, spreading it along the crease, and then added a small white menthol filter. I gave the paper a shake, a quick roll and then licked the edge, sealing the tube and plucking out a couple of loose strands from one end, which I put back in the tin. I rolled the Zippo on my leg, sat back and lit up.

Sucking in the smoke, I felt blood run through my veins. I felt my heart beat. I felt thoughts rush through my mind and heard a low-level hiss in my ears. I looked at the chipped, chapped, shiny reality of my claws and felt the pressure of my backside on the seat, the slight discomfort of the table-legs against my knees. My teeth were sticky and needed cleaning, my bladder was full, there was gas in my stomach and my eyes itched.

Plenty was right. There were too many words in the room.

I looked at each of them in turn: smelled their decay, heard them breathing, watched their tics and twitches. I narrowed my eyes and tried to see them as patterns in a two-dimensional mosaic; a flat jigsaw and nothing else, a coloured drawing if you like. But I couldn't. They loomed towards me, solid, heavy and real. I could hold them, squeeze them, embrace them, grip them, turn them around and view them from every angle.

'What are you thinking?' Plenty said.

'I'm thinking that I could turn you around and view you from every angle.'

'Just try and see what happens,' she said.

'I have a question,' said Billy. 'How come we're so different to other animals? I mean, like, way different – not a bit different but super different. For example, you're a fox that can talk and smoke cigarettes and walk on two legs and has elbows and knees and things. Is that normal? Seriously? Is that the way of other foxes? And we're all about the same size, too, aren't we? Other animals aren't like that. I've not mentioned it before, but now we're having this sort of conversation I thought I'd bring it up. You know what I mean? The graph looks a bit odd – every other species: flat line; this fox, this cat, this hedgehog and even this Pelican: massive spike. Maybe a smaller spike for the Pelican.'

'Have you seen every other species?' I said.

'No.'

I stood up, leaned on the table and without thinking flicked some ash into my saucer. 'Let's go and find the Pelican and check out the hospital and find the hairy man. Deal with the difficult stuff later.' I looked across at the always-angry restaurant owner. 'Can you remember how to get there?'

But the always-angry restaurant owner was staring at the saucer with my ash on it. 'People have to eat off that,' she said.

She got to her feet and it was a bit like a mountain rising from the ground. But all the free-form conversation had loosened me up and I was feeling boisterous, and I missed the multiple warning signs that would have kept me safe and free from physical attack had I noticed them.

'What people?' I said. 'The only time I ever saw any people in here, they were shapes in the window. Shapes like cardboard cut-outs. And the only person I ever actually see in here is you. Where are all your waiters? Your chefs? This isn't really a restaurant, is it? It's a backdrop for our adventures. It could be anything. You could be any-one. It's...'

She hit me on the head with her rolling pin and I fell over.

While I lay on the floor, I watched Plenty jump up and attack the always-angry restaurant owner. I watched them roll around, with Plenty bearing down with her claws out and the always-angry restau-rant owner holding on to her wrists. I watched them thrash from side to side and push tables across the floor and knock over chairs. I watched them catch our tablecloth and pull all the breakfast dishes onto the floor too.

My head hurt.

I saw Billy dance around and then roll up into a ball and land on top of both of them, his quills cracking and snapping. He unrolled between the two and spread himself out, his arms against their bodies, forcing them apart, until they all lay side by side, on their backs, breathing heavily, too tired to move.

'I haven't got the energy for this anymore,' said the always-angry restaurant owner after a while.

'Then don't hit Scraps,' said Plenty.

I hauled myself into a sitting position. 'I think my skull is cracked.'

They looked up at me.

'There is a bump,' Plenty said.

'Just a little one,' the always-angry restaurant owner said.

'It looks like an egg,' said Billy.

'I am dying here, you know that,' I said. But the pain and physical activity had actually gone some way to clearing my head. They had gone some way to breaking it, too.

'I am sorry,' the always-angry restaurant owner said, getting up, and then she added with some curiosity, 'I don't think I've actually done that before, have I? I've threatened to hit you with my rolling pin, and I've definitely chased you, but I've never actually done it, have I?'

'No, and I don't want you to do it again.'

'It was satisfying.'

Plenty jumped up and sat next to me. She looked at her paw. She had lost a claw in the fight. She leaned in and whispered to me, 'Shall I kill her and eat her babies?'

'She hasn't got any babies.'

'If she had.'

'I think we're all friends now.'

'Okay.'

'I'm worried about the Pelican,' said Billy.

'Well, if all the fighting and hitting is over,' I said, 'shall we go on the roof and see what's happening out there?'

We made our way upstairs and again I had an uncomfortable feeling as we passed along the landing that the floor was shifting slightly beneath us. We hurried onto the roof and found a clear blue sky, a warm sun, a balmy breeze. I lit another cigarette and inhaled deeply. 'Nice day.'

'Are you kidding? Take a look down below,' said the always-angry restaurant owner. 'Did a bomb go off in the night? Where is everything?'

'It looks like a kaleidoscope,' said Billy.

He was right. The rooftops and houses of the previous night were gone. Below, the landscape looked like a liquid mosaic with shapes and unfamiliar objects receding into the distance towards the horizon. They seemed to be moving and changing colour, fizzing into existence and achieving a moment of clarity before fading away into something less defined. It was as if scenes from different films were being played and superimposed on each other.

'What is that?' said Plenty. 'What is all that stuff?'

Billy leaned over the parapet and looked down. 'There's the alleyway. See? It's like a path leading off that way.'

The restaurant was the only building left standing. That and the alleyway. One end of which, the end that had once led onto a blinding light, went nowhere. But the far end seemed to continue into the distance, weaving through the strange, new, ill-defined landscape.

'Is that the way to the hospital?' I asked the always-angry restaurant owner.

She frowned, thought and then shook her head. 'Possibly.'

'I'm tired,' said Plenty.

'You've only been awake an hour,' said Billy.

'Fighting makes me tired.'

'I don't think we should wait. I think we ought to get going,' I said. 'Find the Pelican and the hospital and the hairy man.'

'I want to rest first,' said Plenty.

'You can rest later.'

'You're not the boss.'

'I know, but I've been hit on the head. Be nice.'

'I am nice.'

'If you were nice you would go now.'

'I am going now.'

'All right, we'll all go now.'

Billy laughed. 'You're getting better at that,' he said.

'Why don't we deal with this as if it is another adventure?' I said. 'Even if it is a really messed-up adventure. And we'll sort it out like we always do and we'll come home like we always do. And don't forget this time we've got the always-angry restaurant owner on our side.'

'She hit you.'

'We're over that now.'

We went back inside and down to the restaurant, and straightened the tables and chairs and then looked at each other.

'Is this it?'

'This is it.'

'Is there anything we need to take?' said the always-angry restaurant owner.

'Do we have any more bacon?'

'It's all gone.'

'In that case, nothing. Are you ready?' I said.

'No.'

'Me neither, let's go.'

We stepped through the door and went.

17

It was as if a bulldozer had arrived in the night. Instead of seeing walls and buildings, we saw debris. And the sheer scale of it created strange, optical illusions.

'Are we looking down?'

'Or across?'

'Or up?'

'I don't like it,' said the always-angry restaurant owner. 'It's making me feel dizzy. Like I'm going to fall.'

'Just stay on the path,' I said. I thought that sounded good, a calm and terse and authoritative piece of advice; as if I knew what I was doing and was not in any way bewildered, or scared, or confused. We walked and I wondered if anyone was watching, but I didn't think so. I could usually tell when hidden eyes were on me... a shiver ran down my spine. 'Just stay on the path.' After ten minutes of walking, I looked back. There was no sign of the restaurant.

'Has it gone for good?' said the always-angry restaurant owner.

'I don't know.' That was becoming my mantra. Ask me a question, any question, and I wouldn't know the answer.

Plenty walked to the edge of the path and looked down at the changing mass of shapes and objects that ran either side of us. She knelt down and reached out to something she could see.

'Careful.'

She extracted a ball, a pink ball with a bell in it.

'Here it is,' she said. 'I knew it was somewhere.'

'That was odd,' said Billy.

We strung out. Billy and I walked together at the front, the always-angry restaurant owner trudged along at the back, and Plenty kicked her ball along between us. She alone seemed indifferent to the shifting shapes around us and walked without any apparent concern along the edge of the path.

'This is creepy,' Billy whispered. 'And where is the Pelican? What if it got tired of flying and had to land in this stuff? I don't think I could take it if it suddenly leaped out at me.'

'Just take it one step at a time.'

We took it one step at a time for over an hour. Plenty kicked her ball until she grew bored and left it where it was. Billy retrieved it. The always-angry restaurant owner grumbled and muttered and swore. I smoked and looked furtive. We were all in character.

'Hey, look,' I said.

'What?' said Billy. 'Where? Don't freak me out. Is it bad?'

'There. Look.' I pointed. Off to one side, in the middle of the opaque, swirling, changing scenery was a swing hanging motionless, surrounded by railings. 'I know that swing. I know those railings,' I said. 'There ought to be an underpass around here somewhere.'

'Passing under what?' said the always-angry restaurant owner. 'There's nothing here.'

'Just keep walking,' said Billy. 'Jesus Christ. Now what is she doing?'

Again Plenty was kneeling by the edge of the path, reaching into the moving, translucent surface. She pulled a box into view. A small red box with a screen on it, and a button and a speaker. We gathered round.

'What is it?'

'Press the button.'

'Do not press that button,' said Billy. 'Seriously. Do not press that button.'

Plenty pressed the button and a face appeared in the screen. I thought Billy had evacuated his skin. He seemed to be in two places at once, beside us and about a mile down the path. On the screen was a young boy's face; a young boy with a large, lumpy and shy face.

'Hello?' His voice sounded distant and tinny. 'Is that me? Can you hear me, me?'

'Who's me?' said Plenty. And then after a moment's reflection, 'I'm me. He's talking to me.'

'We're all me, you idiot,' said the always-angry restaurant owner.

The face on the box said, 'Don't forget to invent a pill that will keep Mum and Dad and Caroline and me alive forever. You won't forget to do that, will you?'

'Say something,' Billy hissed from the distance.

'We won't forget,' I shouted.

The screen faded and Plenty kicked the box off the path, and we carried on with our walking. The sky remained blue and clear, the sun remained high and warm, and then we saw the underpass. The path dipped and what crossed above was merely a section of road, suspended in the air. We could hear the sound of cars but none could be seen, and as we approached, the smell of urine became stronger.

'Home from home,' Billy said.

'I am not going under that thing,' said the always-angry restaurant owner.

'It's just an underpass,' I said. 'And you've got your rolling pin.'

'There might be mice in there,' said Plenty. 'I like little mice.'

Billy rolled her ball into the tunnel. The bell sounded very small echoing back off the walls.

'Let's go and see,' he said.

'Keep together.'

We walked in. The place stank but I found the coolness and the solidity of the concrete walls and ceiling comforting, and although it couldn't be possible, there was definitely the sound of cars passing overhead. I liked that too.

'Look,' Plenty whispered. 'People.'

Sitting on a blanket halfway along the underpass were an old man and a young girl. Keeping close to the wall on the far side, we walked towards them.

'How about a cigarette?' said the girl as we approached.

'Sure.' I rolled two and handed them over.

'We're looking for a hairy man,' said Plenty.

The girl nodded. 'Aren't we all? Got any change?'

I shook my head. 'No pockets.'

'What about her?' she said. 'The cook.'

We looked at the always-angry restaurant owner.

'Me? I haven't got any money,' she said. She patted her apron pocket. 'Nothing.'

The old man peered more closely at her. 'What's your name?' he said.

'What's it to you?'

'She's the always-angry restaurant owner,' said Plenty. 'Everyone knows that.'

The old man nodded, rocking backwards and forwards as he did so. 'But that's not a name, is it?'

The always-angry restaurant owner ignored him and walked on. We hurried after her and when we emerged from the underpass things were different.

A world similar but not the same as the one he'd known before.

That feeling of my life being stretched over something much bigger was back. Across the road was a hospital. It was a busy road and I had to shout to make myself heard above the traffic that was now visible. I tried to see inside the cars, to see the people's faces, but they were moving too fast.

'Is this it? Is this where you were?'

The always-angry restaurant owner nodded but I could see that her mind was elsewhere. Was she still thinking about those people in the underpass, I wondered? What *was* her name? And then I remembered how upset she'd been the night she showed me the cartoon strip in the newspaper. I put my hand on her arm.

'Are you okay?'

'Of course I'm okay. Why wouldn't I be okay?'

'I was just thinking about what they asked you. In the underpass just now.'

'Well, don't.'

'But—'

'I mean it, Scraps. Don't.'

We crossed the road and entered the hospital. We walked through the reception area, past the shop and the cafeteria and into a long corridor. A woman's face projected onto a plastic head asked us to use the wall-mounted alcoholic gel dispensers situated to her left. We all stopped and gelled up. Clean, lean and green.

'I don't like this,' said Billy. 'I don't like this at all. Look at all these people, and the colours and the sounds. Everything is so vivid.'

'I like it,' said Plenty. 'I can smell food...'

'And the rest. Everything smells. Even the air smells.'

'I've noticed something else too,' I said. 'Nobody is taking any notice of us.'

'Is that bad?' said the always-angry restaurant owner. 'Surely that's good? I think that is good. Is that good? God, I sound like the Pelican.'

'But don't you think it's odd that nobody is taking any notice of us?'

'But why would they?' said Billy. 'We're just ordinary...' he trailed off. 'Things.'

That was my point. I hadn't seen any other talking bipedal animals at all, not even a singing goldfish. So why wasn't anybody taking any notice of us?

'I'll make them take notice,' said Plenty.

A man in blue operating scrubs walked along the corridor. He was young, had dark hair and an expressionless face. Plenty stepped out in front of him and put her paw on his chest.

'Hello,' she said.

He stopped and looked at her. She was a five-foot seven-inch white pedigree cat, standing on two legs, with a tail, fangs and claws like scalpels. She was by any measure an aggressive piece of work. He didn't bat an eyelid. He simply stopped. I walked over and joined them – a six-foot skanky fox with a furtive air, probably smelling of tobacco and urine. He was okay with that as well.

'Are you a doctor?' said Plenty.

Still no reply.

I took a closer look at him. There was something *indefinite* about his features. He reminded me of the carpets and the spare rooms in the upstairs sections of the restaurant. They had given the impression of substance, of something solid and real, but if you looked too hard the patterns would begin to shift as if unwilling to be studied. I looked at his badge. The writing was indecipherable, as if it had been smudged. He looked like a memory of someone; the basics were there but none of the detail, and that thought troubled me.

I said, 'Well, you have a good day. Go save some lives.'

We stepped out of the way and he walked on. Plenty and I went back to the others.

'See?' she said. 'They like us.'

'In the same way that the wind blowing in our face likes us,' I said.

'Does it?'

'Never mind.'

We carried on, along more corridors, until we turned a corner and met another stream of people who passed us by without pause.

'Hey,' said Billy. 'There's your doctor friend again.' A man in blue operating scrubs walked along the corridor towards us. 'Hi, buddy,' said Billy. The man looked at us without expression and walked on.

'Rude,' said Plenty.

'You know, half of these people look the same,' said Billy.

'And how do you know where you're going?' the always-angry restaurant owner said to me.

'I just do.'

I didn't want to tell them that I was simply following the most defined path. Because one other thing I had noticed was that a lot of the corridors we walked past simply petered out to nothing. It was like seeing a pathway that had never been used. I pushed that thought away, too.

We turned a corner and the corridor opened out into a wide waiting area. Seats were laid out in rows in front of a reception area... and there he was.

As simple as that.

What had I expected? Dramatic music? A fade to the credits?

He was about 20 feet away, a large, bulky man squeezed into a blue suit, with an unkempt beard and a substantially wide moustache. I saw him and I knew him. More than that, *I knew him*. We stopped and for a moment none of us said anything. We might have stood there for a long time, but our inaction was broken by the always-angry restaurant owner, who shouted, 'There he is.'

She pointed at him and he turned and stared at us. He had been talking to two women, two nurses, and one put her hand on his arm and I heard her say, *Are you all right, Tom?*

We all looked at each other. Tom.

'Tash,' breathed Plenty. I lit a cigarette and my paws were shaking.

That's not allowed.

The nurses turned and looked in our direction.

Tom? And then we heard another voice calling, *Thomas Hannah? Is Thomas Hannah here?*

Thomas Hannah. I was convinced then. This was Tash. This was our cartoonist. He ignored the voice and continued to stare at us, fiddling with his hand. I puffed on my cigarette and Billy chewed his gum. Plenty picked up her ball, weighed it in her hands and then batted it down the corridor. It landed on the floor and rolled up to the feet of the nurses. One of them still had her hand on his arm. I wondered if they were trying to restrain him.

'He can't take his eyes off us,' the always-angry restaurant owner said out of the corner of her mouth.

'But I wouldn't say he was overjoyed with the view,' said Billy.

Is Thomas Hannah here? Are you Thomas Hannah?

Tom, come and sit down.

But he didn't sit down. Instead he picked up Plenty's ball. I thought he looked stiff and tired and I felt sorry for him. I felt stiff and tired too. He shook the ball and the bell tinkled and then he let it fall to the ground.

That's odd. I didn't think she put the ball in her mouth.

I looked at Plenty and she looked at me. 'I don't,' she said.

I threw down my cigarette. 'Let's go and talk to him.'

We set off along the corridor but Tom was stepping back, turning and walking away. He was picking up speed and by the time he reached the glass fire door that led to the stairs, he was running. I saw him push through a set of glass doors and disappear down the stairs. More than ever I knew we had to talk to him. I ran down the corridor after him with the others following, Billy scooping up Plenty's ball as he passed it. We went through the glass doors and ran down the stairs, along the corridors, through the reception area and out into the fresh air. Our man had gone.

'I can't keep this up,' puffed the always-angry restaurant owner. 'You go on. I'll catch up.'

'No, we should stay together,' I said.

'I can't run all the time,' the always-angry restaurant owner said. 'I'm not an animal. I'll have to walk.'

'No need,' said Billy. 'He's gone. We've lost him.'

We sat on the pavement by the hospital entrance. We could hardly follow his scent, whatever the always-angry restaurant owner might think of our animal abilities.

'What do we do now?' she said.

I was about to repeat my phrase of the week, 'I don't know', when we heard the beat of wings and smelled rotting fish. We looked up and there, descending like a vast, broken kite and accompanied by a fall of maggots, was the Pelican. It came in too fast and I glimpsed the panic in its eyes before it hit the pavement like a sack of rice, its feathers crackling and snapping, and all kinds of crap bouncing upwards. It looked all in. Its skinny ribcage blew in and out like paper-thin bellows. It was getting old. I felt a sudden surge of compassion and of regret, as if there were things unsaid and opportunities missed. I shook my head.

'Want a cigarette?'

The Pelican's eyes seemed to swap places as it focused on the question. 'No. Yes.'

I handed out a few ready rolled. 'So where have you been?'

'I've been to yesterday and the day before.' The Pelican rolled smoke around its throat pouch and blew it out of both sides of its beak.

The always-angry restaurant owner groaned. 'Its brains have gone.'

'We've been chasing the hairy man,' Plenty said. 'But he got away.'

'So we're stuck,' said Billy.

I was finding this place very complicated. There were too many variables, too many things to think about. It wasn't only the physical things that were untidy, random and uncontrolled; it was everything: the atmosphere itself, my thoughts, time. Everything was jumbled up with possible outcomes all over the place.

The Pelican raised its flaking, mottled, decaying head. 'From above I can see below.'

'Someone put it out of its misery.'

'You mean from up there you'll be able to find him?' I said.

'Do I? I saw the dog.'

'The dog? We think the dog's Bullet. Do you remember Bullet? But why would we want to follow the dog?'

'Perhaps she's going back to where she's been all this time,' said Plenty. 'Perhaps that's where the man lives.'

I liked that idea. Why was everyone else having all the good ideas. 'Okay, let's follow the dog,' I said. 'Or rather, the Pelican can follow the dog and we'll follow the Pelican.'

But first we rested. The always-angry restaurant owner insisted – which was another good idea I hadn't had. We waited an hour and set off with the light fading, walking through the darkening streets while the Pelican flapped around overhead. We didn't need to see it, we followed the scent of decomposing marine life.

We walked along empty streets with litter-strewn pavements, past parks surrounded by railings, past pubs with bright lights outside but no sounds coming from within. We passed by an alleyway and I thought I saw the vague shape of a lumpy young boy, dressed in his school clothes, being taunted and tormented by two other children as he hurried along on his way to somewhere. The always-angry restaurant owner shivered and drew her chef's jacket closer around her. Finally, we turned into a cul-de-sac and saw a large house with a cherry tree in its garden, unlit and in darkness.

The Pelican circled the house like a gigantic bat and then landed on the roof.

'Are we here?' I said.

We heard a loud bark from beyond the houses. 'I guess so. She's coming,' Billy muttered. 'So now what?'

'We go in, of course,' said Plenty. 'But it has to be Scraps who goes in first. It's always Scraps. We'll come in afterwards and eat all of the food and kill all of the little mice and rats. We'll go to sleep in front of the fire and always live here.'

'Ye-es,' I said.

I walked up to the front of the house and then followed the walls round to the back.

'Don't eat all the little rats and mice,' Plenty called after me.

In the darkness I could see the outline of an outhouse attached to the kitchen, extending onto the lawn. I tried the windows as I went, but they were all tightly shut. The back door, too, was locked. But when I got to the outhouse I found that the windows were older, and one was cracked: a long line running from the top to the side. The putty was ancient and I dug into it with my claws, gently pushing at the top of the pane, working it loose until I could lift it out. I reached in and unlatched the window.

I climbed into the outhouse and lit a cigarette to calm my nerves, and tried the inner door. It didn't move. I pulled again and then hauled on the handle with all my meagre strength. Still nothing. I looked through the keyhole to see if there was a key on the other side but there wasn't. I checked that it wasn't a door to be pushed, and then tugged sharply on the handle, turning it hard. I felt it give. It wasn't locked; it was stuck.

I kept tugging and as I heaved the door upwards and inwards, it scraped open. Not much of a gap but enough that I could slip into the kitchen.

I liked kitchens. I looked inside the fridge but it consisted mostly of bottles of beer and wine. I found a sliver of cheese and ate it and walked into the hallway. I saw a light beneath the living-room door and, looking up the stairs, a ladder leading to a trapdoor in the ceiling. I crept upwards in exaggerated steps, the carpeted stairs creaking beneath my feet, when a loud commotion kicked off outside. In my experience, loud commotions that include shouting, hissing and the sounds of running feet are best left alone. If only. I retraced my steps and left the house to see what was going on.

18

http://www.tashfanz.com/borkmann%20075interview.htm

A Belgian television interview with Gerard Borkmann from August 2014.

On 26 August 2014, Gerard Borkmann was interviewed by Germaine Kiecke for her late night arts television show *Kiecke In Conversation*. The interview was never transmitted but the following transcript was made available to The Borkmann Creative Agency on request.

Germaine Kiecke (to camera): The Borkmann Creative Agency is one of the largest cartoon syndication agencies in the world and the UK's largest independent agency. It distributes cartoon strips, political illustrations, games and puzzles to over a thousand newspapers and magazines around the world. Its founder, Gerard Borkmann, began syndicating material from a back room in a

London fish market in the 1960s. Now he presides over an international operation with offices in London, New York, Paris and Tokyo. Still working out of his original rooms in London's East End, Borkmann himself is perhaps best known as one-time mentor of the cartoonist, Thomas Arthur Stevenson Hannah, or Tash as he is known publicly, and The Borkmann Creative Agency is the commercial force behind the formidable, and very lucrative, *Scraps* cartoon industry. A man renowned for his firm views and no-nonsense manner, this promises to be a lively interview. Gerard, welcome and thank you for coming in.

Gerard Borkmann: Hello.

Germaine: Gerard, what makes a successful cartoon?

Gerard (pause): I think empathy. The public have to relate to the cartoon and so does the cartoonist.

Germaine: To the characters you mean?

Gerard: To the characters, yes, and to the situation and the storyline. The whole product.

Germaine: I suppose that's true for any fictional narrative. I was wondering if there was something more specific to the cartoon medium. For example, the drawing style.

Gerard: All right. They have to relate to the drawing style too.

Germaine: I can see that. I suppose I'm following a line, exploring, whether or not there is a style common to the more successful cartoons, or rather, is there an approach to cartooning that is more successful than others? I mean, why is *Scraps* successful and other cartoons are not? Do you see what I'm getting at?

Gerard: I don't think there's any kind of dark art to it. If it's meant to be a funny cartoon then it has to be funny, and if it's meant to be a political cartoon it has to be political. A satirical cartoon has to be satirical and a children's cartoon has to work for children.

Germaine: I mentioned *Scraps* and I know you represent many other cartoonists and syndicate many other cartoon strips; but with *Scraps* in particular there is a realistic element to the characters despite the fact that they're talking animals. As you say, people relate to the cartoon, and in that sense the characters can assume a certain veneer of reality. Is that suspension of disbelief essential to a good cartoon, or is it part of what Tom Hannah referred to as the physics of cartoons – we accept them as inhabiting a different reality? Hannah was very interested in this aspect of his cartoons when I interviewed him.

Gerard: Well, I don't go into the mathematics of the stuff. To me they're just drawings; lines on a piece of paper. They're a product that I have to sell, that I want to sell.

Germaine: I sense that it's important to you to maintain a distance, a separation between the art and the artefact.

Gerard: Is that a question?

Germaine (laughing): Yes. Would you say that's the case?

Gerard: Between the art and the artefact... you mean between the paper and the picture, or the imaginary world and the real world?

Germaine: I'll take either.

Gerard: I think it's healthy to keep a separation in both cases.

Germaine: Okay. Let's talk more about the originator. What, in your opinion, makes for a successful cartoonist?

Gerard: A good agent.

Germaine (laughing): I deserved that. And are you a good agent?

Gerard: I think so.

Germaine: What makes you that? What are the qualities of a good agent?

Gerard: A sense of perspective. And in my case, the ability to sell a considerable number of cartoon strips.

Germaine: I can see that's a valuable ability. But I

wonder if there's more to it than that. For example, to what extent are you involved in the creative process?

Gerard: As little as possible.

Germaine: That's interesting... I... just to go back, what do you mean when you say 'a sense of perspective'? In what way is that an important trait to you, the agent?

Gerard: It's a solitary business being a cartoonist. Most of my clients don't work in an office or a studio, they work at home, alone. And if you're going to sit at home all day, spending hour after hour working inside your head, then you need to connect with the real world every now and then. That's what I mean by perspective. Creative people need to be able to compartmentalise, otherwise... it all gets mixed up.

Germaine: And that's part of your job? The agent? To keep them connected? To make sure they don't get stuck in the wrong compartment?

Gerard: I would say so. Yes. To a degree.

Germaine: It's interesting that you refer to the cartoons as a product. I wonder if the term 'product' captures the creative aspect of the work. Is it something that is produced or something created? Do you think that distinction matters?

Gerard: No.

Germaine: But is it a distinction that your cartoonists would make – do they see their product as art? Even if it is a dark art as you called it?

Gerard: I'm sure they do – and I said it's *not* a dark art. I sell cartoons and cartoon strips. It doesn't matter to me whether a cartoonist physically gives birth to a drawing or doodles it into life with his toes. What I want, and what the public want, is a consistent, regular, saleable cartoon strip delivered on time.

Germaine: It's interesting that you use analogies of cartoonists bringing their cartoons to life. That suggests to me that it is something more than merely a product. Do you think that these characters take on a life of their own? That they are, in a sense, larger than life? *Scraps*, for example, is a huge phenomenon. I read in the magazine *Psychology In Action* that Scraps himself has been rated a key influencer on the opinions and moral values of 12- to 15-year-olds.

Gerard: God help us.

Germaine (laughing): Well, I think the ethics of an eco-friendly waste-adverse entrepreneur are quite laudable. You seem resistant to my suggestion that there is more to being an agent than just moving product. I don't understand that. I know that you are far more involved with your cartoonists than just being the middleman and that you are highly regarded and praised, and rightly so, for the effort you put into developing their talent. Let's take Tom Hannah as an example. You spent a lot of time working with him at the beginning of his career, with no guarantee of any financial reward. We've had him on this show, actually.

Gerard: I know, I'm his agent.

Germaine (laughing): Of course, but you mentored him and stayed with him even at a time when animal cartoons weren't selling.

Gerard: I had faith.

Germaine: And what was it about his cartoons that gave you that faith?

Gerard: I thought he had a point worth making.

Germaine (laughing): Is this a glimpse of the real Gerard Borkmann I'm seeing? Tell me it's not just about the money.

Gerard: I thought it would sell and I was right.

Germaine: Do you enjoy cartoons? I mean, are you a fan?

Gerard: I have an interest in them, yes, of course. I would have gone insane a long time ago if I didn't.

Germaine: I want to explore a bit more the extent to which you advise, suggest, *shape* your cartoonists' cartoons.

Would it be fair to say that *Scraps* is your biggest... product?

Gerard: It's the highest earning.

Germaine: And your relationship with Hannah, the chemistry between you two, is that important in the agent-cartoonist relationship?

Gerard: I am his friend.

Germaine: Can we return to your point about whether or not it's healthy to spend too much time in one's imagination? When Tom Hannah was on this show, he mentioned his interest in what happened between the frames, the life of his characters when they weren't captured in the panel – is it a panel or a frame, by the way, I'm always confused?

Gerard: Whatever you want to call it. A box.

Germaine: Hannah was interested in what happened outside of that box.

Gerard: Really?

Germaine: You don't share that interest?

Gerard: No.

Germaine: Not even from a merchandising or spin-off perspective?

Gerard: No.

Germaine: Since I last spoke to him, Tom Hannah has all but disappeared. How hard does it make your role as an agent to have a recluse on your books? I'm thinking about our earlier conversation; about how you see yourself as keeping them connected to the real world.

Gerard: You say recluse as if there's something wrong with that. If he wants to live his life anonymously, that's his business.

Germaine: I don't mean in terms of lifestyle, I mean... well, access. Public access. Isn't part of your job to publicise and promote?

Gerard: The cartoon – not the cartoonist. There is no automatic right-of-way to his front door.

Germaine: I asked Tom when he was here whether

he thought he had any obligations to his characters, to his creations. Do you think that he, and through him, you, have an obligation to the fans, a duty to perpetuate the cartoon strip?

Gerard: No.

Germaine: No?

Gerard: No.

Germaine: Okay. Without dwelling too much on one individual, I understand you were a huge support to Tom Hannah during his… domestic difficulties.

Gerard: I was on hand. But I'm not comfortable with this line of questioning, Germaine. Is this interview about me or Tom Hannah?

Germaine: That's a fair point but I'm trying to explore the dynamics of your role as an agent. *Scraps* is hugely popular; I think it's reasonable to ask how you work with Tom Hannah.

Gerard: Fine, but I am not going to discuss his personal life, or anybody else's personal life for that matter.

Germaine: I understand that and I'm not interested in the details. I'm pursuing the notion of obligations. You have said that there is no obligation to the fans but thousands of readers every week buy newspapers simply to follow the exploits of the *Scraps* characters – and they pay good money to do so. I think that there might be some kind of obligation to them, and I'd like to explore that further. It's your role in the process that I'm seeking to explore – what you see as your responsibilities and how you act upon them.

Gerard: But if you found yourself being relentlessly hounded, how would you feel about those that were hounding you? Would you think it's because they can't live without hearing some new pearl of wisdom drop from your lips, or would it be because they wanted the kudos they'd get if they were the first to successfully flush you out?

Germaine: Gerard, I am not trying to seek out Tom

Hannah, or flush him out, as you call it. I am asking a valid set of questions about your interactions as a business agent with your creative clients.

Gerard: What I would do is leave a man, who clearly wants to be left alone, alone.

Germaine: Gerard, I understand that. I've upset you and I didn't mean to. Can we take the heat out of this conversation? I really do not want to talk about Tom Hannah's private life.

Gerard: Good.

Germaine: I do want to briefly discuss your business, professional, interaction with him during the recent past, briefly, as a means of exploring your role, as an agent, in the creative process. If you don't like the questions, you don't have to answer them – but trust me, I am not trying to exploit your relationship, business or otherwise. Is that all right? Can we resume?

Gerard: Let's see how it goes.

Germaine: Thank you. Okay. So... can we pick it up with Tom Hannah taking a break from drawing *Scraps*?

Gerard: He's taking a break; I think it's fair to say that. And I am fine with that. Fifteen years is a long time with one set of characters. We have a stockpile – a set of unsubmitted cartoons – so there is no immediate syndication issue. Tom has enough unpublished strips to take a year off if he chooses to do so. We are in contact with all of our markets. It's giving him the space he wants.

Germaine: I believe he's worked on another cartoon strip, a new project... can you tell me anything about that? How you feel about that?

Gerard: How do I feel about it? I feel fine.

Germaine: Is it another animal cartoon?

Gerard: That's not for me to say.

Germaine: There's been talk of alcohol-related issues...

At this point Gerard Borkmann stopped the interview.

19

Tom was in his airy eyrie, twitching like an anxious bear and desperate for another drink. He put down the telephone and listened hard, looking first this way and then that, not even blinking. Was that cigarette smoke he could smell? Had the stairs creaked? If so, who was smoking cigarettes while they crept up towards his ladder?

His growing unease had a taste and a texture, a weight and a presence all of its own. It was like a poison running through his veins and clogging up his heart and clouding his brain. He was used to his fear of heights, which was rooted in imaginings of self-destruction. But in the real world he could at least turn away from a tall building and not expect it to pursue him through the streets, and besides, it was always preferable to be alone when choosing not to cross a bridge, because no one could persuade him to do otherwise.

But standing alone in the attic, listening to noises from below, brought with it a different fear. To face confrontation alone, with no one to witness how brave or otherwise he might be, was a frightening feeling in itself. There would be no one to help him, no referee to intervene, no grown-up to step in and stop the fighting, and he knew that the people-pleaser in him – the soft, weak, pliant, leave-me-alone-please Tom – would be unable to overcome that fear, in the same way that he had been unable to overcome his fear of heights. Despite his size, he was not conditioned for conflict. He had no background in aggression, no instinctive desire to hurt anyone. He did not know how to defend himself. He needed a weapon.

He looked around the room and picked up a metal ruler. He tried to imagine grappling with a genuine assailant, being face to face with a violent ruffian who wanted to fight. How could a person who did not want to fight overcome a person who did? It was tempting to roll over and die and get it over with, and avoid all the shouting and running and bleeding.

Tom tried a few practice slashes with the ruler; downwards, upwards, sideways. The Roman legionaries had used short, upward thrusts when they fought, stepping out from behind their shields and disembowelling their enemies with their razor-sharp gladii, and he'd heard that commandos were trained to kill in the dark with only a matchbox. How much better than that was a metal ruler? A commando would be able to wreak havoc with the contents of a stationery cupboard. A commando could probably gut and fillet an enemy with a metal ruler. While he slashed the air, part of Tom wondered whether or not he would be able to gut and fillet his enemy. He doubted it, as he couldn't even gut and fillet a fish. He couldn't even kill a fish. He put the ruler back on his desk.

He listened again for sounds from below and wondered about his mental state. People didn't normally lock themselves in their attic after sharing a takeaway with their wife and children, did they?

'Am I going mad?' he said, and he found the sound of his voice in the silence more troubling than the question.

Was it possible that there had been something in the food, a bad mushroom or an undercooked chicken chunk, or a careless sprinkling of narcotic to spice up the Pad Thai? And if the food had been bad and his senses were not to be trusted, had that been a creak on the stairs? Or was it all nothing more than the normal moans and groans of a house settling down for the night? He wished again he'd kept a store of alcohol in his study. Alcohol was an accepted ingredient in battle preparation, and smoking too. Tom cursed his lack of foresight.

It was only now, listening for sounds in complete silence, that he realised how bad his tinnitus had become: the hissing, humming and throbbing, the occasional pop, the unexpected ping. His head was noisier than a submarine and for a moment he couldn't help but imagine a periscope appearing from his scalp.

'Get a grip, Tom,' he said. 'Focus.'

Now was not the time to think about periscopes emerging from his scalp. He got up and walked as quietly as he could to the trapdoor and lay down on the floor with his ear to the floorboards. The bolt looked puny from such a close proximity; it might deter a weak person, he thought – possibly a child with low strength, or a strong gust of wind – but surely not an adult. Holly alone could reduce that trapdoor to splinters without registering any resistance. Holly alone could reduce the entire house to splinters if she put her mind to it.

He pushed from his mind the thought of Karen, Dan and Holly creeping silently up the ladder, their faces inches from his, separated only by a thin board and a flimsy lock, and found himself instead thinking about how nice it would be to die lying down. He imagined himself at the end of a long and fulfilled life, lying outside on a com-

fortable patch of grass, beneath a tree in an orchard, smoking a cigarette and looking up at the sky, with a light, warm rain drizzling on
his face; his clock winding down, eternal peace building up inside.

A loud commotion kicked off outside. It was the sound of animals fighting. He heard scrabbling claws and feet. He heard something being knocked over, something rattling down the road. He
heard more running and barking; more crying and snarling; a cawing
from the sky. He looked up at the skylight.

His brain felt loosely constructed and he knew he needed to keep
all the parts in place until he could tighten it up again.

'Hold the line, Tom. Hold the line.'

He lay on the floor feeling the weight of his moustache, uncertain of what to do. He couldn't see the road because the skylights
pointed upwards; he didn't dare go downstairs because he was frightened of his family.

'How can you be frightened of your family?'

The noise outside stopped as abruptly as it had begun. Tom held
his breath and listened for a resumption of the fight; for a sniff, or a
snort, or a hiss, or a click, or any sound at all. Had they gone or were
they all dead?

He imagined the scene outside. The cul-de-sac would be a
smoking ruin: cars would be overturned; dustbins and their contents
would be strewn across the road; bodies – mashed and mangled –
would be lying in the gutters or hanging from lampposts. Dazed
householders would be emerging from their houses and gathering
together in fearful groups as they surveyed the carnage. Perhaps one
battle-hardened survivor – weary, battered, broken but unbeaten –
would stand amongst the wreckage and light a hand-rolled cigarette,
blowing smoke into the night air…

The doorbell rang.

Tom awoke with a start. He had nodded off lying on the floor
with his head by the trapdoor. He sat up and listened, waiting to hear
if anyone downstairs would answer it. He wanted to hear the normal sounds of movement; to hear someone call, 'I'll get it', to hear the
front door open, hear voices, and, with luck, the sounds of Borkmann
entering, full of bluster while he took off his overcoat. Instead all he
heard was the doorbell again. A longer, more impatient ring. Surely
it had to be Borkmann pressing that button. Only his gimlet-like fin-

ger could sustain the note for so long. Tom got up, retrieved his metal ruler, pulled back the bolt and lifted the trapdoor, ready to slam it shut if anybody leapt upwards.

Nobody leapt upwards.

He crouched down and tried to see if anybody was keeping out of sight further along the landing. He couldn't see anybody. He climbed down the ladder and listened. The only sound he could hear was his own uneven breathing. The doorbell rang again, followed by a heavy rapping on the front glass. The noise accentuated the silence in the house, magnifying it to the extent that it sounded like a giant's hand rapping on the roof. Tom walked down the carpeted stairs and waited at the end of the hallway. There were two silhouettes on the other side of the front door.

'Who is it?' he said.

'Tom. It's Gerard,' said one of the silhouettes. 'Are you all right?'

Tom opened the front door and peered out.

On the doorstep was Borkmann and a tall, athletic-looking woman with tight, tanned skin and greying blonde hair. She was wrapped in a raincoat and carried a small suitcase.

'Caroline,' Tom said.

He opened the door wider. Borkmann stood next to Caroline. They both looked at his ruler.

'Drawing cartoon panels, I hope,' said Borkmann.

'Tom,' Caroline said. She stepped forwards and hugged him. Tom looked beyond her at the road and the cars and houses that comprised the cul-de-sac, at his father's decaying car, at the cherry tree that seemed to be hitching up its roots as if ready to walk away, and at the darkening sky. Where was the carnage he'd imagined – the mutilated bodies, the sirens in the distance, the smoking ruins, the groups of fearful onlookers, the hedgehog quills still vibrating in walls, the piles of pelican feathers? If he closed his eyes, he could see it. He must have closed his eyes because when he opened them his sister was peering at him, saying, 'Are you all right, Tom?'

'I'm fine. Did you hear anything just now? Like a fight. Animals?'

'No, but we've just got here.'

He looked at her and frowned, as if seeing her for the first time. 'What are you doing here?'

'I've come to see you, of course. I left messages and I emailed.'

'Did you? Are you staying?'

'What Tom really means,' said Borkmann, interrupting, 'is how lovely it is to see you, Caroline, and can I take your case because you must be exhausted after your travels. Is there any chance of you inviting us in, Tom?'

Tom stepped back and took a last look along the road. 'Yes, of course,' he said, and picked up Caroline's case. 'Of course.'

'The telephone call?' Borkmann said as he squeezed passed. 'What trouble are you in?' He leaned closer. 'Have you been drinking?'

Tom ignored him and turned to Caroline. 'When did you arrive?' he said.

'This morning. I've been working on a project in Senegal so I couldn't get away until now. I would have been here even earlier but I went to see Mum's memorial. Gerard called me and picked me up at the station.'

'You didn't need to come,' Tom said and then looked back along the hallway towards the living room. He wondered why Karen or Dan or Holly hadn't come out to see who was at the front door.

'Oh no,' Caroline said. 'I've just seen your tooth.'

'Or lack of,' said Borkmann.

'It's nothing,' Tom said, which was accurate. 'Come on through. We were having a takeaway but I don't know if there's any left.'

'We?' said Borkmann.

Tom led the way to the living room. The side tables were stacked in their nest, the chairs and sofas were all lined up at the correct angles, the footstools were tucked away. There were no wine stains on the carpet; no trays of half-eaten food. The television was off; the curtains were open; everything was neat and tidy, just as Tom liked it.

'They must be in the kitchen.'

'I didn't realise you had guests,' Borkmann said.

As he led the way to the kitchen, Tom thought about those dreams in which he ran as fast as he could but inertia tied his legs to the floor with rubber ropes. The hallway had become one of those dream-like corridors and he was finding it difficult to move forwards. He heard Caroline say, 'Tom, are you all right?'

Why does everyone keep saying that?

'I'm fine,' he said. 'Come and say hello to everyone.'

They went into the kitchen but again there was no one there. Nor was there any sign of their passing: no plates of food or takeaway boxes or glasses waiting to be washed up. Only a neat and tidy and empty kitchen.

'Looks like everyone's gone,' said Borkmann.

'How about in there?' said Caroline, pointing at the outhouse door.

'That's locked,' Tom said. 'Excuse me a minute.'

He left them in the kitchen, looking at each other, and walked down the hallway and up the stairs. The keep-out signs on the bedroom doors were gone. He pushed into Holly's room and saw a bed and a wardrobe and a bedside table with a lamp on it. No photographs, no clothes, no Holly. He opened all the cupboards. He looked under the bed. He even looked out of the window and onto the garden in case his family were hiding in the garden. Nothing.

He crossed the landing and went into Dan's room. It was the same. The laptop was gone; his clothes were gone. Books, magazines and posters had dematerialised. Dan was not there nor were his things. In the bathroom there were only Tom's toiletries, only his towel. In the bedroom, only his clothes.

He walked onto the landing and turned slowly around. Walls, doors, stairway, window and the ladder to the attic passed by his eyes as if he were at the centre of a merry-go-round; at the centre of an always-changing, infinitely varying, dizzying merry-go-round.

He made it halfway down the stairs and then his legs gave way and he had to sit down with his head in his hands, his hair falling forwards and his moustache drooping downwards like a vast dead caterpillar that had been pinned to his lip.

'Tom, where are you?'

They came to him on the stairs and Caroline sat next to him with her arm around his shoulders while Borkmann remained in the hallway, leaning against the wall and looking up. Tom noticed that beyond the window in the front door it was getting dark, but they remained in the gloom without the hall or landing lights on.

'What's happened, Tom?' said Borkmann.

'I don't know.'

Caroline said, 'Would you like some coffee?'

Tom waved the suggestion away as if it were a fly. 'No, thank you. I'm fine. Just a bit tired.'

'Tired?' Borkmann said.

To Tom their voices were like the hammers that rock climbers use to tap into the sides of mountains – a tool that Lawrence would know all about and would probably have stored neatly in his kitbag. Each word dislodged a small piece of his mind and he felt increasingly fragile, as if he might shatter or fall apart – literally fall apart, deconstruct, his arms and legs detaching, his face disintegrating, his ribs crumbling into powder.

Caroline squeezed him. 'I should have come earlier,' she said.

Tom wondered how many people Caroline had sat next to, in how many disaster-torn towns and cities around the world, and of those, from how many had she gently, calmly, kindly squeezed all the life. She had always been good with people.

Borkmann said, 'Who were your guests?'

'Not guests,' Tom said. 'Just Karen and the kids.'

Borkmann looked at Caroline and she looked at Tom. He decided then that he wanted them to go away. Caroline was frowning like someone listening to a bad song. Tom could see questions piling up behind her forehead, questions he was too weary to answer. He felt giddy and he wondered if he was going to pitch forwards and topple down the stairs, break his neck and get some peace. From a long way away, he heard Borkmann say, 'Karen? Not your Karen?'

'Yes, my Karen.'

'But she's in Dubai.'

'How can she be in Dubai?'

'That's where she lives. With Lawrence.'

Tom threw up on the floor.

20

It had been a long time since Tom had done anything like that and it hurt. It hurt his stomach, his chest and his throat. He stared with bleary surprise at the mess on the carpet and then it happened again.

'Jesus Christ.'

His eyes were watering and the back of his throat burned, hot and torn. He wiped his mouth with the back of his hand and his moustache felt thick and sticky. He took a deep breath and waited to see what would happen next. His body had taken over and apparently preferred him to be inside out.

'It's okay,' said Caroline. 'Just stay there until you feel better. I'll clear it up in a minute. How do you feel now?'

'I'm malfunctioning.'

Some of his vomit had splashed Borkmann's trousers and despite Caroline's advice to sit still, Tom stood up and leaned heavily on the banisters.

'Sorry about that. I don't know what's happening to me.'

'It's all right,' Borkmann said. 'Do you want to lie down? Sleep it off?'

'Sleep what off?'

'I'm just saying do you want to lie down for a while?'

'No. I want to clean up.'

'Go and have a wash,' said Caroline. 'I'll clear up here.'

'I think it was something I ate.'

Tom went to the bathroom, washed his face, rinsed his mouth, cleaned his teeth, dumped his stained and ruined suit in a plastic bag which he threw into the back of a cupboard, and put on his dressing gown. If there was one item of clothing that Tom truly loved. Borkmann went to the cloakroom and sponged his trousers. Caroline retrieved what cleaning equipment she could find and sterilised the stair and hall carpets.

They reconvened in the living room, where Tom sat quietly in an armchair and nursed a glass of water. Borkmann sat in the chair opposite, his damp legs crossed, and Caroline sat on the sofa. Tom looked around. It was a different scene to earlier and a different atmosphere. The room seemed cooler and larger than it had when he, Karen, Holly and Dan had shared a takeaway. He made a mental note to call the restaurant and complain. He wondered if the others were suffering or whether it was only him, but mostly he wondered where they had gone.

'Well,' said Borkmann. 'That was exciting.'

'I didn't expect it to happen.'

'How are you feeling now?' said Caroline.

'Embarrassed.'

'Oh no,' she said. 'Don't feel like that. You looked peaky when we arrived.' She had made coffee for herself and Borkmann. It was now dark outside and the curtains had been drawn and the table lamps were on.

'But really, how do you feel?' Caroline said.

Tom tried to find a way to answer that question.

'Do you remember Dad once told us about two railway engineers who started building a single railway track from opposite ends of the country, and when they met in the middle the track didn't join up? I feel like those two engineers.'

'Confused? Frustrated?'

'No. Like I'm two parts of one thing.'

'Tom,' said Borkmann. 'Tell me again. Who were your visitors?'

Sitting in his chair, his immense head pointed towards his glass, his bulk once again wrapped in his dressing gown, Tom wondered why, when people wanted to talk, they didn't bother to listen. He said, 'This Lawrence – was he one of Karen's work friends? A willowy, weaselly, sandy-haired creature? Older than me.'

Caroline looked at Borkmann. Neither of them said anything for a moment and then she said, 'Well, I'm not sure. They live abroad. He works in Dubai, as Gerard says. But I don't know if he looks like that. I don't know if any of us ever met him. I think they did work together, though. At the beginning. He might be a bit older.'

At the beginning. As if anything ever really begins. There is always something before, never a first frame unless you're a cartoonist.

Borkmann stirred. 'Tom, just so you know, I called Karen and told her about your accident and I said you were all right. I thought she'd read about it anyway. She was relieved. She was in Dubai when I called her, and she's in Dubai now almost certainly. I'm just saying.'

Tom thought about Holly and Dan's empty bedrooms. He thought about the empty spare room, the men-only toiletries in the bathroom. His clothes and his clothes alone in the bedroom. But still he remained unmoving in his chair, a giant statue, immobile, his thoughts locked deep inside.

Give me your hand. Let me hold your hand.

The lights in the room seemed over-bright to him, heavy on his eyelids. Tom sat inside his head as if he were at the centre of a vast surveillance operation, the flight commander at mission control. He stared at the living room from behind his eyes while everyone on the late shift in his brain sifted through the incoming information and images and sounds and signals and a million tiny data feeds, trying to make sense of it all.

He looked across at Caroline and at Borkmann, and seeing their long legs crossed and bent like arranged sticks, he wondered what would happen if he closed his eyes and imagined them in a different position. Would they be like that when he looked again? He knew what they were thinking: that he was drunk. He wished he was. Who were these people who had arrived in his house? Had he made them up? Had they once been sketches that he had coloured in with his imagination? He felt the edge of his seat. What if this was the illusory moment, the waking dream? What if all this were a piece of film stretched from wall to wall behind which the real world of Karen, Holly and Dan existed, asking each other where he was or perhaps even staring at him and wondering what he was thinking, or why he was talking to people they couldn't see.

Tom heard Borkmann say, 'I don't know what's been going on or who's been here or... what. But we're here now and you're here and it doesn't look like anybody else is here. You say that a woman called Karen and her children were here?'

'Our children.'

Borkmann paused.

'Tom,' he said gently. 'Are you talking about Karen, your exwife, who doesn't have any children – or are you saying something else I don't understand? You are worrying me. What do you mean, children?'

Her face was calm and serene and she looked up at him from behind the bars of her lacquered eyelashes. She was perfectly still, silent, unblinking, scarcely breathing, and then she laughed and reached out to him.

'Tom...' said Caroline.

'What?'

'Tom, tomorrow I think we should maybe talk about seeing the hospital people again? Just in case there are any... left-over issues.'

'What kind of left-over issues?' That would never do, he thought. Waste not, want not. Tom stared at the water in his glass. He could hear a whining in his ears, an endless background noise that might have been the keening of a dog or the howling of a wolf, or only his loosely held-together brain rustling against his eardrums. He wanted these people to go away so that he could have a few drinks and take his time tightening it all up.

'Are you all right, Tom? You're very quiet. What are you thinking?' said Caroline.

Things aren't always what they seem. Like those optical illusions. One moment it's an old woman's face, and the next it's a young woman looking away.

What are you thinking, Tom wondered? Are you thinking about thinking or are you actually thinking? And what does that mean? Thoughts behind thoughts, above and below thoughts, over here and over there thoughts.

'Like black bags piled up all around me,' he said.

'Pardon?'

Tom tapped his head. 'The world is in here, not out there,' he said. 'I once said that.'

'Did you?'

'I did.'

Neither Caroline nor Borkmann looked comfortable. Perhaps they thought he might vomit again. Borkmann sat forwards and leaned with his elbows on his knees and his hands steepled against his chin. 'Tom,' he said, 'do you remember much about how things have been for you recently?'

'How things have been for me?'

'Yes.'

'Like in the last couple of weeks?'

'No. Before that. Before your accident.'

'You mean pre-bananas?'

Tom saw in his mind's eye the knotted ball of thoughts and memories that seemed to exist in the days leading up to his fall. Was it a bigger ball than he'd realised? Were there more than hours and days in there? Were there weeks and months and years? Tom held onto his seat and hoped Borkmann's suit was out of range.

'Tom,' said Caroline. 'None of us knows why you were on that roof or what happened.'

'I know that.'

Borkmann looked at Caroline and unfolded and refolded his legs, exactly as Tom had imagined he would. 'I'm not talking about why you were on the roof, at least not directly. I'm talking about before. I'm talking about you and Karen and everything.'

Tom lay back in his chair. 'Everything?' he said. 'I don't know what you mean. What are you saying. You're not making any sense, Gerard.'

'I'm just saying that it took you a while to get over Karen leaving. That's all. Her meeting this Lawrence. That was a big thing. It took its toll. She was honest, you have to give her that. But it was hard. I don't think you saw it coming. I can imagine it's tough when you think you're going to live happily ever after and then pow, you find out that you're not. At least, not in that relationship.'

She's in Finance; I'm in Marketing. We are ships in the night.

'Maybe it would have been different if you'd had children.'

'But I did have children.'

'Tom, you didn't.'

'When was this? When was it that I didn't have children?' Tom felt like an observer, a curious tourist not personally involved in his own life.

'Karen left you about two years ago.'

Tom thought about what he was hearing. Two years ago. It wasn't a missing Sunday; it was a missing two years? But that couldn't be right either. Holly and Dan were teenagers. This story didn't sound right at all.

'It was springtime,' said Caroline. 'Remember you stayed with me for a while in the Gambia. It did you good. Got you out of yourself.'

Got you out of yourself.

Tom imagined himself stepping out of his body, his ghostly figure leaving the room, leaving the house, leaving London, and finding Karen in another time and another place on the beach, lying on the pebbles, the salty smell of her skin and the wetness of her lips making his skin tingle. And then he saw himself finding Lawrence. Travelling to the deserts of Dubai and seeking out that willowy weasel with his hat and six-guns, and making him dance a jig with his own bullets.

'You drank,' Borkmann said. 'Afterwards. Much too much.'

'I know it was hard for you to accept,' Caroline said. 'I just wanted you to find happiness again. We all did. And of course it wasn't just you and Karen,' she said. 'Mum died that July, about a month after you went home. It was an awful time for you, for us all.'

Tom closed his eyes. He hadn't thought about his mother's death since he'd left hospital. Was that wrong? He studied the carpet and in its contours he saw images of the hearse, of him sitting in a car staring out through the window as the roads and people passed by, standing at a lectern, people watching him, a terrible, terrible feeling of unhappiness throughout.

'Do you not remember any of this?' said Borkmann. 'Do you remember burying yourself in this house? You threw away your mobile phone, cut all contact with the outside world, and stopped drawing *Scraps*. Did you know, you are officially a recluse? The newspapers say it, so it must be true.'

I don't want this. I don't need this.

'We've been keeping the syndication going but, as I told you last month, the stockpile of *Scraps* cartoons is almost exhausted. Unless you draw more we'll have to come out of contract with all of our markets. We're at the crossroads, Tom. The press have been all over it, of course. Even that Kiecke woman, and I always thought she was very straight. Gave me a tough time about your so-called disappearance. I walked out. Wouldn't discuss it with her. I think she's stalking us on social media, by the way. Calls herself Harrock or Padlock or something.'

'I don't remember you mentioning anything about a crossroads.'

'Well, I did. God, if I'd known you were in this state I would never have left you alone. You seemed perfectly fine in the hospital. How could they let you leave?'

'I am perfectly fine.'

'I went home to the Gambia after the funeral,' said Caroline, as if speaking to herself. 'What else could I do? But I kept in touch. Gerard kept in touch. We owe Gerard a lot, Tom.'

'It's all itemised,' Borkmann said. 'I'll send you the bill. And then you came up with another cartoon strip. It was called *Happy Family*. Want me to tell you about that too? It stank. Reeked to high heaven. Awful. Too cutesy, no punch, no edge. Ghastly. A husband who was obviously you; a wife who was obviously Karen; two kids…' Borkmann trailed off. 'Ah.'

Her face was made-up and her hair was tied back in a businesslike fashion. Beside her was Holly, a heavy 15-year-old, looking beefier than she might with her hands in her pockets and her hips pushed forwards. And Dan, two years younger than Holly and built like his mother: slim and cat-like.

Tom wanted them to go now.

Borkmann said, 'I told you, get it out of your system and then get back to *Scraps*. And don't hawk that stuff around under your own name or you will be dead in the market. Sorry Tom, but there it is. Caroline's right. We need to get you back to hospital –'

'Do you think I jumped?' Tom blurted it out and for a moment Caroline and Borkmann could do nothing but look at him.

'Tom,' said Caroline, finding her voice. 'Of course not.'

'Why not? According to you I am abandoned, bereaved and drunk.'

'Nobody mentioned jumping, Tom,' Borkmann said. 'And anyway, it doesn't matter what we think. The point is, you've had a traumatic accident and you're still in recovery, and here you are rattling around in this house with just you and Otto. No wonder you're on edge.'

Tom looked up. 'Pardon?'

'I said, you've suffered a trauma. I think that you need –'

'Otto.'

'Yes. Where is he, by the way?' Borkmann looked around, letting his hand trail over the side of the chair as if he were expecting something to come to it.

The phrase 'an icy hand gripping your heart' is very accurate. An image of his heart as a cold ball of ice isolated from the rest of the meat in which it sat overrode every other thought in Tom's head. It was a physical sensation, enough to make him gasp. Tom lurched forwards. If earlier his body had tried to turn him inside out, now it sought to move him through space and time away from that moment, to move him away faster than the awful, burgeoning memory could emerge. His head tingled from neck to scalp and part of him wished more than anything that he was dreaming or in a coma, or possibly even dead. Again the planet was spinning too fast and he put out his hands to steady himself. He wanted the ground to give way beneath him and the floor to reveal a bottomless chasm into which he could fall. He wanted a meteorite to strike; a bomb to go off; a collision of planets; anything, anything that would be bigger than the awfulness that was now engulfing him. Because inside his head, a small but significant landslide was taking place. A section of his mind was falling away to reveal a clean and shiny memory, a nugget of gold from the motherlode. He stared with horror at Caroline and Borkmann.

'Oh God.'

'What is it?' said Caroline. She was scrambling away from his expression. 'What is it? You're frightening me.'

He stood up and swayed on shaky legs.

He had forgotten he owned a dog.

'Otto.'

'What?'

'I forgot all about Otto. The whole time. All this time. I forgot Otto.'

Tom, you need a companion. Get a dog. You used to have a dog didn't you? It will take your mind off things. Give you reason to get out.

He ran out of the room with his dressing gown flying behind him. He ran into the kitchen and rattled the outhouse doorknob. 'It's locked,' he said. 'Karen's put the key somewhere.' He called through the woodwork. 'Otto!'

Caroline and Borkmann were behind him and she put her arms around him to pull him gently away.

'Are you sure it's locked,' said Borkmann. 'When I've been here in the past it's just been stiff. You need to lift the handle up and give it a good thump with your shoulder.'

'Do it. Break it down. Smash it to pieces.'

Tom was beyond action. He was back in mission control, an observer of unfolding events, back in the vast metropolis in which teeming thoughts and sensations buzzed endlessly backwards and forwards, attending to their own business, independent of him. All sights and sounds, tastes, touches and smells were now welcome at his borders. He would receive them all – unvetted, unchecked, real or bogus. He would be the fixed point in a moving universe; he would succumb to the cosmic merry-go-round. He would do his penance; be good; do anything.

'Just open the door.'

Borkmann put both hands around the outhouse's doorknob and with a grunt gave it a heave and a push – and the door swung inwards, scraping against the floor. Piles of papers and miscellaneous bric-abrac that should have been thrown away years ago were stacked up on the floor. The smell was musty, stale and biscuity. Beside the door was a dog bowl and a water bowl; a dog basket and blanket; bags of dog food and old, half-chewed soft toys; and a ball and a couple of old, chewed leads. All the paraphernalia of a dog without the dog itself. Tom looked at Borkmann and Caroline.

'Gone,' he said.

21

I climbed out through the window and stood on the grass. It was a beautiful night: a clear sky, moonlight, stars, a cool breeze, the scent of gardens going to sleep, flowers hauling in their petals and, perhaps, night creatures coming out to play. At least that was how I suppose it was meant to look. But the only night creature coming out to play in that garden was me, and I was a six-foot fox smoking a cigarette. And now that I was becoming accustomed to questioning everything around me, those stars didn't look too convincing, either. They were up there but I wasn't sure they formed any known constellations. As for flowers hauling in their petals, well perhaps, but I would have bet that they would turn out to be strange and enormous multi-coloured plants. Like drawings on a sketchpad.

Have you ever had that moment when you believed something to be true for your whole life and then it turns out to be wrong? I don't mean when you've been deceived or lied to. I mean when you've worked something out for yourself but the whole premise was wrong. Like a song lyric. For years I thought the words 'find me someone to love bite' made up the closing line to a song that really ended 'finally someone I can love right'. Even though I liked my words better, the actual lyrics made a lot more sense and the world fitted together a bit better. That's a minor example. Here's another: when I was young I always thought that dogs were male and cats were female. It didn't make sense but it sort of worked for me. When I found out the truth I couldn't believe how wrong I'd been and I marvelled that I'd actually thought that. My world changed. The cogs fitted the grooves.

That's how I was feeling when I walked into the garden. I had a strong intuition that my premise was all wrong. I didn't know what that meant but I had the feeling that the cogs were realigning. I suppose all along I had been wondering about things – big and elusive things. But when you're stuck in a box it's hard to tell what's outside. It's hard to believe that there is an outside.

I walked round to the front of the house and, as I had thought she would be, Bullet was back. The echoes of her barking were still bouncing around the houses. She was standing in the middle of the road, her legs wide apart, her head down, snarling and barking and dribbling, her eyes burning like coals in her superheated head. She was a caricature of a dog: her teeth were tusks pushing out from her cavernous mouth; her head was as big as a beach ball but her body was a tiny bundle of muscle and energy – a bantam body driving a bulldozer of a skull. She looked like a ferocious dog should look. I wasn't surprised at that either. Isn't it funny how everything is always as it should be?

On my side of the road, ranged against her were Plenty, Billy and the always-angry restaurant owner, their backs to the garden wall, spread out so as not to create a single target. Bullet's head moved from side to side as she regarded them and she made me think of those car ornaments I'd seen, a nodding dog in a rear window.

I remember I was driving home one night and the car in front was going slowly and kept braking, and I thought they had a dog on the back seat, and I don't know why but I started waving, and I poked my tongue out and waggled my fingers and did everything I could to make it do something.

I waggled my fingers at Bullet and she turned her massive, angry face towards me. The road was lit like a play: street-lamps cut through the gloom, creating bright oases of light, a mist drifted through the air, and the calmness of the back garden had given way to a more dramatic atmosphere now that battle seemed inevitable. Huge shadows fell across the pavements and gardens as if a crowd of giants had gathered to watch from the sidelines.

I looked up and saw the Pelican, hovering above like a vast, unstable dirigible, drifting occasionally into the reach of the street-lamps' glow and showering the road with lice and fleas and feathers and bits of horrible goo, its legs dangling beneath it, its mighty beak pointing downwards, its wings so outstretched that they seemed to reach from rooftop to rooftop, although that couldn't be possible.

I looked at my friends: peaceful creatures forced into this unnatural situation by a turn of events that had little to do with them and everything, or so I was beginning to believe, to do with the dog and this place – and me.

Billy, the least aggressive of us all, had slicked back his depleted stock of quills and taken two which he now held loosely, one in each hand, like two short, stubby stiletto daggers. The always-angry restaurant owner had produced her heavy rolling pin from her apron pocket, its ability to stun something I could vouch for, and between the two stood Plenty, perfectly balanced, leaning forwards slightly, utterly still, unblinking, her eyes fixed on the dog, possibly the only one of us anticipating the fight with any kind of pleasure. And I joined them, a threadbare bag of bones, meat and gristle; a scabby, skinny, scrawny eco-friendly urban fox with coked-up lungs and dreams of a quiet life.

There is no joy to be had in describing a fight, nor in fighting. There is nothing noble or worthy or good. It demeans us all. But fight we did, for a short time, and when it was over I was the only one who was injured, and Bullet was no longer our enemy, although she was a long way from being our friend.

It went like this. Bullet attacked first because that was the way of dogs. Bereft of a pack and left to fight alone, they have no strategic outlook, no patience. Chase it away or shake it to death is their natural approach. And as I thought she might, Bullet pawed the ground and bellowed like a bull before she charged, running straight at Plenty with steam blasting from her nose.

From a participant's perspective, it's difficult to take in all that happens around you. Things move fast. Sounds are mostly your own: ragged breathing and blood pounding in your ears. The cries of others are secondary, spurs to adrenalin rather than meaningful communication – no one expects to join a discussion group during a fight. It is enough to make sounds, to expel air, to turn fear and aggression into cries that drive you forwards.

And so began the strange, hesitant dance of lunge and withdraw, lunge and withdraw, until the awful moment of engagement when you grapple with your opponent and feel their strength, feel their desperation to do to you what you want to do to them, and it becomes a matter of determination, a desire to survive and the strength and composure to do so, and luck. Luck more than anything. Luck and strength and determination. And speed. And teeth. Especially teeth. And claws. Luck and strength and speed and determination and teeth and claws. And rolling pins.

Plenty was lucky. She waited until the last moment before jumping to one side, turning as she did and raking her claws across Bullet's ear, shredding it and sending a fine line of blood droplets into the air. Billy jabbed with his quills and the always-angry restaurant owner swung with her rolling pin. I ran forwards with no plan other than to cling on until one of us died. I was utterly useless in these situations.

Bullet turned on me and, lacking Plenty's agility to avoid contact, Bullet sank her teeth into my thigh. The pavement rose up and hit me and then I was dragged down and under, with Bullet's massive presence on top of me; her smell, her sweat, her short-cropped fur devouring me.

The others tried to pull her away while the always-angry restaurant owner's arm rose and fell as she beat Bullet's body with her rolling pin – short grunts escaping her mouth as she bent to her work. Bullet released me and turned on her, trying to bite through her blows, but as she did so, something vast and awful fell from the sky: a huge, oily blanket riddled with stench and sickness landed on us, and an unyielding beak struck Bullet on the side.

The Pelican had entered the fray.

Bullet was being overwhelmed, but somehow with a wriggle and a roll she broke free, running back across the road and turning to face us, snorting heavily, a dull expression of pain in her eyes. The Pelican flapped its wings and with great effort rose shakily into the air. Bullet watched its rising with little expression. What were her thoughts, I wondered? Did she hate us? Did she wish she was far away in front of a fire, or on a blanket in her basket? I know I did.

I tried to stand up but when I did my left leg gave way. I was bleeding and I could smell the redness of it. I knew that Bullet would too and she would be drawn to me, drawn to my blood and my weariness and my weakness, and my general air of foxiness. I limped to a low garden wall and sat down.

The others regrouped, spreading out in a semi-circle, ready for the next instalment. Bullet faced us and we faced her. I caught a glimpse of Plenty circling around until she was beside me, her claws extended, while the always-angry restaurant owner stood close by, her rolling pin held behind her head like a baseball bat. Billy had lost both of his stilettos and was kneeling down in front of me, ready to ball up.

And then the Pelican dropped out of the air again and landed in a clump of feathers and scum in the middle of the road, unable to maintain a flightless hover any longer, and we all instinctively shielded our faces in case we were covered in anything glutinous. The unexpected expansion and contraction of feathers released an odour that rose into the night air like a malign living organism. It spread out and then descended on Bullet.

'That's not fair,' she said, and hurried across to our side of the road. 'There are rules, you know.'

I tensed, ready for any new onslaught, but the madness had left Bullet's eyes and the violence was gone from her body and I sensed, and I hoped, that the fight was over. I held out a spindly cigarette from my tin, the last of the batch I had rolled earlier.

'Smoke?'

Bullet looked at it, looked at me, looked at the others and then took it. She remained on the pavement, still breathing hard, watching us while the others joined me on the wall, the Pelican trailing a noxious smear in its wake. I looked at my wound. A flap of skin and fur hung down from the side of my thigh. I peeled it back. It was deep and dirty. I spat on my hand and rubbed saliva into the gash, wincing when it stung, and then pulled the skin back up and held it in position while I lit the cigarette for Bullet.

'Poor Scraps,' Plenty said. 'Always fighting with dogs.'

The always-angry restaurant owner took off her apron and wrapped it around my leg. It was starting to throb.

'I'm sorry about your leg,' Bullet said.

I nodded. 'That's all right.'

There was a general shuffling of feet.

'You're Bullet, aren't you?' said Plenty.

Bullet contemplated the road for a moment or two. 'Yes.' Her voice was hoarse, presumably from all the barking and howling and baying she'd been doing recently. 'Surprised to see me?'

'You've been away a long time,' I said.

'Away. That's a nice way of putting it.' She looked at the always-angry restaurant owner. 'Remember me? You abandoned me. Left me on my own. Out there.'

'That's not true. You slipped your lead. You ran away.'

'You know it wasn't like that. You let it happen. You all did. You wanted me gone. I wasn't part of the gang. So you all let me go and were glad, and never thought about me again, or looked for me, or cared at all.'

None of us said anything. She was right.

'Well, I'm sorry – that I hit you so hard just now,' the always-angry restaurant owner said. 'With my rolling pin. I was angry.'

Bullet shrugged. 'You are always angry. It's what you do.'

'But I'm not. I'm not always angry. I don't want to be always angry. Why does everyone think of me as always angry?'

'The clue is your name, honey,' said Bullet.

'What did you do after you… ran away?' said Billy. 'What was it like out there, away from the alleyway?'

'I don't know. What's it like when you dream?'

'Is that how it is when you're not here – like a dream?' said Plenty. 'I would like that.'

'But you weren't asleep, were you?' Billy said. 'You were doing things, being a dog, being a Bullet?'

'Was I?'

I see what's not this.

'Are we done fighting?' I said, wheezing through the pain. 'Because if we are, I've got two things to do. Go find the hairy man and clean up my leg.' I looked at Bullet. 'Are you coming?'

'Are you asking?'

'I am, but just so you know, we have a no-claws rule. And that means no biting, too.'

'I've never heard of that rule,' said Plenty.

'Yes, you have.'

'What about a no-abandoning rule?' Bullet said. 'That would be nice. Can you add that?'

'It's up to you,' I said. 'Stay or go.'

The Pelican was too tired to fly, so it waddled along next to us as we made our way round the back of the house, me limping and surprisingly being supported by Plenty. Bullet followed us.

'She's got nowhere else to go,' Plenty whispered in my ear. 'She wants an owner. She's our friend now but if she ever bites us again I will eat her eyes while she sleeps.'

'Have you ever actually eaten anybody's eyes?' I said.

'Yes.'

We made our way along the side of the house, keeping to the shadows.

'There's the window,' I said. 'We'll go in that way.'

From the front of the house we heard a doorbell ring. We didn't move. We listened and waited. The bell rang again, a longer sound this time. I looked around, my night-sight scarcely helping me. A path ran down the garden from the house. A glass shed was on one side of the path amongst a patch of plants suffused with the smell of urine. I had to check my own urge to mark that place as mine. At the end of the path, furthest from the house, was the shape of another building, not glass but wood. A wooden summer house.

The bell rang again, this time followed by an urgent rapping on glass.

'Someone's moving,' Plenty said. 'Inside.'

I heard a low rumbling sound, as if someone had switched on an engine. It was Bullet growling.

'Shhh.'

I could hear movement now, cautious movement from inside.

Who is it?

Tom. It's Gerard. Are you all right?

'Let's wait down there and see what happens.'

I limped and led the way down the path to the summer house. We crouched down behind the bench on the narrow verandah and waited. We could hear sounds and voices from inside the house and then, suddenly, from an upstairs window we saw the face of the hairy man looking out. Even though we had come to confront him, we all instinctively ducked down – all except Bullet. She stared through slit-like eyes at the face in the window and said, 'I know him from somewhere.'

'We all do,' I said.

The hairy man went away from the window and we stood up. The always-angry restaurant owner sat down on the bench and Plenty and Billy joined her. The Pelican flopped down on the lawn, laid out like a soiled serviette that someone had thrown away, and

I leaned against the wooden building. I rolled a cigarette and lit up again.

Bullet said, 'When you sent me away…'

'When you slipped your lead.'

'When you sent me away… I sometimes saw that face… reflected in things.'

'What things –' I began and then stopped. Behind me the wooden door that led into the summer house was creaking on its hinges. Doors usually creak on their hinges in that way when they are opening very slowly. The fur from the top of my head to the tip of my tail stood on end. I heard footfalls on the wood. I stared at the faces of Billy and Plenty and the always-angry restaurant owner and Bullet, and then together we stepped onto the grass and into the shadows as the door opened to its full extent.

'What are… what is…' said the Pelican, coming to life and seeing us huddled on the lawn in the dark. And then it saw what we saw. 'Oh.'

Stepping out onto the summer house verandah, one by one, were a tall woman buttoned up and belted in her overcoat; an older, willowy weasel of a man; a heavy-set teenage girl and a slim teenage boy, his face mostly obscured by hair. They stood in a line and looked at us. It was too dark to see them clearly, but I could see that, like us, they were threadbare; unhealthy; unclean. Bullet wandered over, sniffed them and wandered back to us. They watched her with disinterest. They seemed disinclined to talk, to do anything other than stand there and look at us, as if awaiting direction.

'Who are they?' said the always-angry restaurant owner. 'Why do they look so dopey?'

'You might say they've slipped their leads,' said Bullet. 'I would use the word abandoned – until further notice.'

'What are you talking about?'

I was impatient now. 'Come on. Forget them. We're going in.'

Leaving the forlorn four to stand by the summer house and watch us, we crossed the lawn and returned to the open window that led into the outhouse.

'This is it,' I said. 'One way or another, this is it.'

Trying not to catch my loose flap of skin on the woodwork, we climbed inside.

22

Tom sat at the kitchen table. Beside him was Caroline, and at the counter making coffee was Borkmann. The kitchen light was on, and beneath the upper cupboards, concealed halogen bulbs lit the counters, illuminating the kitchen in a way that the flat overhead light couldn't and creating shadows with textures and depths that on another occasion would have pleased Tom.

'I'm not well, am I?' he said. 'That's what you're both thinking.'

But he couldn't be sure if what he was saying was because it seemed to fit the circumstances, or because he believed it. Every time he tried to think, he felt tired. He felt tired and weary and life was becoming too difficult. He wanted to be alone to think whatever he wanted and to forget whatever he had forgotten without guilt.

He tried to picture Otto, his beloved Labrador, his beautiful pet, and saw only the words, epithets that floated in the air because he knew that some of the time he was confusing Otto with Bullet, and what did that mean? He had forgotten all about a living, breathing dog that had looked to him for care and love and attention, and now he was probably dead because of Tom's neglect, or feral, or starving, or being skinned alive by Cruella de Vil.

There was guilt, and fear that he had so easily forgotten something so real, but those emotions seemed to be one step away from his feelings, as if they were bubble-wrapped or behind a window: seen but not felt.

'It's a terrible thing when someone says you did this or you did that and you have no recollection at all,' he said. 'It's like being lost in a maze...' And then he stopped. 'What am I talking about? Actually, it's nothing like that. It's just very, very annoying.'

Caroline squeezed his hand. 'But you remember things now?'

Tom looked at his hand in hers, his paw. He said, 'From the moment I woke up in the hospital, I've been trying to remember things, trying to remember and trying to *imagine* what happened to me. Every waking moment has been about that – and quite a few unwaking moments, too. I've thrown my whole mind at it. I've put so much effort into trying to imagine what happened, that now I'm not sure if I can actually tell the difference between what's true and what's not. And I'm not sure I even care anymore. I've been haunted by my missing memory, Caroline, and I wonder if I've been haunted by Otto, too. And yes, I have been drinking. I admit it. But that's how I work. I need a drink to lubricate my mind, to fire up the engines, to get the images rolling.'

'Well, that's one way of putting it,' said Borkmann.

'It's not like there's a cupboard I can look into and rummage around until I find something. Imagine a page in a book that has been folded over and stuck down. I read that bit and that bit and I never knew that there was something in the middle. I forgot I had a dog. What else have I forgotten?'

But still Tom had the sense that he was constructing a description that had no root in how he felt. It was as if there were two Toms: one who lived on the surface where everyone could see him, and one who lived deep underground, an unseen mass of rolling thoughts and emotions that was neither able nor willing to be articulated.

He had held Karen's hand in the hospital. He had felt it; he had felt the skin and the bones and the flesh. He had felt the warmth and the familiarity of her hand. How could that not be real? He looked at Borkmann. 'Do me a favour, Gerard. Let me hold your hand.'

'What?'

'Let me hold your hand.'

'Hold your own hand. I'm making coffee.'

'I'm holding your hand,' said Caroline. 'See?'

Tom saw. She was. But it wasn't the same.

Borkmann poured coffee and fetched milk and added sugar and busied himself in the up-lit corner of the kitchen while Caroline watched Tom. He wanted a stronger drink than coffee. It was lubrication time.

'Imagine a world,' he said. 'A world where there is only ever now. No past, no future. Wouldn't that be nice?'

'You've just said how awful it is not to be able to remember,' said Caroline. 'You're describing dementia. You wouldn't be able to remember all the lovely things that had happened to you.'

'That's not what I'm saying. I'm describing a state of being, a way of life, a different perspective. It would be a bubble in which everything you needed was with you. Forever. Like that moment when you're about to wake up. Or maybe that moment just before you die.'

Borkmann brought the coffee to the table. 'Tom, can we park all the fun talk for a moment?' He sat down and rubbed his face. He looked tired, too. 'Let's keep it simple. All this talk about bubbles and Karen and children and living in the now, what are we meant to do with that? How do we process all that information? It doesn't sound like a normal person talking.' He put his fingertips together and created a steeple. The three of them studied it as if it were a structure in which the answers to everything were contained. 'Let's focus on Otto,' he said. 'I thought when I brought you home that he was here. I should have checked. You haven't seen him since you came home from the hospital?'

Tom stared at Borkmann's hands. What was the right answer? He didn't know what he thought now. Had he seen Otto in the house? He had heard a dog. He had heard a dog the first night he woke up in the hospital. Was that Otto calling for him? Or tinnitus? Or a dream? Or a wild demon hunting him down?

'I don't think so.'

'You don't think so?'

'No.'

'When was the last time you saw him?'

'I don't know. Look, I get it. I forgot him and he must have been lost and bewildered and died alone and it's my fault.'

'Was he chipped?' said Caroline.

Tom groaned. Was he? He couldn't remember.

'I don't think he was. No.' He shook his head. Idiot.

'Okay. So we need to phone around the dog centres, the police, the RSPCA. I can do that, Tom. A big dog like that can't just be –'

'Left to die in the gutter?'

'Tom,' said Borkmann. 'There's no blame here. It's not your fault. Just shut up a minute and let me develop this train of thought. Otto's not here so what does that mean?'

'It means I'm bad.'

'No it doesn't – it means: if he's not here then why is he not here?'

'What are you getting at?'

'Well, Otto hasn't got a key, has he? So he didn't let himself out. Presumably Tom did – and that was probably to take him for a walk.

And if you took him for a walk and he's not here, then it's because you didn't bring him home; because you couldn't bring him home.'

Tom sat up. 'Because I fell off a roof,' he said. 'Good point, Gerard.'

Borkmann stared at Tom. 'Which is why I don't think you did jump.'

'Gerard.' Caroline looked anxious, as if using the word 'jump' might invoke some new terrible incident.

But Borkmann wasn't deterred. 'On that Sunday you probably went for a walk with Otto. A Sunday morning walk. And if you took Otto for a walk then I would say it's unlikely that you intended to jump and leave him loose. Even you're not that selfish. If you had intended to jump, then you would have made provision for Otto.'

'Not if it was a spur of the moment thing.'

'But you're not a spur of the moment sort of person. You're a planner, a draughtsman, you make things neat, not messy. There are no loose ends in Tom Hannah's life. It is all there because it's needed. No passengers.'

'Perhaps I did make provision and I've forgotten. Perhaps Otto is staying with a friend or something.'

'Tom, you have no friends. The only person with whom you would have made provision is me. The only four people in your life are you, me, Caroline and Otto – Caroline lives in the Gambia, you are you, and Otto is the missing dog. Which leaves me, and I haven't got him. So, for whatever reason you ended up on the top of the car park, it wasn't through self-pity – hard though that may be to believe right now.'

'So I didn't jump?'

'It doesn't seem likely.'

'I never thought I had jumped,' he said, looking at them both.

Borkmann finished his coffee and stood up. 'I don't know why you were up there, but at least you probably weren't alone. I think Otto was with you. So it's still a conundrum, Tom, but one I will have to leave you and Caroline to ponder. I have to go. Early start in the morning.' He looked at Caroline. 'I'm glad you're here now. Call me if you need anything.'

Tom stood up too. 'Sorry about your trousers.'

Borkmann sighed. 'Just get drawing again, Tom. And do us all a favour – lay off the booze. It doesn't suit you.'

'I'll see you to the door,' said Caroline.

Tom wondered what whispered messages they might exchange in the hallway. When Caroline returned, she sat opposite him and held his hand again, a bridge between two people that spanned the table.

Poor Caroline. Tom's borders were now closed. No more connections would pass across that bridge that night. The black hole in his head was beginning to shrink and everything in orbit around it – Karen, Holly, Dan, Caroline, Borkmann, dogs, foxes, nurses, hospitals, alleyways, the past, the present, the future – were spinning in ever decreasing circles towards the centre of his mind. It didn't matter what was real and what was fiction, what was imagination and what was memory. All that mattered to Tom now was to bring them all home safely, neatly, orderly, and to put them in the right compartments.

He looked at his hand and at Caroline's hand, at their stillness and their shape, at the flesh and the creases and the hardness of their nails. The blood and bones and tendons and sinews.

'He might still come back,' Caroline said. 'Somebody might still take him to the police station.'

'Who, Gerard?'

Caroline laughed. 'No, Otto.'

'I doubt it.'

'Can I ask you a question?' she said.

'No.'

'Please. Just the one. And then I promise I'll go to bed.'

'There is never just one, Caroline. What is it?'

'Did you really think it was Karen? That she was here. Did you really think that?'

Tom looked down at the table. Did he think that?

Did he?

Really think that?

The police came this morning. We wondered where you were.

This morning?

We weren't there yesterday.

He looked up. 'Does it matter?'

'Of course it matters. Gerard said that Karen is in Dubai.'

'I know.'

'And children. Did you think there were children here?'

'That's more than one question.'

Caroline squeezed his hand again. Was it to comfort him or to wring out the answer she wanted to hear? They sat there for a while, Caroline squeezing his hand and looking at him with a soft, puffy expression while Tom waited for her to stop doing that and to go to bed. Perhaps if he closed his eyes she would be gone when he opened them.

'Have you seen other people here?' she said.

'Other people?'

'You know, other people. Like Mum and Dad?'

Tom saw for a moment a hungry wolf sitting opposite, a hungry wolf with greedy eyes, searching his face for food.

'No, Caroline. I haven't seen Mum and Dad here.'

'No, of course not. Sorry.'

The wolf was gone and Tom saw his sister again who, like him, was alone. 'I'm not crazy,' he said, gently. 'I might look it, but I'm not.'

'I know.'

'They did scans and all sorts of tests. They said I was fine. They said I was very lucky.'

'You are very lucky. You could have died.'

'I know. So you must expect a few wrinkles. I'm getting better, I'm getting better every day. I'm just trying to piece it all together in my own way, that's all.'

He smiled at her and knew that with his missing tooth and wild moustache, it would not be a reassuring look. She nodded and laughed, sniffed and sighed.

'But you can't just go from being not all right to all right. You thought that there were people living here. You talked to them.'

'But now I've got you to keep me company. And everyone talks to themselves.'

'Not everyone.'

'Most people. Let's not look for things to worry about. Let those things find us.' He extracted his hand. 'We should get some sleep. Talk about everything in the morning.'

'Okay. I wish I knew what you were doing on the car park.'

'Me too.'

'I'm glad Gerard said what he did about you not jumping. That was nice of him.'

'I know. Let's talk some more in the morning.'

'It's just because I care, you know that. All this nagging.'

'That's what big sisters do.'

She looked at him and squeezed his hand again. 'I am your big sister, no matter how big you are.'

Tom hugged her but even as he did so he wondered if she was really there.

23

Caroline slept in the spare room, the room that until recently Karen had been using. Tom lay awake in his own bed across the landing, the moonlight from outside casting shadowy stripes across the wall opposite his window. He thought about the little boy he had once been and the trajectory that had led from then to now. 'Hello me,' he said, and his voice in the dark sounded small and pitiful.

His thoughts roamed across the open landscape in his mind and he saw, for a moment, a scene, a flashback to a time at school, a heavy, beefy girl with matches, taunting him, her unpleasant brother flying through the air. Tom winced and closed his eyes and buried that scene in the swirling mass of half-forgotten images..

He thought instead about Holly and Dan and tried to remember if he had ever met Karen's sister, Sylvia. Surely he had. He imagined them all standing in the shadows somewhere, staring at him, waiting for him to wake up and return them to his life, to bring them home from the darkness of his broken memory. Had he now abandoned them, too? Is that what he did? Was it out of sight, out of mind with him? Or was he now locked in a psychotic prison, unable to see the very people who loved him most, trapped inside his head and blind to the real world? He wondered if, in the morning, when he knocked on the door of the spare room, Caroline would be there or if the room would be empty, the bed unslept in, the cupboards bare, the curtains wide open. Or would he find Karen waking up, looking at him from behind the bars of her lacquered eyelashes, laughing and reaching out to him? Or Maggie, Maggie turning sleepily in the bed, the covers clinging to the curling, curving shape of her body?

Sleep seemed unlikely now. He got out of bed.

You came up with another cartoon strip. It was called Happy Family. It stank. A husband who was obviously you; a wife who was obviously Karen; two kids...

Tom climbed the ladder to his study. It was cold on the floorboards and he hoped his footsteps wouldn't wake Caroline. He went to his filing cabinet and searched through his archived drawings.

He found the *Happy Family* cartoons in a section of their own at the back of the bottom drawer. Two folders, perhaps a dozen or more completed cartoons, a few practice sketches. And they were all there, beaming out at him: Karen, Holly, Dan and himself – and Lawrence: Lawrence the bad guy dressed in black, his face even more weaselly than Tom remembered.

Tom studied the cartoons. Borkmann was right: they stank. He thought if he drew it again, he might put Maggie in as his wife, and maybe have Karen and Lawrence working for the always-angry restaurant owner. That would be fun. He could retire Scraps, give him time to smoke his cigarettes and ponder life; and meet up with the old gang from time to time. Billy could open a quill salon and the Pelican could be hired as a weathervane. People would have to learn not to walk directly beneath the perch. And what about Plenty – send her back to Nanny's? That would never last. Or maybe it was time for new characters and a new type of cartoon. *Happy Family II* or something, with a harder edge.

He put the drawings down.

Enough.

Enough thinking. He put his face in his hands and tried to shut out the light. What would he give simply to *be*, to be free of thoughts and images; to have a clean slate on which to start again, to travel lightly through life and to leave no footprints. Clean, pure, uncluttered.

He sat up, shivering, and leafed through his drawings, and as he did so he became aware of sounds: low-level murmurings beyond the whispering hiss inside his ears. He thought it might be Caroline stirring but he listened harder, staring into the unlit corners of the attic, and realised it was coming from deeper in the house, from the kitchen. An image of Otto returning made him stand up and make his way quickly and quietly down the ladder, down the stairs and along the hallway. Surely it couldn't be, he thought, not after all that time, not on the very day he had remembered him, as if in the act of remembering he had somehow made real Otto's presence.

He switched on the kitchen light and went straight to the back door and opened it. He looked out into the night. There was nothing there, and no barking either. For once he wished he might hear the plaintive sound that had followed him since hospital. He closed the door and felt a weight of disappointment, as if Otto was a ghoul lying across his shoulders.

He found a bottle of gin and poured himself a large glass. He added some tonic and drank deeply, topped it up with more gin and sat down at the kitchen table. The lights were heavy on his eyelids and he felt sleepy, no up-lit halogen lights this time, only the stark ceiling lights flattening everything into two dimensions. He rubbed his face with both hands and imagined himself as a rough sketch of a sleepy man with a large, drooping moustache sitting in a kitchen late at night.

And then he heard voices. Tom looked at the door to the out-house. There was no doubt about it: a subdued conversation was taking place on the other side of the door. He stood up, crossed the kitchen, put his ear to the door and listened. And then, remembering Borkmann's technique, he lifted the handle and heaved. The door scraped open and he looked in.

And he saw us.

We had been debating whether one or all of us should go and find the hairy man when the hairy man found us. We stopped talking and stared. There was absolute silence. None of us moved. The man hung on the door and pushed his massive hand through his hair. He was an enormous figure. A goliath with a huge moustache and wildly curling hair, standing in his pyjamas and fluffy blue dressing gown and gazing down at us with baggy, bleary, cold-lidded eyes. He stared at us for a long time and then looked over his shoulder, looked back at us again, and then stared some more.

'What's he doing?' hissed Plenty.

'I don't know,' Billy said.

'He's being surprised,' said the always-angry restaurant owner.

Without taking his eyes off us, the man's hand fumbled along the wall until he found the light switch. When he found it and switched it on, the room became instantly smaller, the long shadows shrinking into dusty nooks and crannies, corners and edges. There was no light shade, only a bulb hanging from the ceiling, and we blinked, unaccustomed to such stark brightness.

With small, uncertain, unsteady steps, he walked into the room and closed the door behind him. He smelled of hair and skin and soap and alcohol. We made way for him and, taking a deep breath, he moved a pile of newspapers onto the floor and sat down on an old chair. He had brought a glass and a bottle of alcohol with him, which he put on the floor. He leaned back and sighed, put his feet up on the pile of newspapers and held up his glass to us as if in a toast.

'Last time I saw you, you scared the shit out of me. You still do. Proof that I am insane,' he said, laughing, and drank it all. He closed and opened his eyes twice, turning his head quickly in an exaggerated double take, and then laughed again. 'You're not quite as I imagined you.' And then, 'Actually, no, scratch that. You're exactly how I imagined you.' He rubbed his face and stared at his glass. 'Dear God.' He closed his eyes again.

Was I being fanciful or did his voice sound like my thoughts? I probably was. Anyway, now that we had found him, I wasn't sure what I wanted to say or do. So I said, 'You don't seem surprised to see us.' But he didn't say anything.

The always-angry restaurant owner was more bullish. 'Hey,' she said. 'Wake up. We've been looking for you.'

He looked up and around, as if searching for the voice.

'Are you Tash?' said Plenty.

Again he searched the room until his eyes settled on her. He looked at her long and hard and then sat back and stroked his moustache. It made a rasping noise that reminded me of the sound my fur made when I scratched it. He poured some more gin into his glass and looked towards her again, but not exactly at her.

'Call me Tom,' he said. 'I insist.'

'Do you have any food?' she said.

Tom didn't answer. Plenty wandered off and I watched her roam amongst the old boxes and the stacks of newspapers. I took out my tin of tobacco, rolled some cigarettes and handed them around. I lit up and blew out a long stream of blue-grey smoke. And then Plenty, having searched the outhouse for mice and rats, leaned on Tom's shoulder and said, 'Why have you been drawing us?'

I felt a pull, some kind of instinctive warning that I couldn't place, like opening a door and finding yourself standing on the roof of a very tall building. Tom turned in his chair and looked up at Plenty in an intense way and then said, 'This can't be good for me, can it? I must be burning out all my synaptics. Perhaps I am having a stroke.' He touched his face. 'How would I know?' I didn't know what he was having but he didn't look healthy. He looked around as if searching for something.

'What are you looking for?' I said.

A wide expanse of shimmering white concrete.

I was about to say that we had been looking for him. I had wanted to ask him if he knew why things were changing. I had wanted to ask him if he knew why we weren't having any adventures anymore, if he knew why we were falling apart and looked like shit, like those people outside. Instead, I said, 'My leg's bleeding. Mind if I sit down?'

He didn't say anything so I sat down on a stack of newspapers. I said, 'Are you still drawing us?' But, of course, he wasn't. I knew that as soon as I said it, although I didn't know what that meant and nor, I suspected, did the shambling mess in front of me. So I said, 'When was the last time you drew us?' But that was pointless too. And then I wondered, what did it matter? Why was I bothering? I felt a reckless sense of self-awareness, of independence, of freedom. I had hoped to find answers, to find a connection, but now I felt that we didn't need him or his answers or anything else he had to say. Why had I ever thought we did? To hell with aligning cogs. I looked at my arms and at my chest as I had done in the restaurant and I felt the life flowing through them. More than that, it was my life that I felt flowing through them. I put my hand against my bitten leg. That was a real wound and I was losing real blood.

'Let's go,' I said. 'We're done here. I need to find a vet.'

'But what about food?' said Billy. 'I'm pretty hungry, too.'

'We'll find our own food from now on.'

'I thought we always did?'

'Exactly. We always did. That's my point.'

'Are you all right, Scraps?'

An unpleasant gagging sound cut through our conversation. It sounded like a washing machine that had broken mid-cycle. It was the Pelican clearing its throat. 'Ahem.' It crossed its eyes a few times and released a yellow cloud of noxious gas into the room.

'Here we go again,' said the always-angry restaurant owner.

'The people from the garden are at the window,' the Pelican said. 'Shall I let them in? Or perhaps not?'

Billy skipped several steps sideways.

It was true. There were four gloomy faces peering in. Tom looked at them and then got up and walked to the window. There was an old rattan blind rolled up at the top. He jerked the string and it unrolled in a sudden drop, covering the glass.

'Later,' he said.

He sat back on his chair and said, 'A shape moving across an expanse of shimmering white concrete, a bird flying over the edge of a wall, a cold punch of something hard hitting my face, blood in my mouth. Does any of that mean anything to any of you?'

We looked at each other. Plenty shrugged, Billy stared, the Pelican crossed its eyes and the always-angry restaurant owner frowned. Bullet, who was skulking in the shadows, simply growled.

'Not really,' the always-angry restaurant owner said.

Tom closed his eyes. 'Shame.' His voice became a mumble, a slur, as his chin fell onto his chest, a barely intelligible stream of sound. 'I thought, you know, given that you're on the inside… I thought you might shake it up, if I imagined you trying to find…' He trailed off.

Where do ideas and notions come from? Those sudden thoughts and illuminations; the answers to riddles – and the riddles themselves. Do they find their own way through some mental undergrowth; developing, learning, maturing until they suddenly pop up and say hello? Or are there signposts? Does one part of our brain give them a helping hand while the other part isn't looking? Do they simply materialise, dressed, fully formed, and ready to go? Like giving birth to an adult.

Or does someone put them there?

'It wasn't shimmering white concrete at all,' I said. 'It was ordinary grey concrete. It was the warm air rising from a patch of dried oil that made it shimmer, and the sun made it look lighter than it really was. Is that the memory you're looking for?'

Tom lifted his head and moved it from side to side as if he were searching for the source of a smell. He drank some more gin and laid back in his chair.

'You should take it easy on the sauce,' said the always-angry restaurant owner.

'The always-angry restaurant owner,' he said quietly, and smiled. 'Always so angry.'

I looked at her and she looked at me. And then she said, 'I really do not like being called the always-angry restaurant owner all the time. It takes forever to say and I'm not always angry.'

'But that is your name,' said Plenty.

'No, it's not. It's a description, a label, a tag or something. It is not a name. Plenty is a name. Scraps is a name. Billy is a name. Even the Pelican is sort of specific. The always-angry restaurant owner is not a name.'

'Well, what is your name?' said Billy.

'It's... it's—'

'Barbara,' Tom muttered.

'What?'

'Barbara.'

Nobody said anything for a moment, but we all kept an eye on her rolling pin.

'Yes,' she said, suddenly and defiantly, looking at each of us in turn. 'That is right. That is what my name is. Barbara.'

'Barbara?'

'Barbara. And I am not always angry.'

'But you are a restaurant owner,' Plenty said. 'Aren't you?'

'Yes, but I am not always angry,' she shouted.

I thought about the lost people in the garden, trying to see through the blinds and about us, standing before this tired man who was slumped in his chair, and I had a momentary image of moons revolving around a planet in erratic orbits. I looked at the others – Billy, Plenty, the Pelican – and I thought, were we all formed from the same dust cloud? Satellites made from the same matter as a host planet? The always-angry restaurant owner hadn't known her name, but Tom had.

Oh dear. That really is too much thinking even for you. A little less brain, a little more body – that's what I always say.

I gave up. I said, 'Great. Barbara it is. We're all sorted. Let's go.'

There was movement in the shadows and a hoarse voice said, 'Ahem. I hate to break up the love-fest but anyone remember the comedy dog?' Bullet lumbered forwards. 'You know, the big ugly bitch that nobody wants as a pet? I'm not going anywhere.'

With a colossal effort, Tom poured another tumbler of gin. It was touch and go and required all his concentration not to miss the glass. When he'd filled it to the brim and taken a large sip he looked up and said, 'I had another dog once. I let it down. I let it down and now it's gone. A lovely yellow Labrador called Otto. All gone.'

'There was another dog,' Billy said. 'A big, ugly, yellow thing, all meat and muscle. We saw it chasing a ball. That's what kicked off this whole thing.'

The room seemed much smaller now.

'We saw it,' Plenty said. 'On an expanse of shimmering white—'

'It wasn't white,' I said. 'It was the sun making it white.'

'It chased Scraps onto the roof.'

Tom tilted his head back and sighed. 'Oh, that's right,' he said to himself, his voice scarcely a whisper. 'Chased a fox. And I followed.'

Oh, clever Tom. We were like pinpricks of light that must not fade. The dots would join, the connections would be made. If we were thoughts inside his head, then he wanted ours. And I didn't know how he would take them or what would happen to us once he had, but take them he would. He would extract his lost memory like teeth from a gum. We were his mechanism of remembrance and always had been. He had used us to find his way in and to light the darkness. Tom drank his gin and closed his eyes. He heard sounds and smelled smells and felt the seat beneath him. He breathed and the breath from his nose flowed over his moustache. And then somewhere inside his head, images began to form.

24

Tom opened his eyes. He was in the First Frame. There was no darkness at all. Instead there was white, and what wasn't white looked clean and clear and precise. He looked around and saw that he was leaving his house with Otto. It must have been the Sunday morning, *the* Sunday morning, because he had liquorice sweets in his pocket. Otto always remained close to him if he could smell liquorice sweets.

They walked along the streets, cut through the empty underpass and paused by the mismatched couple sitting on the floor, so that Tom could give them some change.

'Got a cigarette?' the girl said.

'I wish.'

They took a short cut through the children's park, where the swing hung motionless and a bird sat on a tree and looked down at the passing man and his dog. Otto walked ahead, pulling the lead as far forwards as he could. They came upon the car park and the market. Across the road, a man was working with a hoe along the edge of a patch of grass. Tom and Otto walked down a side road beside the car park and found a wide expanse of shimmering white concrete. Tom unhooked the lead and Otto ran free.

Otto was having fun. Tom lobbed the ball and Otto chased it, taking it farther and farther away, running along the top of a grassy verge alongside a cluster of industrial units. But then he stopped and looked intently at something. Tom couldn't see what. He waited, calling and whistling, and then he walked along to see what was up. But Otto had forgotten his ball and now he was chasing something.

It was a fox. A skinny, red, urban fox and it ran fast. It ran around the corner and up the car park's exit ramp pursued by Otto, who was ignoring Tom's calls. He ran after them, dropping the lead and breathing heavily. Tom wasn't built for that form of exercise. He was hot and discomforted in his heavy-knit cardigan and woollen overcoat.

They ran up the ramps, zig-zagging upwards until Tom noticed that they were dangerously high – at least, dangerously high for him. They were almost on the roof.

'Otto,' he shouted, but his dog was out of sight, barking madly somewhere above. With reluctant feet, Tom walked up the final ramp, came out onto the roof of the car park and walked into the Second Frame.

On the far side of the roof, the fox had somehow got up onto a low wall, a parapet that ran around the edge of the roof; a wall that was below chest-height for Tom; too close to his centre of gravity for comfort. Otto was barking and trying to scrabble up as well. The fox stayed on the edge, six floors up. It made Tom shudder. It made him want to crouch down and hold on to the floor. He wanted to go down.

A fear of heights is a very common thing. It's easy to worry about what might happen but who says it's going to happen?

Up there, up anywhere he supposed, the sky was all around; the big sky, infinite and untouchable. There were no cars parked anywhere, only empty bays and the low wall that ran around the entire edge of the roof, topped with its white concrete cap. Otto was becoming insane trying to reach the fox. Tom could see it clearly: a ruined and threadbare waif; an urban fox living off rubbish. It was terrified, skittering on the edge. Tom couldn't bear it. He had to do something. But he was scared.

He thought *this is ridiculous. People walk around up here all the time. Old people, young people, children, all sorts of people.* It was simply a car park. But it felt too high. Tom closed his eyes and walked forwards. One step, then another, and then another. Three steps, four steps, and then he had to open his eyes again.

He was halfway across the roof.

Away from the shelter of the ramp, the breeze blew harder and louder. It pushed and jostled him towards the edge. A bird flew past and dropped out of sight and seeing it do that, seeing it disappear downwards so easily and so naturally, struck a blade of panic through Tom's heart.

He thought that if he narrowed his peripheral vision and blocked out the wall and the emptiness beyond, and didn't listen to the sounds of traffic down below, he might be all right. If it was his imagination that was scaring him, then perhaps he could try to imagine himself out of his fear; imagine that he was walking over to Otto, grabbing his collar, dragging him back to the ramp and walking briskly down to safety. He would imagine himself walking outside and looking up at the car park. He would imagine himself joyous with relief.

'If you imagine something happening, it might actually happen,' he said. But the wind snatched his words away and his legs were trembling so much that he couldn't move them. He called for Otto again in a voice that was thick and slurred, and that scared him even more, hearing his own voice sounding so strange. So he made a sudden decision and ran across the roof towards the edge.

Into the Final Frame. This was it.

The wind rippled through his hair and moustache like the parting of a corn field. Close up, the white cap of concrete was dazzling in the bright sunlight. The wall seemed very low and some wayward aspect of his brain questioned whether the safety of children had been adequately considered. He could see the cracks where seasons had expanded and contracted the cement, and layers of acidic bird-shit washed by the rain and dried by the sun.

Beyond the wall was a long drop to distant cars, pedestrians and tarmac, and the hard south London street. He could feel a vast cushion of air between him and the ground and he had an urge, a frightening urge, to lean out and fall into it to see if it would take his weight; to fall into it and get the fear over with; to drop like a stone and create a puff of dust far below as all the best cartoons do; to face his fear by dying.

He saw the market stall down below and a splash of black spots appeared and disappeared in front of his eyes like a firework display in negative. It felt as if bits of his brain were operating independently.

'Come on, Otto. Come on. Come here.'

His head felt tight, sounds were muffled, and the black spots reappeared, joining up and spreading darkness across his mind. He was malfunctioning. He was fainting. He grabbed hold of Otto's collar and tried to haul him away but the dog jumped, brutally bending Tom's thumb. The fox ran along the wall and Otto tried to follow him, dragging Tom with him. He tripped and fell on his knees, shuffled along and then threw himself onto his dog.

I was dragged down and under, with Bullet's massive presence above me; the smell, the sweat, the short-cropped fur devouring me.

Otto wriggled and slipped away, and bounded towards the fox. Tom managed to grab his back legs, shouting with pain as his thumb was bent further back. And then the fox ran back along the wall, past Tom, and he lost his grip as Otto changed direction.

Otto tried to run through Tom and his slab-like forehead smashed into Tom's mouth and knocked him senseless. Tom staggered upwards, rising to his feet, blood in his mouth, put out his hands to steady himself and found he was leaning on nothing. He was looking at the street below, hanging over the edge of the low wall.

He tried to recover his balance but instead lurched further forwards. Tom's heavy head looked outwards and down over the street-scene, like an ancient gargoyle, and for a second he saw that other ancient gargoyle his student housemates had once sculpted. But he was leaning too far outwards. More weight was over the wall than behind it. He hoped for a friendly hand to pull him back but of course there was none. He twisted and turned and tried to grab hold of something. Anything.

And then he fell.

His fingertips squeezed the wall and slipped off and he was gone, his legs following him over the side like eels slipping into water. It turned out that it was very easy to fall off a roof. There was no cushion of air to carry him safely to the ground and, if there had been, it would have been too thin to take his weight. Instead, he saw the concrete cap above him recede at speed and felt the warm wind push past him in an upward rush. There were no thoughts and no past life flashing before him; only a tumbling and a reaching out for what wasn't there.

Epilogue

Tooth Returned to its Rightful Owner

By Robert de Moor – Tuesday, 12 July 2016

SOUTH LONDON – In a touching scene yesterday, Parks & Open Spaces gardener Peter Hobbes, 28, presented a fragment of tooth to Tom Hannah, the former cartoonist. Readers may remember that, just over a year ago, Mister Hannah was involved in a fall from the roof of a multi-storey car park and sustained, amongst other injuries, a broken tooth. Hannah, the creator of *Scraps*, has since declared his retirement from cartooning, much to the dismay of his many *Scraps* fans. However, his new reality game, *Happy Family Plus*, developed by Borkmann Augmented Realities, is scheduled for launch this autumn and will feature a completely new set of characters.

Mister Hobbes presented the tooth in a resealable plastic bag at the scene of the tooth's recovery. He said, 'I was just turning over the soil and saw this little glistening thing. I thought at first it was a piece of chewing gum. But it turned out to be a tooth and I thought, I know exactly who that belongs to.'

Mister Hannah was unavailable for comment but his agent, Gerard Borkmann, said that earlier in the year the cartoonist had been reunited with his dog, Otto, who had run away and been found at a local dog rescue centre.

Which meant that this was the second time in 12 months that his client had been reunited with a missing canine.

Acknowledgements

I owe a lot of people a lot of thanks for helping me get this story out of my head and into the real world. Those people include: all the wise, and discerning (hem) patrons who pledged their support and made it actually possible; Unbound, who took me on and took the risk; Whitefox, whose editing rigour and professionalism smoothed out the wrinkles; Mecob, who took the design brief and turned it into something special; the Unruly Writers, who listened without complaint to endless variations on a theme; tutors and lecturers who patiently explained why nested voices might prove tricky.

And, finally, thank you to all those great strip cartoonists whose art, humour and philosophies shaped my world.

Patrons List

Gail Anderson
John Auckland
Helena Bondy
Joseph Brady
Natalie Browne
Anita Burnett
Janine Casey
Lauren Cass
Frank Colligan
Alexandra Coulton
Esmé Coyne
Nicoletta Demetriou
Yvonne Dewing
Joe Ellis
Brenna Ewing
Brooke Fell
Abby Gibbon
Sarah Gibson
Ben Gourley
Jenny Green
Gretel Hallett
Imogen Harris
Sarvat Hasin
Chantal Havard
Jasmine Hawkins
David Hebblethwaite
Rhian Heulwen Price
Verity Higgitt
Katy Jones
Edwin Kayes
Sylvia Ladunga
Jing-Jing Lee
Claire Lever
Jenny Lewis

Stephen McGowan
Erinna Mettler
Lindsey Moore
Jamie Nuttgens
Jamie Nuttgens
Laura O'Connor
Kizi Padden
Matthew Parker
Michael Peters
Chris Price
Tricia Rogan
Isla Rollason
Tansy Round
Suprit Roy
Rebecca Rue
Nemat Sadat
Haiya Sarwar
Phil Scherb
Mike Scott Thomson
Jim West
Alex Wilson
Stephanie Wiltshire